W9-BFK-796

"You don't want to sleep on the couch," Andy whispered as Penny opened the buttons of his shirt, his mouth next to her ear, his head buried in the fluffy curls of her hair. She shook the curls gently.

"Not unless you'll be there, too," she answered softly. On unsteady legs Penny stood and pulled her dress over her head, leaning forward to finish tugging it off, exposing, as she did so, the line of her back underneath a loose satin teddy trimmed with lace.

In one motion Andy lifted her gently and carried her to the darkened bedroom, where he put her down on the bed.

"I knew this was going to happen, didn't you?" Penny asked him.

"No. But I'm happy it has...."

Dear Reader,

We're so proud to bring you Harlequin Intrigue. These books blend adventure and excitement with the compelling love stories you've come to associate with Harlequin.

This series is unique; it combines contemporary themes with the fast-paced action of a good old-fashioned page turner. You'll identify with these realistic heroines and their daring spirit as they seek the answers, flirting with both danger and passion along the way.

We hope you'll enjoy these new books, and look forward to your comments and suggestions.

The Editors
Harlequin Intrigue
919 Third Avenue
New York, N.Y. 10022

In For A Penny

DEIRDRE MARDON

Harlequin Books

TORONTO • NEW YORK • LONDON
AMSTERDAM • PARIS • SYDNEY • HAMBURG
STOCKHOLM • ATHENS • TOKYO • MILAN

For Gale,
whose enthusiasm and
long-term support are priceless.

———————————◆———————————

Harlequin Intrigue edition published August 1984

ISBN 0-373-22002-2

Copyright ©1984 A. Mardon, Inc. All rights reserved.
Philippine copyright 1984. Australian copyright 1984.
Except for use in any review, the reproduction or utilization of
this work in whole or in part in any form by any electronic,
mechanical or other means, now known or hereafter invented,
including xerography, photocopying and recording, or in any
information storage or retrieval system, is forbidden without
the permission of the publisher, Harlequin Enterprises Limited,
225 Duncan Mill Road, Don Mills, Ontario Canada M3B 3K9, or
Harlequin Books, P.O. Box 958, North Sydney, Australia 2060.

All the characters in this book have no existence outside the
imagination of the author and have no relation whatsoever to
anyone bearing the same name or names. They are not even
distantly inspired by any individual known or unknown to the
author, and all incidents are pure invention.

The Harlequin trademark, consisting of the words
HARLEQUIN INTRIGUE, with or without the portrayal of a
Harlequin, are trademarks of Harlequin Enterprises Limited;
the portrayal of a Harlequin is registered in the
United States Patent and Trademark Office and in the
Canada Trade Marks Office.

Printed in Canada

Chapter One

Penny Greenaway opened her eyes at last, coming slowly to the surface from the dream in which a rhythmic jungle drum had inserted itself into her consciousness. The last wisps of sleep evaporated, but the rude repetitive beat continued, wrenching her into the morning light that filtered down through the windows of her brownstone apartment half a story below MacDougal Street in the heart of Greenwich Village.

The demanding knock on the door of her studio apartment continued. She stared at the cracked ceiling and pulled the damp sheet away from her naked body. No wonder she dreamed of steaming jungles, she mused, since at barely ten in the morning the temperature must already be in the nineties on this, the sixth day of a record heat wave that had clenched New York City in its humid fist the entire first week of August.

Penny swung her feet out of the Hollywood bed and onto the bare floor, standing to wrap the sheet tightly around herself and, at the same time, blowing her bangs out of her eyes before crossing the cluttered studio to the front door. She put one eye to the peephole.

"Who's there?" she called through the door, interrupting the peremptory knock which had just begun again.

"Is this Greenaway and Ackerman, Art Restorers?" asked a man's voice.

"Yes, who are you?"

Penny looked him over through the peephole—young, thirty-one or two, perhaps—which would make him five years older than Penny's twenty-seven. His gray plaid summer suit and crisp white button-down shirt quietly insisted their origins at Brooks Brothers or J. Press, haberdasheries to the right people; subdued striped tie, cotton because of the summer weather; dark brown hair freshly cut much too short for her taste; and deep blue eyes, so deep that if she were to paint them, she would reach without hesitation for the tube marked Copenhagen Blue.

"Andrew Keller of North American International Underwriters," he replied, holding up his business card to the peephole, so she could read it. "Are you going to open the door?"

He looked legitimate enough, she decided as she began to undo the chain which protected the studio. She opened the door.

Andrew Keller stared at Penny's attire, a crumpled, blue-and-white striped designer top sheet which her mother had given her after her first—and last—visit to the Greenwich Village studio her daughter maintained.

"Come in, Mr. Keller," she said graciously, enjoying immensely the shock written on his regular features. Apparently Andrew Keller wasn't accustomed to greeting sheet-clad strangers. Penny smiled mischievously at his discomfort.

"I can wait until you're dressed," he stammered. "I'll wait here in the hall."

"Am I immodestly covered?" she asked him innocently, looking down the length of her petite, sheet-wrapped body to the floor where only her bare toes peeked from the once crisp folds of the blue-and-white stripes.

"N-no," he agreed.

"Then, come in," she advised, backing into the disorderly square room which served as her studio. Slowly he followed. He carried a briefcase and wore wing tipped shoes, just as she had anticipated. The way he dressed reminded her of her father as he left the house each morning to commute from Wilmette to the Loop in Chicago where he maintained his law practice. Penny didn't know anyone in New York who dressed like Keller, all her friends being of the same artistic bent as she, but she was familiar with his attire from her acquaintances in one of the most affluent of the Chicago suburbs where she had been raised.

"Those shoes must be very hot in this weather," she commented. "Why don't you take them off?"

"Take off my shoes?" he repeated, blinking. She might as well have asked him to take off his trousers, she realized from the blush that stained the angular bones of his cheeks.

"I just thought you'd be more comfortable."

"Is Mr. Greenaway or Mr. Ackerman here?" he asked, choosing to ignore her comment.

"I'm Penelope Greenaway," she explained. "Ackerman retired, and there is no Mr. Greenaway. What can I do for you?"

He looked doubtfully at Penny, then glanced around the studio at the unmade bed, the coffee cans of solvent on the floor circling the paint spattered easel in the middle of the room, the stacks of primed and unprimed canvases leaning against two of the walls, and the overflowing bookshelves made of wood planks and concrete blocks under the windows.

"Is something wrong, Mr. Keller?" she asked. Clearly he had expected a much more formal establishment when he called on the firm of Greenaway and Ackerman, Art

Restorers. "Did you think you were going to find the curators' room at the Metropolitan Museum?"

"Uh. . . you are the restorer?" he asked.

"I am the restorer. Did you want to talk to me?"

"I tried to call you, Miss Greenaway—"

"Penny. You can call me Penny. What shall I call you?"

"Andrew," he answered automatically, having been caught off guard, and making Penny feel certain he preferred to be called Mr. Keller. "But there seems to be something wrong with your telephone."

It's been cut off because I didn't pay the bill, she said to herself. "Oh, really?" She crossed the room in tiny steps, and picked up the receiver, holding it to her ear. Letting go of the sheet for a second, she tapped the button repeatedly. The sheet slipped several inches, exposing the tops of her breasts.

"It's dead all right. I wonder what happened."

Keller cleared his throat and said nothing. He seemed to be studying the cracks in the ceiling with great concentration. Penny smiled inwardly, but kept the expression on her face placid.

"Would you like a cup of coffee? Come into the kitchen." She held the sheet close to her chest and walked toward the doorway behind him which led to a tiny kitchen in the back of the apartment. He studiously avoided looking at her.

"No, no thanks," he replied. "My, it's hot in here." He ran a finger under the starched collar of his white shirt.

"Yes, it is. And it's only morning. You should feel it by three in the afternoon." She flipped the switch on a table fan as she passed. With a low hum, the fan began to rotate back and forth, blowing some papers, which Penny ignored, onto the floor. She went into the kitchen with Andrew Keller behind her. She indicated a stool. He set his briefcase on the floor and perched.

"What happened to Ackerman?"

"Janie? Oh, she got married and moved to Philadelphia," Penny answered casually, opening the refrigerator and pulling out a can of Coke which she opened immediately and put to her mouth, swallowing without stopping for several seconds. She had been so angry with Jane when her friend abandoned their business, angry because she feared just what had come to pass—that she alone would not be able to keep her head above water financially. But she was over the anger now. Janie had the right to fall in love, to marry, even to move to Philadelphia if that's what she chose. Penny had simply resigned herself to the reality that she would have to close up shop in the fall, and she knew she would have to begin trying to sell her business soon, if she hoped to salvage anything from her equipment.

"I'm from Philadelphia," he said.

I could have guessed, she thought. "How smart of you to leave," she said dryly. "I went to see Janie once; I wasn't too thrilled."

"Well, not the city," he hastened to explain. "I grew up in Bryn Mawr on the Main Line which is quite lovely—"

"That's where Janie lives." A dead silence followed.

"Do you always have Coke for breakfast?" he asked finally.

"No, sometimes I drink Sprite. It depends on how I feel."

Penny glanced quickly at him to gauge his reaction, but his head was down as he picked up the black briefcase and balanced it on one knee. He was handsome, she decided, quite handsome. But much too staid and formal for her taste. She sat on the other stool, hooking her sheet shrouded feet behind one rung, and sipping at the second half of her Coke. Every so often, she blew her bangs out of her eyes.

"I have a proposal for you, Miss Greenaway," he said as he pulled a sheaf of papers from the open briefcase.

"Please call me Penny."

"Penny it will be. North American International Underwriters needs the services of a restorer for a large job. Are you interested?"

Is the sky blue? she answered inwardly. "How large?" she said aloud, feigning indifference.

"One hundred paintings," he replied. "Water damage."

Penny's heart flipped over. *A hundred paintings! Much, much more than a whole year's work, maybe two year's work.* She could get her phone turned on again, pay her bills, buy some new clothes. She wouldn't have to return to Wilmette with her tail between her legs and face that I-knew-she'd-get-over-this-stage look on her mother's endlessly tolerant, perfectly made-up face. She could buy the books she had been eyeing at Barnes and Noble—the Monet book, the Rauschenburg book, the monograph on...

"Well, are you interested?" he prodded.

"I don't know, Andy, I'm pretty busy right now—all those things I'm working on in my studio." She gestured with the Coke can toward the outer room, causing the sheet which covered her breasts to slip slightly. He looked down at the papers quickly. "But I'd like to consider the commission. May I see the art?"

"Certainly," he assured her. "It's in a warehouse not far from here. I'll take you there right away. As soon as you are ready to go, that is." He eyed the striped sheet somewhat awkwardly.

"I'll get dressed."

"Don't you want to eat breakfast first?"

"I just have," she answered, hopping down from the

stool and returning to the outer room where she went to the single closet and pulled out something gauzy which she took into the bathroom.

"Just make yourself at home," she called through the closed door.

Penny was washed, dressed, and ready in two minutes, but she purposely dawdled in the tiny bathroom, not wanting Keller to know how anxious she was to obtain the commission. As she ran a wide-toothed comb through the short curls that framed her head with a cloud of brown tendrils, the thought crossed her mind that his proffered job was too good to be true. She wasn't the only art restorer in Manhattan, far from it, and not only that, she wasn't well-known or considered to be the best, by any means. One hundred paintings! She simply had to get the job! But if he saw that she was hungry, he would make her restore them for a pittance. She had enough professional self-esteem to play the bargainer's game right to the last note; she wouldn't bring up money until she had inspected the paintings, assessed the damage, and perhaps made him wait two or three days for her answer. She ran a light pink lipstick across her lips and pressed them together. Well, maybe twenty-four hours.

On a wicker shelf stood a large bottle of Laura Ashley perfume, a birthday gift from her doting father who was aware how much Penny loved the romantic fragrance. She took out the round glass stopper and sprinkled herself with the floral scent, and the close room filled with the essence of rose and iris and jasmine. Today might be only business, but it never hurt a woman to wear perfume when she was near a man.

"I'm ready," she said, coming out of the bathroom to be greeted by a blast of cold air. He had turned on the air conditioner and its effectiveness was evident in the small confines of the studio. She crossed quickly to the window and shut it off, knowing that her electricity bill was on the edge of outer space already, and she couldn't afford to have Consolidated Edison turn off the power just now. After all, she didn't have the commission yet; perhaps Keller had bids out with other restorers already.

"It was so hot," he explained, standing as she entered the room and staring wide-eyed at her outfit which consisted of gauzy, almost transparent, harem pants and an embroidered Indian shirt which she had tied around her waist leaving three inches of her midriff exposed. On her feet she wore sandals. But he recovered quickly. "I thought perhaps the air conditioner was broken, but it works perfectly."

He had removed his jacket and, much to her surprise, he sported bright red suspenders underneath. The suspenders pleased her inordinately; perhaps he wasn't as stolid as she had first imagined. In his hand he held one of her books, Stout's *The Care of Pictures*—one of the bibles by which she worked.

"I can't afford to run—er, I mean, it's not good for the art works," she fabricated quickly, indicating the half-finished canvas on the easel.

"I would think just the opposite," he said, and he was correct, but she did not have to acknowledge his accuracy because he continued immediately. "I was looking at that painting. You're very good. You did paint that, didn't you?"

"Yes," she answered. He knew nothing about art, that much was clear from his comment. Not that the painting was bad, but if he had known anything at all, he would have recognized at least its familiar style. Penny crossed to the easel and eyed the painting critically, unconsciously sticking out her lower lip to blow upward and ruffle her bangs as she noted that the hind legs of one of the horses were definitely out of kilter. She would have to paint them out and redo them.

"It's a fairly well-known Degas," she explained. "*Aux Courses, Les Jockeys.* I'm copying it on commission for a decorator friend of mine." She indicated a large color reproduction of the original painting which was tacked up on the wall behind the easel.

"Can you just do that?" he asked surprised. "Copy a painting, I mean. Is that legal?"

"Yes, as long as you don't make the reproduction the same size as the original. You see, the Degas is forty-five by thirty-six centimeters. My painting is square and much larger. And then, of course, it will be sold as a reproduction; there'll be no attempt to pretend the painting is original. I'll sign Degas' name, but on the back I'll put my own."

"It's a very fine likeness," he complimented her, looking from the photograph to the canvas on the easel. "Do you paint much?"

"I like to paint. That's how I got to be a restorer actually, but I'm not very good. Copying—I'm very good at copying, and part of my business is doing reproductions." *The only thing I'm getting paid for at the moment, in fact.* But the work was laboriously slow and wasn't enough to keep her in groceries and phone calls, let alone to pay the rent and buy clothes and books.

"Good, then you'll like the job I offered you."

"Reproductions?" Of course, they had to be. Who else would have one hundred paintings all in one place unless a museum had been flooded? And if a museum were flooded, they wouldn't be coming to Penny Greenaway for restoration; they'd be using their own curators.

"Yes, reproductions," he said quickly, "but we can discuss them later when you see them.'' Penny looked at him closely. Was he trying to hide something from her? He seemed nervous and most anxious to change the subject.

"Am I to bid on the project?" she asked quickly, nervous herself that she might lose the opportunity to have such a large commission. "How many others have you approached?"

"There is no one else at present," he answered, choosing his words carefully. "If we can come to appropriate terms, the job will be yours. If you think you can handle it, that is." She was certain he was warning her subtly not to price herself out of the market, which she had no intention of doing.

"How extensive is the damage? Was there a flood?"

"No, the paintings were stolen from a European shipment we insured. We were forced to buy them back from the thieves, ransom them, I suppose you'd say. That's not something insurance companies care to discuss too much, but, of course, it goes on all the time. Anyway, the thieves treated the cartons carelessly and they were water damaged. Not all of them, we are certain, but the entire shipment will have to be gone through and restored to its original condition for the consignee."

"But how did they get water damaged?"

"The thieves left the cartons in a swamp off the New Jersey Turnpike. After the payoff, they instructed us to pick them up there. It appears the cartons were there for up to a week."

"Oh," she said.

She couldn't believe how carelessly some people treated original art, hanging fine oils above the fireplace for decorating purposes when every restorer knew that, except in direct sunlight, there was not a worse place in the house to hang a work of art which was then constantly exposed to carbon soot. It broke her heart to know of such outrages, not to mention the well-publicized purposeful vandalism of masterpieces such as Michelangelo's *Pietà* which had been attacked by a madman in the Vatican several years before and had been years in restoration, hidden from public view afterward.

"You have a lot of equipment, Penny. I had no idea restoration was so complicated." He picked up a thin, flat sculptor's spatula from a table and examined it closely. She, in turn, examined his hands, noting that they were clean, strong and capable looking, the fingers long like those of an artist and the fingernails trimmed closely. Penny always looked at people's hands, perhaps because she disliked her own, which were often stained from the paints and chemicals she worked with, and whose fingernails were bitten to the quick, a hateful habit she had been fighting unsuccessfully since she was a child.

You should see the studio of someone who's really outfitted, she thought. Jane had taken all her own tools with her when she went back to Philadelphia, and one of the reasons Penny was so broke was that she had been forced to purchase her own ultraviolet unit and Omega studio camera. In addition, she was paying Jane, little by little, for her share of the vacuum hot-table that they had purchased together, which was used for relining paintings. The hot table had been a mistake; too expensive for Jane and Penny to buy together, and much too expensive and sophisticated for Penny to own, considering her present circumstances. She had been advertising to sell it in several of the art supply stores she patronized, and she had asked her former art restoration teacher, Henry Ostrov, to ask around at his school if anyone was interested in purchasing a hot table.

"What's this?" asked Andy, indicating the ultraviolet unit.

"That's called an Illuminator. You can look at paintings in both white and ultraviolet light. Yes, you're right—the work can be complicated," she agreed, "but I love it. Before we leave, Andy, I have to feed a neighbor's cat. She—my neighbor, not the cat—has gone to Europe for the month of August and asked me to take care of her pet, but I can't have him in here because of all the chemicals. Would you mind? The apartment is just upstairs."

"Not at all," he answered politely. He put on his jacket, picked up the briefcase, and was ready when Penny had turned off the virtually useless fan and all the lights. She led him upstairs to the second floor and unlocked the door to a sunny apartment which looked out over the sunbaked garden in back of the building. She knew he couldn't fail to notice the difference between the sunlit, sparsely furnished two rooms of Winnie, her compulsively neat neighbor, and her own dark, cluttered studio room below. The cat ran to her and nuzzled against her gauze-covered legs.

"Now *this* is a nice place," he said in a friendly tone, but Penny took his remark as criticism.

"I can't help it if I have to live where I work," she answered testily. "I prefer working for myself rather than punching a clock for a big company." *Like yours,* she added silently. She couldn't imagine a fate worse than being just another employee number on a computerized paycheck as Keller must be.

"I didn't mean—"

"No, I know you didn't. Sorry," she apologized. "The heat makes me irritable. Have you worked a long time for—what's the name of your company again?"

"North American International Underwriters. Yes, since I got out of the service."

"And you like it there?" She opened a can of cat food,

turned it into a clean bowl, and ran the tap for a fresh bowl of water for the cat.

He hesitated before answering the question. The pause was long enough that she looked over to where he stood at the kitchen door and studied the glorious blue color of his eyes, the best feature of his earnest face which seemed to reflect that he was weighing the forthcoming answer carefully. He looked taller somehow in the confines of the small kitchen, and his shoulders were broader than she had first noticed.

"I've always liked the company," he said. "But lately things are different. I have a new boss who has changed the way we operate. Guess I just have to get used to him."

"That's why I like working for myself," she explained. "You have to answer to the client, it's true, but ultimately you answer only to yourself. Wouldn't you care to have a job like that?"

"But there's no security," he objected. "You never know where your next meal is coming from."

His assessment was so accurate, she decided to change the subject.

"How did you get your present assignment? I don't mean to be offensive, but you don't seem to know too much about art. Why are you in charge of this restoration project?"

"Just the draw," he answered, but something in the tone of his voice made her believe he wasn't being entirely truthful. "In the insurance business you take care of the client, no matter what he has insured—his racehorse, his yacht, his paintings. Even if you aren't interested in the project."

"You weren't interested? Why didn't you ask to be put on something else—something like a sunken cargo ship, or an airplane crash. You insure that kind of disaster, don't you?"

"Yes, of course we do. It isn't that I didn't want to be on

the project; it's that there were other claims that were more my specialty, at the time. My specialty is ships, as a matter of fact. Mainly oil tankers.''

''Then why art?'' she persisted.

''Well, my boss assigned the case to me because there was no one else available, at the time. It doesn't matter,'' he insisted, but she had the idea that it did indeed matter to him, that he was disappointed in an assignment he apparently had been forced to accept, and that he did not want to discuss the matter further. His face was so simple to read, she mused, like a pane of clear glass. ''Besides,'' he said earnestly, ''you don't turn down the company when they ask you to handle a project; that's business. Anyway, I don't mean to sound conceited, but I'm a very good adjustor no matter what the problem is, and I don't need to know anything about art when there are experts like you around.''

He was trying to be polite, to compliment her, she realized, probably to atone for the unflattering comparison which had emerged from his comment about Winnie's apartment. She thought he was very sweet, if a bit naive for a man his age, and more than a bit pompous. A good adjustor, indeed, as if such a thing mattered in the scheme of life. He was shy and serious, exactly the opposite of Penny, and because he was so diffident, he was the perfect target for her sense of humor. To tease him was irresistible.

''I like your red suspenders.'' She smiled at him and was gratified when her comment made his blue eyes wince in embarrassment. ''They're such a surprise after that straight Brooks Brothers suit you've got on. I bet your underwear is wild, too.''

This time, to her glee, he actually blushed, a quick flash of red that covered his neck above the starched, white collar of his shirt, and shot up to his cheeks to turn them a mottled pink. Penny loved his discomfort. She wasn't a cruel person, but rather one who hated stuffiness and pomposity, and she relished forcing people to look at themselves in a new light. He was so easy to embarrass she decided to make every effort possible to make him blush again. "Are they? Am I right? Little ladybugs? Red and yellow and blue boat flags?"

"Really, Penny," he sputtered. "That's an outrageous comment. You don't even know me! You let a virtual stranger into your apartment when you had no clothes on, and now you're making comments about my underwear. You're taking a terrible risk, don't you know that? You'll get yourself killed with such behavior!" There was a thin film of perspiration on his upper lip, which she did not ascribe to the still, airless atmosphere in the closed up apartment.

He was right, of course; she had lived in New York City long enough to know that with anyone else she would have been taking a patently foolhardy risk. But her instincts told her that Andrew Keller was different. He was a gentleman through and through, a prep-school product from Bryn Mawr, Pennsylvania, who probably still held doors for strange women in office buildings, insisted on seeing a woman into a car first, and did not consider the most strident parts of women's liberation a viable alternative to the good manners he had been taught when young. Although if she asked him, she knew he'd answer forcefully and honestly that he believed in equal opportunity for both sexes. She thought he was terrific, a throwback to the fifties, when life was simpler and people knew what was expected of them in all situations. She thought he was a refreshing change from the men she had been dating for the past few years; struggling artists and out-of-work actors who moonlighted as waiters—men so serious about their careers that all they wanted to talk about was theory and their own fragile egos, but not in that order.

She could not resist teasing him a bit more.

"A risk with *you*, is that what you're saying? You mean your suspenders indicate a man barely in control of his passions? I thought that's what they meant, and it's always satisfying to have your intuitions confirmed, don't you think?" She smiled impishly.

"Penny! Is that cat taken care of? We have to get to the warehouse soon." He leaned back and looked ostentatiously at his wrist watch, a thin, gold affair in quiet, good taste.

She crossed the room in two steps and stood close to him. She had to tilt her head back to look him in the eye, not that he was terribly tall, not quite six feet, she imagined; but she was very short, an inch more than five feet, and she was in flat shoes. One of the reasons she wore her hair in the unkempt fluffy curls that had made her mother blanch when she first saw it, was to give herself a bit of height. And to nettle her mother, of course.

"You're really cute, Andy. I love the way you blush. You remind me of a big, squishy teddy bear."

Chapter Two

Teddy bear, indeed!

This Greenaway woman's behavior was incredible, Andrew Keller mused as he followed her down the narrow, creaking stairs of the gloomy brownstone building in which she lived and out onto MacDougal street where the air hit him like the flames from a blast furnace. The blistering heat of the sun had already melted the tar between the square pieces of concrete that made up the sidewalk.

Woman, he had called her, but girl was a more apt description. He assumed she was a woman, however, estimating her age to be somewhere in the mid-twenties, basing his guess on the quality and quantity of the equipment in her studio, and certainly not on her physical appearance. Clearly, her restoration business was a serious pursuit, the equipment alone probably worth thousands of dollars, most especially that big, complicated and mysterious machine that had dominated one corner of the square room. Such a business took time to establish and an education to run, so he figured she had been out of school for a while and in practice for several years at least, despite the fact that he suspected that her financial state was precarious.

But if he had met her somewhere else out of context,

seen her on the street perhaps, he would have put her age at no more than seventeen or eighteen years.

Just a dash of pale lipstick, that was all the makeup she wore. Andy liked that; he liked it very much. One thing he cared little for was a woman who slathered her face in cosmetics—orange skin, purple cheeks, brown lips, silver eyelids, and eyelashes any conceivable color of the rainbow. He saw those women all the time in Manhattan, both in the Wall Street area where his main office was located, and in midtown where the firm maintained smaller quarters, and he knew they thought themselves chic, well-dressed, and *au courant*, but they were too thin, too artificial and too hard-edged for his taste.

Pink lipstick—a soft, tender pink like the petals of peonies—that was the perfect color for Penny Greenaway whose very name seemed exceedingly romantic and reminded him of what? Something long ago. Pictures of English gardens and children playing happily in an uncomplicated world.

"Is your real name Penelope?" he asked, and she confirmed that it was. She was walking on the inside of the sidewalk, apparently trying to catch the erratic drips of air conditioning units two and three stories above. She told him, when he asked if the water bothered her, that, to the contrary, the artificial drizzle provided a measure of relief from the heat. Her hair was sprinkled with water which shone like so many diamonds in the blazing sun. Andy shook his head at her eccentricity.

But the way she dressed! The outfit she wore right now was more like a Halloween costume than clothes in which to be seen on the street. For one thing, he was able to see the outline of her thighs through the gossamer thin layers of fabric that barely covered her legs. He supposed they were pants, but not like any pants he had seen on a woman since his stint in Lebanon when he had been a Marine ten years before. That woman had been a belly dancer. He didn't remember much of the evening, it was true, but he remembered the woman's costume. The cream colored pants fit tightly around Penny's very trim ankles, but ballooned out as they traveled up to her tiny waist, actually showing nothing, he admitted to himself, but hinting seductively at the petite, but fully formed curves of her calves and thighs beneath.

It had come as no surprise to Andrew Keller that the hard-hatted men who were supposed to be excavating at the first corner they came to on MacDougal Street, but in fact were drinking coffee and eating paper-wrapped danishes, had whistled at her and called out benignly suggestive comments as she passed. But Penny hadn't shown herself to be perturbed in the slightest, had smiled in fact, and had waved one tiny hand in acknowledgment as she walked by.

"Save it for your wives, boys," she had called with a smile, causing Andy to look away into the shop window at his right.

He chanced a sidelong glance at her waist which was naked for all of MacDougal Street to appraise, there being two or three inches of her smooth midriff exposed between the gauzy pants and a wildly embroidered shirt of undyed linen covered in blue and green and rose flowers and serpentine vines, and spangled with miniature mirrors. The shirt was tied casually around her ribs. He noticed that she had a tiny mole on her stomach.

Quickly he looked away and his eye caught a display of fresh peaches piled artistically on the sidewalk table of a Korean green grocer they were passing, making him recall the unsuitable meal with which Penny had begun her day. Andrew Keller believed in God, the American flag, and a hearty breakfast, in that order, and he had been shocked by Penny's nutritional failing.

"Penny, would you care for a peach? All you've had is a Coke today. That's not good for you," he blurted out, to his great surprise.

He hadn't meant to suggest such a thing, but the words had slipped out of his mouth before he had a chance to stop them. Buying a peach for her was something he would have done on a date, and today was business, strictly business; he didn't want to leave her with the wrong impression. He was certain she would turn down his offer of fruit—she drank Coke for breakfast, after all—but, to his consternation, she agreed readily and he found himself standing in the welcome shade of a green awning and fumbling for some coins in his pocket while negotiating with the shopkeeper whose command of English was faulty at best. Andy wanted the peach washed, and the salesman either could not or refused to understand.

Penny waited patiently, poking at a pile of exotic, dark purple South American fruit balanced on the next table, extending her lower lip to blow her breath up in order to make her wispy bangs flutter and relieve her forehead, he assumed, from the effects of the morning's heat. She was always blowing on her bangs, and Andy wondered why she didn't do something with her hair—get it cut or pull it back, or something. Her hair was cut fairly short, but there was a lot of it, a mass of curls and tendrils that clouded around her small face like a fuzzy helmet. It looked as if she combed it with her fingers.

Andy was unaccustomed to such casual dishevelment in a woman. The only woman he saw regularly was Caroline Potter whom he had been dating with serious intent for the past year. Caroline's hair was always sleekly pulled back into a low bun or a perfect ponytail which was tied with a ribbon that inevitably matched the tailored dress she wore. Caroline never had a hair out of place. Even on a day such as today, when the humidity had to match the temperature exactly, not a single hair on her head would have dared spring loose from her coiffure whose studied informality was maintained by the pink ladies behind the red door of Elizabeth Arden of Fifth Avenue.

He flushed with guilt just thinking of Caroline, wondering what he would say if he ran into her here on MacDougal Street while in the company of the half-naked Penelope Greenaway. Half-naked was an exaggeration, he admitted; Penny's body was covered except for her hands, her face, and her toes at which he glanced quickly while the Korean, who had finally understood his eminently logical concern with hygiene, went somewhere in the back of the dark shop to wash the peach. Small, dark marks stained each one of her toenails. Under the pretext of tying one shoelace, Andy crouched and examined them. A perfect little butterfly sat in the midst of the pale pink enamel which glistened on each toenail, the butterflies becoming smaller and smaller as they fluttered between the largest and smallest toe.

"If you like my toenails, you'll love my tattoo," she said, making him flush and rise to his full height quickly. The sudden change in blood pressure made Andy momentarily dizzy, and he put out a hand to steady himself, inadvertently knocking over the apex of a pyramid of ripe, red tomatoes which sat on the table.

The Korean, who was just returning from the back of the shop, shouted something unintelligible in a high singsong voice, and rushed to Andy's side with the peach in one hand and a plastic bag in the other. Pushing the peach into Penny's hand, he began to shovel the smashed tomatoes which stained both the pavement and Andy's black, wing tipped shoes into the plastic bag. With a grunt, he held out the bag which looked like the first stages of spaghetti sauce on a Boy Scout cookout, and said in perfectly clear English. "Three-fifty!"

"But, but—"

"Three-fifty. You break, you buy."

Andy looked at Penny who was nonchalantly biting into her peach, trying, he could tell, to smother a giggle, and with a shrug, he took his wallet from his back pocket and handed the green grocer a five-dollar bill. The man smiled and slowly counted out six quarters in change.

"Let's get out of here!" said Andy when the shopkeeper had finished his smiling transaction, taking Penny by the elbow, and walking quickly toward the corner where they had to wait for a traffic light. He dropped the bag of tomatoes into an overflowing trash can.

While they stood on the corner he bit his lower lip. He couldn't help himself; he had to know.

"Do you really have a tattoo?" he asked finally, knowing he was going to regret the question.

"Maybe," she answered. She looked up at him and smiled enigmatically, and he felt his heart do a flip as his imagination kicked into overdrive. He wouldn't ask, he swore to himself. She would not provoke him into asking.

"Don't you want to know where?" she asked.

"No!" he sputtered.

He realized he was still holding her by the elbow, and he let his arm drop to his side. He ran one finger under the collar of his shirt in which the laundry had put too much starch and wished he could remove his jacket. The temperature seemed to have shot up about ten degrees, but perhaps it was only because they were standing on the crowded corner waiting for the light to change and being buffeted by other warm bodies in the same situation.

From the corner of his eye, he saw Penny pluck the front

of her blouse away from her skin and blow down into its dark and mysterious recesses. He took a snowy white handkerchief from one pocket and wiped his forehead.

"Eeek!" she said, jumping six inches toward him.

"What is it?"

"Someone pinched me!" She was looking around at the group of people on the corner, straining to see who was standing behind her, and sidling even closer to Andy as she craned her head. She took his arm tightly as if to seek his protection. "On the behind," she confided in a stage whisper.

"If you wore normal clothes, Penelope, you wouldn't be subject to such harassment," he said automatically, but he was concerned for her and drew her arm through his, gently pulling her away from the spot where they had stood. The light changed and the crowd began to surge forward across Seventh Avenue. They stepped into the street which sank mushily beneath his heels, having already nearly melted to the consistency of molasses under the August sun.

"Let's take a cab," Andy suggested. They were within walking distance of the warehouse, although it would have been a considerable trek, but the morning was so hot and her outfit so shocking that he, who usually loved to get exercise by walking, finally decided to give in to the obvious.

"Are you implying that I asked to be pinched? That it's my own fault?" she exploded, ignoring his suggestion. Her hazel eyes were shooting sparks of indignation and anger, and there was a sheer glow of perspiration on her heart-shaped face. The fringe of lashes around her wide-open eyes was so thick he would have assumed they were fake on anyone else, but she had come to the door with those incredible eyelashes already in place, and he doubted that she slept in them. "I suppose you think women like the attentions of the perverts who bother them? Asked to be raped, asked to—"

"Hold on, I never implied anything of the sort," he said quickly, standing near the curb and surveying the flow of traffic in search of a cab whose white top light was on, indicating that it was empty and cruising. He held her arm firmly. "But you have to admit you enjoyed the attentions of those construction workers back there. You even answered their lewd suggestions."

"Andrew Keller, you're really weird, do you know that? You think those were lewd suggestions? That's a game they play, and I hope I'm dead and buried before the comments stop coming. There's nothing dirty about their remarks; they're flattering and they make a girl feel good." She tossed the peach pit over her shoulder without thought for who might be standing behind her. Fortunately, there was no one.

"You're an attention grabber, that's what you are," he sputtered critically—attention grabbing not being one characteristic held in the highest esteem in the towns on the Philadelphia Main Line. *Exactly the opposite of Caroline,* he thought, who herself would have been silently indignant if a group of street workers had called out to her. Caroline would have put her subtly aquiline, Main-Line-perfect nose up into the air as if she had smelled an indescribably terrible odor, and walked off with her head held high. Caroline was a real lady, a product of the best prep school on the East Coast, two years at a highly regarded—if not academically stringent—college for women, and the would-be future mother of his children, if everything went according to plan in their protracted courtship.

He waved at a cab coming down the street, but the driver ignored his signal and sailed by without a look in their direction. He spotted another cab and waved more forcefully, to no avail.

"We'll be here all day if this keeps up," said Penny, putting two fingers in her mouth and letting out a shrill whistle. A yellow cab pulled up in front of them with a squeal of its tires.

"And, by the way," said Penny as Andrew opened the door to the cab, "you're a stuffed shirt." She wrenched her arm, which he hadn't even realized he was holding, from his grasp and jumped into the ample back seat of the Checker cab.

The entire conversation was getting out of hand, thought Andrew as he followed her into the taxi. He had to get back to business since the most difficult part of the delicate negotiations with her was yet to come. When she saw the so-called art work, she would probably turn down the commission, and he couldn't afford to lose her, given the current state of affairs at the office.

Penny hugged the far corner of the back seat, first pulling open the jump seat with a thud and resting her butterfly bedecked toes in front of her. She leaned her elbow on the door handle, her chin on her hand, and she stared out the window as the cab made its way west toward the warehouse on the Hudson River not far away. Andrew stayed on his own side of the back seat, musing about the office. He took an antacid tablet from the roll he had lately begun to carry in the pocket of his suit jacket and popped it into his mouth. He was taking several tablets a day now, ever since Dieter had replaced his immediate boss.

Andy had been with North American International Underwriters since being mustered out of the Marines seven years before. Slowly but surely he had climbed the executive ladder at NAIU, his career on the uneventful and prearranged schedule which pleased him. Everything had gone according to plan until his current boss, Frank Dieter, had been called back to New York from his position in South America and had tried to impose the rules which had made his southern outpost run smoothly, but which were so difficult to follow in New York that two of Andy's fellow adjustors, including the resident expert on art matters, had already been fired. Luckily, both of his colleagues had been able to obtain positions at NAIU's major competitor, but no one, including Andy, wanted the blot of being fired on his record.

Andy didn't think of himself as a conceited person, but he knew he was good at what he did, good enough that Caroline's father, one of the most successful insurance men in Philadelphia had hinted through her that he would be welcome in his business when he and Caroline married—which, it was assumed, they would.

Andy was taking his time, not because he wouldn't jump at the opportunity to join her father's firm, but because he believed that since marriage was forever, he and Caroline should get to know each other well before making the long-term commitment to each other. They had dated every Saturday night for the past year, and he had spent a long weekend at her parents' farm in Gladwyn, outside of Philadelphia, the previous June. He liked the way the Potters lived; he liked the role of gentleman farmer that Mr. Potter played; and now, in serendipity, he had an unexpected opportunity to marry into that family and aspire to the same quiet elegance which comprised Caroline's native habitat.

But if Dieter fired him, would Mr. Potter be as interested in Andrew Keller as a son-in-law? And Dieter was on the verge of firing him.

Although convinced the man was jealous of Andy's superior workmanship, fearing that Andy would surpass him in the ever-upward climb at NAIU, he knew Dieter had the power to let him go. Dieter's present tactic was to make Andy quit, a subtlety which Dieter had not bothered to apply with his fellow adjustors, but Andy would not play the game. When he had been assigned to this ridiculous restoration project which had been insured for a mere hundred thousand dollars, he had swallowed his pride and accepted what amounted to a demotion, knowing that the assignment was the type usually handed out to a mere trainee. He had thanked Dieter with false enthusiasm while cringing inwardly at Dieter's hostile, mirthless smile.

"I don't see any reason that we should fight," said Penny suddenly in conciliation, breaking into his distressing reveries. She moved a scant two inches away from the window and closer to him. She fluttered the fringe around her hazel eyes. The lashes were so thick that they cast a smudgelike shadow on her upper cheek right across the sprinkling of freckles that lay on her cheeks and marched across her pertly turned-up nose as well.

"Neither do I," he answered quickly, happy that she had made the first attempt at friendliness.

Her good will was important to him. She was the fifth restorer he had contacted; all the others had turned him down as soon as they realized what was in the crates. He didn't understand why they were so huffy and filled with pride, but they had all said the same thing: "I don't work on pictures like *that*" as if the pictures had been pornographic, or worse. The few paintings he had actually seen looked all right to Andy who admittedly knew nothing about art, but the other restorers had sneered at them. Two of the restorers had been kind enough to suggest he contact a firm called Greenaway and Ackerman.

Andy was fairly convinced Penny would take the job, and for very little money, too. She was broke, after all, although she was trying valiantly to hide the fact from him. Despite her transparent theatrics with the telephone receiver, he knew her number had been disconnected, having been told so by the operator. Since she was his last hope, he had taken the chance of going directly to the studio in hopes that the firm of Greenaway and Ackerman was still in business, but he hadn't expected to meet a tousled teenager wrapped in a sheet. He decided to offer her slightly more than half of what the firm was willing to pay for restoration, knowing that the cheaper he brought in the job, the less reason Dieter would have to find fault with his work.

"How old are you, Penny?" he asked in an amicable tone.

"I'm twenty-seven," she answered. "Why?"

"You look much younger," he said.

"I know. I was asked for identification in a bar last week," she replied.

A hint of jealousy pricked Andy somewhere in his upper stomach. He wondered immediately about the man she had gone with to the bar, but then, knowing her the few short minutes that he had, he realized she might have gone alone. She certainly seemed to be the independent type. He shook his head slightly in wonder at the unfamiliar emotion. He had no right to be jealous; he had a fiancée himself. Maybe she did, too. Caroline wasn't *really* his fiancée, he amended. He and Caroline were engaged to be engaged—yes, that was the proper expression for the understanding he had with Caroline.

"Are you married, Andy?" she asked, almost reading his mind.

"No. No, I'm not."

"Why not? You're straight, aren't you?"

"Yes, yes I am. Of course," he choked, but he was saved from continuing the conversation by their arrival at the warehouse near the ramshackle piers of the turbid

Hudson River. He got out of the cab first and held the door as Penny slid across the seat toward him and extended her butterfly toes to the street. He paid the driver and then extracted a small, black leather book in which he wrote the cab fare and tip in neat numbers while still standing next to the curb.

"What are you doing out there in the sun?" she called from the narrow sliver of shade cast by the ancient brick building. Her gauzy pants fluttered in the slight breeze that blew from the river and she squinted, although one arm was raised across her brow to shade her eyes from the glare in the street. He thought she looked particularly vulnerable, if outlandishly dressed, but in this part of town there was barely a soul to see her.

"My expense account," he explained, nearing her and smelling the romantic fragrance that he had lost in the stale cigarette scented air of the cab. Roses, he decided. No, jasmine.

"You're so methodical, Andy. I bet your socks are lined up like little soldiers in their own special drawer. Or do they have to share a drawer with your ladybug shorts?"

She reached up and pinched his cheek. She broke into a musical giggle that had the sound of crystal wind chimes on the hot, still air of Christopher Street.

"Really, Penny!" he exclaimed. He ran one finger under his collar again. He definitely had to speak to the shirt laundry about the starch; it made the collar feel so tight. And clearly the city was just as hot down here by the river, he noticed. Even hotter, if that were possible.

Penny giggled, and then she laughed the high, musical laugh that had infected so many of her friends and acquaintances for most of her life. She had never met a man so easily nonplused as this Andrew Keller who was the epitome of Wall Street conservatism. His face flashed a dull red as soon as she pinched his cheek.

She watched with glee as he ran a finger under the collar of his shirt, something she had noticed he did with endearing frequency. If he didn't wear those tight, starched collars and neatly knotted ties, he'd be cooler in the damnable weather that was ruining this particular August—usually one of her favorite months since the city was not as crowded as during the rest of the year. Everyone with two cents to rub together was on vacation in the Hamptons or Block Island or Cape Cod and not stuck with a useless air conditioner in a hotbox half-a-story below MacDougal Street.

Remembering that she had an opportunity to turn the air conditioner back on and that Andy held the key to that opportunity, Penny decided she had better watch her behavior with him. She hardly knew him; she might inadvertently cross the line between having fun and being obnoxious, leaving him with the impression that she wasn't as professional as she knew she could be. She thought she might already have gone too far in the discussion of the construction workers, but he had been amenable when she apologized.

He had already commented on her youthful appearance, the bane of her existence, although she did nothing to make herself look more mature, shunning the artifice so many of her girlhood friends thought was necessary to be an adult. She couldn't be bothered with lots of makeup, structured clothes, and the ever-changing dictates of *Vogue* magazine. Even her mother had finally given up sending the packages of dresses from Bonwit Teller and Lord & Taylor, Mrs. Greenaway's two favorite stores, and had resorted to a check for five hundred dollars every Christmas to be used for new clothes. Penny always blew her mother's check at the January sales at Laura Ashley, the only good store whose clothes definitely appealed to her. The rest of the year she filled in with Indian cottons and even an occasional foray into her three favorite thrift shops, but even there pickings had been slim in the past two years, reflecting the depressed state of the economy.

"Well, where are these fantastic paintings, Andy? Let's get to work."

Andy held the heavy, metal door open, and Penny walked into the instant gloom of a cavernous warehouse. She stared at the high ceiling as Andy signed them in at a glass-enclosed, air-conditioned office, although the temperature inside the enormous building was a blessed relief after the shimmering heat of the street.

An attendant took them up three stories in a large elevator which gave Penny a case of instant vertigo since there was no door to hide the brick construction between the floors, but only a folding metal gate to separate the passengers from the wall. She closed her eyes against the unreasonable fear which was almost a nausea that crawled into her stomach and made her head swim.

"Are you all right, Penny?" Andy touched a clenched fist that hung at her side.

"I hate this kind of elevator," she said without opening her eyes. She felt his arm rest around her shoulder in a tender, protective gesture which surprised and pleased her.

"It's all right; we're almost there. I'm certain we can come back down by the stairs when we've finished here," he said gently. The attendant confirmed Andy's speculation at the same time he rolled back the flimsy gate with a clatter.

Penny opened her eyes and sighed with relief, blowing her breath up on her bangs automatically, and they walked out into an enormous room with dirty windows set high in the walls, a light source which did little to illuminate a series of chicken-wire enclosures crisscrossing the room. Andy led her to the enclosure that sported a hand-lettered sign that meant to say North American International Underwriters, but which had been written by someone who had inadvertently misspelled three of the four words. He took a key from his pocket to open the seven-foot high gate of the enclosure.

"That's not a very secure arrangement," she commented, thinking of the probable value of one hundred oil paintings, even paintings done by lesser-known contemporary artists.

"This warehouse suits our purposes just fine," he answered quickly. She looked at his profile as he swung back the door, thinking he seemed slightly nervous, and unable to imagine what would cause *him* to be jumpy. *She* was the one who would have to go back to Wilmette and its predictably dreary suburban lifestyle before the snow flew, if she didn't get this job. Long before the snow flew.

A sense of anticipation had been building in Penny's breast ever since they had left the cab. She plucked at her blouse, pulling it away from the damp skin of her breasts, although the warehouse was fairly cool. She couldn't wait to see the art work, doubly excited because she both loved the challenge of bringing something beautiful, but flawed, back to a pristine state, and was in such dire need of the potential commission. She could barely contain her enthusiasm as Andy walked to the back of the enclosure and pried the side off one of the ten wooden crates that stood three inches off the ground on weathered skids.

Too bad there had been no skids available in the New Jersey swamp, she mused. The side of the crate was mud-spattered and marked with a discernible water line about six inches from its base.

The wooden side came off with a screech, revealing the

edges of ten framed paintings, correctly packed in a neat arrangement of horizontal mesh screens on which each hung.

"These seem in pretty good shape," he said, "except for the frames, but they'll give you an idea of what happened to the shipment. You do restore frames as well, don't you?"

"Sure," she answered, coming up behind him just as he slid the first screen out for her inspection. The painting, a portrait of a misshapen, dark-haired nude woman who looked out doubtfully at the viewer, glowed luminously even in the dim light of the warehouse, making Penny's heart flip over. She blinked in surprise and looked at the curvaceous nude again.

"But that's a Modigliani!" she exclaimed. "*Seated Nude.* That's a very famous painting."

"This is a reproduction," he reminded her.

"Of course," she answered, attempting to recover her composure. At first, she had thought the work original; it had that magic light that only a genius knew to impart to his work. She comprehended the difference between ability and genius; she painted reproductions to keep her body and soul together, and she had always been able to copy the line and structure of any work she cared to attempt. But like all copyists, she was incapable of recreating the light. "And what a reproduction!" she said under her breath. She wondered at the nameless, faceless painter who had been able to capture the essence of the tragic Italian post-Impressionist whose fleeting career had been a brief, brilliant flash of perfection cut short by his thoroughly dissolute life in Montparnasse.

"You certainly know your art," said Andy with admiration.

"Well, the work is well-known."

Andy still stood between her and the Modigliani, making it difficult for her to see well. She reached into her handbag and felt around for the magnifying glass she always carried there, jostling Andy slightly as she moved around him and approached the glowing reproduction. She leaned down and examined a spot picked at random, a deep dimple in the chin of the nude.

Her heart sank. *I knew this was too good to be true,* she thought, referring as much to the Modigliani as to the entire job offer from NAIU.

"This is a photographic reproduction," she said with evident disappointment. "Just a photograph." No wonder the light had been so perfectly duplicated. A painted reproduction of such obvious quality was rare, so rare that the reproduction itself would sell for much more than all but the better known artists received for their oil canvases. "I don't handle photographic repros. I don't kn—"

She was about to admit she knew nothing about them, but she stopped just in time. The restoration job was nothing like what she had let her imagination hope it would be, but if it were a case of fixing up a bunch of damaged frames, she could stay in business another month or so, and perhaps a real job might come along, enabling her to eke out another month.

She looked at Andy who was biting his lower lip in nervous consternation. A thin line of perspiration glowed above his lip and under his eyes.

"Couldn't you make an exception just this once, Penny? We'll make it well worth your while."

It was Penny's turn to bite her lower lip. Certainly she planned to accept, but not wanting to make the negotiations too easy for him, thereby lowering the price he was willing to pay, she hesitated for a long moment.

"You're insulting me, Andy," she said mildly. "This

isn't an art restoration job; it's more like house cleaning, which is an honorable profession, I'm certain, but not what I'm trained to do." She felt she'd struck the right note with him—firm words, strong words even, but delivered in a pleasant tone which showed no anger, or insult.

He chewed his lower lip. He was most anxious to win the negotiation, she realized, thinking his concern was totally out of place. She imagined his company was enormous, with enough assets to be able to drop this shipment of photo-repros at the bottom of New York Harbor, pay the claim, and get on with business without even noticing that some small change was missing. Andy was worried, that much was obvious to her. He took a deep breath of the stale, dusty air in the warehouse.

"But you can't afford to turn us down, can you?" he asked with a small smile on his face. Penny looked at him in surprise. Here was a firm, businesslike, almost ruthless side to him which she had not previously suspected. Yes, he was a company man. Yes, he was staid and serious. But he was a bargainer, too, and not as easily manipulated as she had thought.

He watched her closely for her reaction.

"Well, they *are* pretty good repros; in fact, if they're all like this Modigliani, they're the best I've ever seen," she said hesitantly.

"Now, can you?" he prodded softly and waited for the wheels to turn around in her head. The telephone, the air conditioner—he had figured out everything.

"Correct. I'll take the job," she said, immediately regretting her hasty capitulation and certain that he would now offer her half of what he had planned. "But at a decent price," she added. "You'll never be able to find another experienced restorer in town who'll work on photo-repros, Andy, and I think you know it already. Don't you?"

"I do," he admitted. "But I'd like very much to work with Greenaway and Ackerman. Especially Greenaway." He smiled triumphantly, mentally rubbing his hands together, but shoving them into his pockets instead.

"I thought so," she said, consciously batting her eyelashes at him. Maybe the situation wasn't hopeless, after all. Maybe they would reach a price he'd be willing to pay that, at the same time, wouldn't insult her professional esteem. Photo-repros, indeed! She hoped none of her colleagues found out what she had agreed to restore.

Chapter Three

Andrew went out of the chicken wire cage and waited while Penny occupied herself by pulling the other identical Modiglianis from the open crate and looking them over carefully. At a summons from his stomach, he glanced down at his watch and noted that it was already past his usual lunchtime.

Should he invite her to have lunch with him? Why not, he asked himself, excited by the prospect. He had good reason to invite Penny to lunch, he rationalized, since they had not yet discussed a fee for the job, nor the mechanics of delivering the crates to her studio. Her acceptance of the commission hadn't really surprised him, he decided in retrospect, although she had hesitated longer than he had anticipated, but he had read her financial situation correctly.

Broke she might be, but she came from a good background. Hippiestyle clothes and the disorganized clutter in which she lived could not hide a certain breeding from his eyes, or rather from his ears for it was her diction that gave away her background. Although there still remained a trace of midwestern flatness in her speech, there was also the telltale perfection of pronunciation that belied a careful and probably an expensive education. He wondered why she chose to live in such haphazard chaos.

He was pleased at the prospect of eating with Penny, although he had an idea that she and he did not share the same taste in food. In fact, it was obvious to him that they shared little in common, but she had begun to fascinate him, nonetheless. He knew no one like Penelope Greenaway, and he wanted to become better acquainted with her. His sudden interest both surprised and confused him.

Penny came out of the cage slapping her hands together as if to free them from dust.

"They really are extremely good reproductions," she said, closing the gate behind her. "If it weren't for the magnifying glass, I could never have told in this light. Hanging on a wall in a softly-lighted room, anyone would think he was looking at a Modigliani. Are all one hundred of them the same, the *Seated Nude*?"

"No, I have a list of contents of the entire shipment somewhere." He patted the breast pocket of his jacket and inserted a hand inside, pulling out a neatly folded paper. "There are ten Cézannes, ten Modiglianis, ten Monets, ten Seurats, ten—"

"That's all right, Andy, I'll look at it later. Right now I'm starving. Let's get a slice somewhere."

"A slice?"

"A slice of pizza."

Andy frowned. "There must be someplace better than a pizza stand to eat. Let me take you to lunch."

"I'd love that," Penny answered with too much enthusiasm, leading him to wonder when she had eaten her last decent meal. She might be broke, but she certainly didn't look like someone who was starving. In fact, although she was what he would describe as petite, she had curves in all the right places and she looked as if she'd be soft to the touch, unlike Caroline who could charitably be called fashionably angular.

"I know just the place," she smiled, and he realized he had been staring at the tiny mole on her stomach where the skin was exposed between the harem pants and the spangled Indian shirt.

He usually frequented a family-owned restaurant downtown that specialized in seafood prepared in the Italian manner, but they were on the edge of the Village here, too far uptown to visit his favorite place, and he was unfamiliar with the restaurants in this part of the city. The problem annoyed him slightly. He hated feeling at a disadvantage; Caroline always allowed him to choose where they would eat.

He felt a little guilty when he caught himself comparing the two women for the second time in as many minutes.

They used the echoing metal stairs to descend to the first floor and then they walked northeast on Christopher Street, not even looking for a cab in the warehouse district where few drivers cruised for fares. She took his arm each time they reached a corner to cross, a gesture he liked because it seemed so unrelated to her usual independence, somewhat like her fear of the elevator which had surprised him and impelled him to put his arm around her shoulder to comfort her. He hadn't meant to touch her like that; he had meant to be businesslike and professional, but there was something about Penny that made him want to protect her.

She said she knew a restaurant that served interesting salads, and that accepted credit cards, as well, which she assumed was important to him, since he was on an expense account. The thoughtfulness implied in the observation surprised him, too, and made him forget his earlier irritation with her. He agreed that a salad was just what he wanted on such a hot day. In fifteen minutes they were seated across from each other at a table covered with a blue-and-white checked cloth in a French bistro style café whose name he had missed.

"Wine, Penny?" he asked her, looking over the menu. If there was one area in which Andrew Keller excelled, aside from actuarial tables, it was wine.

"No, thanks. I'll have the tabouli and an iced tea."

"Is that all you want?" He was slightly disappointed, having wanted to show off his expertise with the wine list which actually was not that spectacular, relying heavily on California jug wines.

"Really. It's so hot." Large ceiling fans stirred the air in the café, but the room was stifling nonetheless.

A waitress brought them their iced teas immediately, and Andrew watched Penny drink half of hers before she set it down on the tablecloth and played idly with the glass, a pensive look on her face. Gazing at her hands on the glass he realized for the first time that she bit her fingernails, so perhaps she wasn't as relaxed and carefree as she would have the world believe. Her forehead was creased right then, a frown that belied a worry that hadn't appeared there before.

"Is something wrong, Penny?"

"I'm curious, Andy. All those Modiglianis are backed with brown paper. That's quite unusual. You'll probably want me to replace all the paper."

"If it's damaged, of course. Why? Is that a problem?"

"No, no problem. You don't usually see brown paper behind a canvas; it's used mainly to protect lithographs from dust. I've never seen brown paper used like that, but of course with photographic reproductions, perhaps the process is different. I'll check into it right away. They look so real! I can't get over it," she said, apparently still surprised at the quality of reproduction. "Who are they for?"

"No one exotic, I'm afraid. They're to be used in the refurbishing of a hotel chain on the West Coast. They were insured for a hundred thousand dollars," he told her.

"A hundred thousand! That's way too much, in my opinion. That makes them worth a thousand apiece, and no photo of a painting, even framed, has that much value unless someone is smuggling diamonds or drugs in the frames."

"I hardly think NAIU is part of a smuggling ring, Penny," he laughed. "Apparently they were worth that much to the consignee." A hundred thousand seemed like play money to him, considering what a fully laden oil tanker out of the Gulf of Aden was worth. "Couldn't one of those reproductions be passed off as the real thing?" he asked.

"No, never," she assured him. "One look under a magnifying glass and I could tell they weren't real. To pull off a forgery, you would need an authentic oil painting exactly the same size as the original, perfectly painted by a master forger. That kind of painting is expensive to come by, ten or fifteen thousand dollars minimum. Even so, with all the sophisticated methods used these days to detect forgeries—X rays, chemicals, special lights—you wouldn't dare show it to an expert."

"What's the point of a forgery if the imitation costs as much as the original, and an expert can spot a fake immediately?" he asked.

"Hardly as much as the original! Not long ago a modern work by Piet Mondrian sold at Christie's in London for more than two million dollars, making Mondrian an artist well worth copying. Do you know his work?" she asked, obviously forgetting that he knew as little about art as she did about insurance.

Andy shook his head. As she warmed to the subject he watched her eyes and her hands, fascinated by the sparkle that lit the depths of her gold-flecked pupils.

"Mondrian is a modernist, very abstract. That means the shapes of his work are not difficult for a decent painter

to copy, although that's not to say that a copyist can capture
the magic that makes the artist's work worth two million
dollars today. Of course, to do a great copy, one that would
pass inspection by a fairly knowledgeable appraiser, you
understand, one would need the type of canvas and paints
Mondrian worked with in the twenties and thirties.''

"Go on," he said, digging into the salad the waitress
had just set before him. Penny ignored her tabouli and
gestured with the tiny fingers of her hands. She wore no
rings, which surprised him. He pictured her as the type of
woman who collected exotic jewelry from places like
Kenya and Afghanistan—tribal necklaces and elephant
hair bracelets. Caroline, in contrast, wore only gold. In
fact, she had maintained, since she was eighteen years old,
her own charge account at Bailey, Banks and Biddle, the
finest jewelers in Philadelphia, although it was her father
who paid the bills she ran up there. Sometimes Andrew
wondered how he was going to maintain Caroline's lifestyle after they married.

"That type of supply, old paint and canvas, is difficult
to find, but not impossible," Penny was saying. "So you
paint a great copy of a Mondrian, one that isn't too well-
known, or is lost or something. You paint a really authentic looking duplicate, and you take it to a bank to use as
collateral on a loan. The bankers know that Christie's just
sold a Mondrian for two million bucks, but all *you're* asking for is five hundred thousand to upgrade the equipment
in your widget factory. They tell you they'll think it over.
They call in the local appraiser who may or may not be any
good, and after his glowing verification—because you, of
course, have not chosen a bank in a city that is a major art
center, and would be dripping with expert art appraisers—
very pompously they allow you to do business with them.
As you walk out the door with half a million dollars less

the fifteen thou you paid the forger and the three thousand dollars you spent to have phony stationery and a phony annual report printed up, the fat bankers are rubbing their hands together and telling each other how smart they are to back their loans with such blue-chip collateral. You see?''

"While you, of course," he continued, wiping his mouth with the napkin, "laugh all the way to the beach in Rio where you go into tax-free, heavenly exile without fear of extradition."

"Exactly!" She took a bite of her salad. "Not enough mint," she pronounced.

"You have a larcenous mind, Penny," he laughed, delighted with the intricacies of the plot. He took out his black notebook and wrote a quick memo to himself.

"Not at all. You asked why forgery is worthwhile and I told you. It's done all the time, but you don't read about it in the newspapers because bankers aren't fond of looking stupid and greedy in print.

"Did *you* ever think of trying a stunt like that?" he asked.

"Don't think it never occurred to me, Andrew Keller, but that's for big crooks, folk in the major leagues. I'm just a nice girl from Wilmette, Illinois. Besides, I don't paint well enough."

"I thought your Degas was very fine," he said sincerely, "and we should talk about your fee now. Then you won't be tempted to paint a forgery."

She laughed the delightful, musical notes he had heard before. "What did you write down just then?"

"Just a note about what you told me. As an insurer, it bears looking into for the future."

"Why?"

"To make me better at what I do, that's all."

"Oh, you're so serious, Andy," she laughed again, this time rolling her eyes. "Don't you ever relax?"

"Sure, sure I do." He belonged to a team of Wharton Business School graduates who met weekly to play softball in Central Park on Saturday mornings, but his real passion was sailing, something he seldom was able to pursue since he had neither a boat nor a car with which to escape from New York on weekends. Caroline hated the idea that he loved to sail, and had told him he would have to give it up if they should decide to marry someday because she worried too much for his safety, and besides she was easily seasick.

Andrew and Penny settled on a mutually agreeable fee before they had finished their salads, and then they moved to the logistics of transporting and storing one hundred reproductions. Penny was satisfied with the figure arrived at, an amount slightly more than what she had hoped to receive, and she knew Andy was pleased from the smile on his face so she assumed she had agreed to take on the work for sightly less than he was willing to pay.

"I can't handle ten crates in my studio," said Penny. "One will strain my facilities as it is."

"Suppose we deliver the crates one at a time, then. When you're finished with the first ten paintings, call me and I'll have the next sent over and the first picked up. And so on." He insisted on calling the photographs "paintings," she noted impatiently, but she decided to say nothing. Why should she be interested in re-educating Andrew Keller?

"Good idea," she concurred with his plan to deliver the crates. That way she wouldn't lose touch with him. He wasn't her type, she told herself again, but he was so nice, nicer than any of the other men she knew right now. And so serious! His quiet manner had begun, unbelievably, to grow on her. He was methodical, it was true, probably too methodical, but Penny's life had been chaotic enough lately that she welcomed him into it like a breath of fresh air. She wondered why he, at thirty-one or two—she would have to ask his age—was still available. She had been single in Manhattan long enough to know that a straight, unmarried man whom a girl could take seriously was hard to find. Almost impossible to find.

She wasn't looking for a husband, but it would be nice to hang around with someone like Andrew Keller for a while. However, as soon as she admitted her growing attraction to him, she realized to her dismay, that Andy was exactly the man over whom her mother would chirp with happiness if she ever brought him home to meet the family. Mrs. Greenaway, whom her two daughters called Mrs. Clipboard behind her back, would like nothing better than for Penny to settle down, preferably in one of the correct suburbs north of Chicago, and begin producing Greenaway grandchildren according to the schedule she had worked out for her daughter's life long ago.

Penny shook her curls in disbelief. How could she suddenly find this quiet man so attractive? She had spent the last six years rebelling against the expected, and she wasn't about to capitulate now. Even if she had to go back to Wilmette, it certainly wasn't going to be on the arm of an insurance broker or agent or whatever he was.

"Andy, I'm invited to a party on Saturday night. Would you like to come with me?" The words were out before she had even thought about them, and immediately she regretted the invitation. He was the type of man who, once interested in her, she would never be able to shake. *Oh, well,* she thought, *he'll turn me down anyway. I'm sure he thinks I'm crazy.* Penny tended to be impulsive at times, and spent ten times as much time and energy extracting herself from awkward situations as she did falling into them.

He hesitated a long time before he answered—indecision

written all over his transparent features. He hesitated so long, in fact, that she felt compelled to question him again, although she had already asked the same question before.

"You're *not* married, are you? I withdraw the invitation if that's the case. I don't go out with married men." For some perverse reason she wanted him to accept her invitation, although she was certain she would be sorry afterward.

"No...no, I'm not married. Saturday night, well, let me see." He took out the small black leather book that seemed to serve as his diary, his watch, and his set of rules and made a great show of consulting the page for Saturday. She thought the book was silly, but she also realized that if she had a book like this, she wouldn't forget the promises she made to others, she wouldn't forget the items on her grocery list, she wouldn't forget to show up at functions she had agreed to attend. She made a mental note to pick up a little notebook like Andy's. She promptly forgot.

"I'm free for Saturday," he said, somewhat doubtfully. "What time?"

"It's for dinner. Why don't you pick me up around seven? We'll have to bring something, some wine I think I said."

"I'll bring the wine," he said quickly. "I have a bottle of 1977 Beringer Reserve Cabernet Sauvignon I've been saving for a special occasion."

"Is that a good wine?"

"Yes, very fine. I laid it down three years ago, but I'm certain it's ready now."

"You're really into wines, I see," said Penny, with a gleam in her eye. On a good day she could tell a red from a white.

"I fancy myself somewhat of an oenophile, yes," he answered.

"Oenophile? Does that mean an expert in wines?"

He agreed.

"Maybe you'd better keep your Cabernet Sauvignon for a while longer. I was thinking more along the lines of a gallon of Gallo chablis, but if you want to be fancy, you can bring Almaden instead." She giggled at the tiny frown that creased his forehead. "I can't wait for you to meet my friends, Andy."

Penny had her telephone hooked up as soon as the computerized retainer check from North American International Underwriters arrived by commercial messenger shortly after nine the following morning. She had to go in person to the telephone company to settle the bill.

With unaccustomed efficiency, she cleared a space on her worktable as soon as she had returned to her apartment studio, and she sat down to pay the entire electric bill and one half of the outstanding balance of her accounts at Sam Flax and Arthur Brown's, the two art supply houses she patronized. Both stores had carried her debt for months without so much as one dunning notice.

As soon as the checks were written, she turned on the air conditioner and stood in front of its vents to feel the cool air blow on her. She even left the machine running when she went out to mail the letters.

At four in the afternoon there was a knock on the door.

She checked the peephole and saw a dark-skinned young man, no more than twenty years old, who wore a pale blue shirt with the initials of NAIU embroidered in red on the breast pocket.

He introduced himself as Mercurio Gutierrez, told her that he would be bringing and picking up all the deliveries from the warehouse, and announced that he had the first crate ready in the van outside on the street. She had already cleared an area in the corner of the studio for the crate and directed him to place the stenciled wooden box which he wheeled in on a dolly in the space provided.

"I thought you were coming at two," she chastised him gently, having stayed in to wait for him when she wanted to be out buying groceries with her newly found cash. He took a crowbar which had been resting atop the crate and pried off one narrow side of the box.

"I know. I was on my way, but I stopped for a red light on First Avenue and the most beautiful Madonna with the biggest brown eyes came up to the truck and asked me for a ride to the Port Authority Bus Terminal. How could I turn her down? It was so hot and she looked so tired—"

"All right, Mercurio," laughed Penny, "but call me if you're going to be late next time. Did you get her name?"

"Yeah, but she lives in Jersey City and I live in the Bronx. It's too far for me to travel without a car."

"That's too bad. Maybe you'll meet someone closer to home."

"Mercurio is always looking," he said, and he winked at Penny as he went out the door and up the stairs to the company's van which he had left double-parked in front of Penny's brownstone.

She pulled one of the mesh screens from the box and lifted the work, one of the Modigliani reproductions, off its hook, laying it face down across four padded blocks on her work table. She used the corner pads, which were simply eighteen inch blocks of wood to which mattress padding had been stapled, to protect the frame from damage that the weight of the picture might cause as it rested on the table. She removed the hanging wire and eye hooks from the wooden frame, and with a wallpaper knife, she cut away the unmarked brown paper which had been glued to the frame. She already knew the Modiglianis were in good shape, and that only their frames needed to be checked for stains and warping, but she planned to take this one apart to ascertain how it had been constructed in order to know what supplies she would have to buy to complete the job.

She left the table and went to the telephone, joyous to hear the dial tone when she put the receiver to her ear. She dialed a number she knew by heart, that of Henry Ostrov, the man who had taught her and Janie to be restorers when they first came to New York from two years at the Virginia college where they had met while fellow students in the art department. Ostrov had a large studio on the top floor of an old building on West Fifty-seventh Street where she and Janie had studied under the grime-coated skylights of his establishment for two more years before opening Greenaway and Ackerman with high hopes on their part and limited backing on the part of their doubt-filled parents.

Penny identified herself, which wasn't really necessary because she and Henry had kept up a close friendship since her student days, but people who started a telephone conversation without giving their names irritated Penny to distraction, and she tried never to do the same. She thought their assumption that you knew who they were was the height of arrogance, implying that you received phone calls from no one else but them. She often consulted Henry about technical questions which arose in her work. After the necessary preliminaries, she went directly to her question.

"On photo repros, is there any need for a kraft paper backing?"

"Could be. What are the photos mounted on?"

"It looks like museum board. I'm not certain because the work is still in its frame."

"There's no need, Penny, but it's an extra touch, I suppose. You don't need it for a dust backing because the photo is literally laminated to the museum board on a hot press so no dust would ever permeate from the back. Perhaps it's done so the casual observer won't realize the backing is museum board?''

"You call someone checking out the back of a painting a casual observer? What's a serious observer then?'' They both laughed. Changing the subject abruptly, Penny asked, "Have you found a buyer for my hot table yet, Henry?''

"Such an expensive machine," he lamented. "No, not yet.''

"If I don't find one soon, I'll be asking you to find a buyer for my entire business, I'm afraid.''

"Are things so bad, Penny?''

"Yes, they are. Business is abominable. Why else would I be working on photo-reproductions, Henry?''

"You're serious about looking for a buyer?''

"You might make some discreet inquiries," replied Penny. "Maybe some of your students want to set themselves up in business like Janie and I did. I have all the equipment a restorer needs, and my lease gives me the right to sublet my studio, too.''

"There may be some students who are looking. I vaguely remember a discussion some time ago. I'll ask around,'' Henry said sadly. "But I'll miss you, Penny.''

"I'm not gone yet," she laughed, and she hung up, satisfied to know that her teacher had verified her first thought and relieved that he had not commented on why she was working on photographic reproductions. Henry was professional enough to realize that a restorer took what work she could get when business was slow.

She started to make a list of necessary supplies. She would have to buy a wide roll of kraft paper to replace any stained backing, although as a dust cover, the paper was unnecessary. She needed several cans of Minwax to mix in order to match the stain that had been damaged on the wood frames. She would have to check her supply of Photoflat, the paper that was heavily waxed on both sides and had probably been used to laminate the photographic reproductions to the museum board in the first place, because, if some of the frames had been water damaged, it was possible that the photographs had begun to peel away from their backing, and would have to be tacked down again.

She blew up on her bangs as she wrote, tapping her foot to the beat of the music that came from the radio on top of the book shelves, and humming under her breath. The apartment was cool, she was back in business, if only temporarily; and she was happy.

On Thursday she called the switchboard at North American International Underwriters and asked for Andy. He came on the line immediately.

"This is Penny. I'll be finished with the Modiglianis by tomorrow morning. Could you have the next crate sent over?"

"So fast! You really know your business, Penny," he said with admiration.

"Thanks for the compliment, but you know as well as I do that there was almost nothing wrong with that crate. All I had to do was touch up the frames and put new backing on the pictures. The crate nearest the door in the warehouse showed a lot of water damage, and so did the one behind that. Why don't you have Mercurio bring me one of those? Then I'll have the weekend to get started on the works that really need some attention."

"I'll call him right away. Tomorrow afternoon is all right for a delivery?"

"After two would be best. Are you still coming to dinner with me on Saturday?"

"You bet I am," he answered with more enthusiasm than he had evinced when she first invited him. "I'll be there at seven. And Penny—"

"Yes?"

"I had a very nice time at lunch the other day." Andy's voice was shy and, even though she couldn't see him, she suspected he might be blushing slightly. She wondered what his office looked like, if perhaps he had a nice view of New York Harbor from the window. She tried to imagine that he took off his jacket when he worked and showed his red suspenders to the other personnel in the office, but the picture would not come clearly to her mind.

"So did I, Andy," she said in a quiet voice.

When she hung up the telephone, Penny experienced a tiny thrill of anticipation. She hadn't felt excitement before a date in quite awhile and the feeling was pleasant. It made her feel like a teenager.

"Cool it," she told herself. "He's not your type. He's a stuffy old insurance man." Nevertheless, she looked forward to Saturday, and she hoped her friends wouldn't be too outlandish in front of Andrew Keller.

All of Friday afternoon passed without a sign of Mercurio Gutierrez. With growing irritation Penny waited for him, not wanting to call Andy and get Mercurio in trouble with his employers, but also not pleased to be stuck waiting for a delivery that seemed less and less apt to arrive as the hour grew later. It never crossed her mind that Andy might have forgotten to pass along her request for a fresh carton of photoreproductions. Andy wrote everything down in his black notebook; unlike Penny, things did not slip his mind.

Finally, at half past four she called NAIU's switchboard to find out what had happened, but Andy wasn't in the office either. The operator informed her that the office closed at three on Friday afternoons in the summer, and to call back on Monday morning if she wished to speak to Mr. Keller. Penny resigned herself to a weekend without any work to do, not an unpleasant prospect. She could always pick away at the Degas copy she was working on, she supposed, but she thought she'd go uptown to the Central Park Children's Zoo instead. The zoo was a much more fascinating place to spend a Saturday morning than her cluttered studio.

Then, after lunch, which would probably consist of two soft pretzels studded with coarse salt and eaten in the acrid smoke of the pretzel vendor's pushcart, she thought she might go down to the Seaport Museum on the East River and wander around the complex of stores where there was a Laura Ashley Shop. Maybe there would be some dresses on sale. She doubted it, even though the end of the summer season was near. Too many tourists with money to burn went to the Seaport Museum for the merchants there to bother with sales. She knew the Seaport Museum would be jammed with visitors from all over the country, but the wind that blew off the always turbulent East River was refreshing, and one food store there carried a wonderful selection of the freshly-baked cookies she loved.

She didn't mind making plans to spend a Saturday alone. Although she had a great variety of friends she could have called to join her on her outing, she was a loner at heart, and had passed many a weekend exploring her adopted city by herself. Tomorrow shouldn't be any different. But she wondered as she straightened up the studio, which, suddenly and disconcertingly, seemed in much greater disarray than usual, what Andy did with his Saturdays.

Chapter Four

With the exception of the winter season, Andrew Keller played softball in the park every Saturday morning on a team of University of Pennsylvania graduates—all Wharton men like himself, who had been meeting informally since long before Andy had worked his way through college. Dressed in a school T-shirt and warm-up pants, he was poised to go out the apartment door when the telephone in his neat, modern kitchen rang.

"Drat!" he said out loud, continuing to open the door, but hesitating with his hand on the knob. What if it were Caroline on the line? He flushed uncomfortably at the thought of Caroline. Never before had he lied to her; never before had there been reason.

The phone rang again. And there was no valid reason for him to have lied to her, he told himself guiltily, except that he had wanted to accept Penny's invitation to dinner. When he explained he would have to be out of town for the weekend, tying up some loose ends in the art reproduction case he was handling for the firm, Caroline had been understanding and gracious. She hadn't questioned him at all and had only commented that Tampa seemed a strange place to send him when the stolen shipment had come from Germany. He had agreed, and they had gone on to discuss other matters.

The telephone shrilled once more. Andy wasn't a man to let a phone ring, no matter what the consequences. Taking the chance that Caroline trusted him implicitly, he let the heavy door slam and ran to the receiver which hung on the wall next to the stove.

"Dieter here," barked a curt voice.

"Yes, sir?" replied Andrew, mentally snapping to attention and practically saluting, but with a successful attempt to keep the surprise from his voice. Dieter had never called him at home. No one from the office ever called him at home. He steeled himself for bad news.

"There's been a break-in at the warehouse. Get down here immediately!" Dieter slammed down the phone.

"Yes, sir," said Andy to the dead receiver. He dropped his catcher's mitt on the counter and ran to the bedroom to pull on a pair of slacks and a striped cotton shirt with a button-down collar. He slipped his wallet into his pocket and was out the door in three minutes.

The warehouse district seemed completely deserted that Saturday morning. In front of the building in which NAIU rented space, two automobiles—a dark limousine with tinted glass and a nondescript panel truck—sat in the already blistering sunshine. But aside from the two vehicles, the street was empty of movement—with the exception of the multicolored scraps of litter that blew lazily in the hot wind from the river.

Letting his cab go, Andy rang the night bell at one side of the door and was admitted to the darkened building almost immediately by a uniformed guard who told him to go directly up, using the stairs he and Penny had descended the time he had brought her to the warehouse. Rounding a corner at the top of the echoing stairs, he saw Dieter, elegantly dressed as always, engaged in conversation with a small, dapper man with thinning, gray hair. Spotting

Dieter's attire, Andy flushed with irritation, wishing he had taken two more minutes to don tie and jacket. Dieter was a short man, muscular and compact, and he dressed nattily, almost seeming to strut as he walked. That morning he wore a somber business suit which fit him like a glove, but he had made a concession to the weekend—he sported a neatly tied ascot. Dieter was given to terse, forthright, and usually opinionated statements and was not the least interested in another's opinion.

Whenever he was around his boss, Andy always felt as if he could do nothing right.

"What took you so long, Keller?" barked Dieter, without preliminaries, as soon as he spotted Andy coming toward him. Despite his fluency in English, Dieter was still unable to pronounce his *W*'s. Andy ignored the question as unworthy of answer since a scant twenty minutes had elapsed since Dieter's imperial summons. He approached the two men, wiping his right palm which was damp with nervous apprehension, on his slacks. He hated to present a perspiring hand for a shake of introduction, but Dieter did not acknowledge the presence of the other man who stepped back a pace or two into the gloom as Andy neared.

"What happened, Mr. Dieter?"

"What does it look like? As any fool can see, the cage has been entered," responded Dieter impatiently.

"How did this happen? How did they get in? Is anything damaged? Have the police been informed?" asked Andy.

"Those matters have been attended to," said Dieter curtly. "You are not to worry. We need from you the disposition of the shipment. The crates have been counted, and two are missing. Those that remain have been, as you see, vandalized."

Andy entered the cage where the crates were stored. The floor was strewn with splintered wood and brown paper.

All the crates had been pried open, the frames pulled out and thrown haphazardly on the floor of the large cage, and the brown-paper backs of the works had been methodically slashed. The pictures themselves appeared to be unharmed.

"There doesn't seem to be much damage," said Andy, slapping his hands together as he emerged from the cage to the aisle where Dieter awaited, tapping one shiny black shoe impatiently on the gray cement floor. "There must be a book in which they log the deliveries and pickups. Have you asked to see the log?"

"Go downstairs and find out," ordered Dieter.

Andy raced down the stairs to the office where he found the guard seated with his feet up on a desk. At Andy's request, the guard shoved the log across the scarred oak surface toward him, and Andy quickly paged through until he came to the warehouse activities of the previous week. There was a small smile of satisfaction on his lips as he took the stairs, two at a time, back to the third floor where Dieter, now alone in the cavernous room, awaited him.

"Nothing missing," Andy announced triumphantly, only slightly out of breath. "The restorer has the other two crates. The second one was delivered on Friday."

"Who is the restorer?"

"Greenaway and Ackerman, in the Village."

"Very good, Keller. Take care of this mess," said Dieter, and he headed for the stairs without another word. Andy stared after him. His Saturday was ruined. Where would he find workmen to clean up? Were there employees here at the warehouse to fix the torn and gaping chicken wire? And how about a new lock for the door? The old one had been twisted and battered, before the thieves had given up and cut the chicken wire. Then, on Monday, he would have to locate a new warehouse. This one, as Penny had told him in the beginning, was hardly secure.

Andrew Keller knocked on the door of Penny's apartment at exactly seven o'clock on Saturday night. It had been a race to arrive on time, considering that most of the day had been spent supervising the cleanup of the warehouse, but he had made it. Andy believed in rigid punctuality.

As he waited for her to respond to his knock he shifted the gallon of Almaden wine he carried to his left hand and touched his throat self-consciously with his right. He was unaccustomed to going out on a Saturday night without wearing a tie and, even though he had a feeling a tie would be inappropriate among Penny's friends, he felt almost naked with his shirt left unbuttoned at the collar.

Andy never had trouble choosing what to wear. Never before, he amended, until that evening. If he and Caroline had gone out to dinner that Saturday night, he would have worn a suit, a tie, even a vest if the weather had been cooler. Tonight he had chosen a madras sports jacket and coordinating slacks, but somehow he didn't feel that the madras would meet with Penny's approval. Well, if it didn't, he was certain she would tell him.

The door to the apartment opened, and Penny stood there dressed in a lacy white cotton nightgown. He had just checked his watch, so he knew he wasn't early. Obviously, and not to his surprise, she was one of those women who was never on time for anything. Andy believed in punctuality, but he knew he wouldn't mind waiting for Penny. He wouldn't mind waiting as long as she needed.

"Come in, Andy," she said with a welcoming smile that lit up her hazel eyes clearly, despite the thick fringe that surrounded them. "I'm all ready to go, but if you'd like a drink first, I have some wine."

"You are?" He stared at her attire. He was certain the gown she wore was meant for sleeping, but she really did seem ready to leave. She wore subtle makeup—a bit of pink rouge that matched the color of her lips, and a touch of muted turquoise eye shadow. The waistless gown was white with a lacy, square neckline through which a pale turquoise ribbon had been threaded. The dress, if that's what it was, stopped midcalf. On her legs she wore sheer white stockings, and on her feet tiny turquoise silk shoes with matching bows. She had the most incredibly small feet.

"Isn't that. . . isn't that a nightgown?" he choked.

"Yes, but I shortened it. Do you like it?" She pirouetted around in the narrow hallway to show him the full skirt of the cotton gown "I bought it this afternoon. I was looking for a dress, but everything's so expensive at Laura Ashley, I thought I'd try a nightgown instead, not that they were giving away the nightgowns either, I might add." She took him by the hand and drew him into the studio. "I know you gave me a nice retainer, but I had a lot of bills to pay. I'm trying not to spend it all before I take care of my obligations."

"It's lovely, Penny. You look lovely." She *did* look lovely, like a model in the out-of-focus pictures they used to advertise romantic perfumes. In the cloud of curls on her head, she had affixed a large white bow that made her look like a Victorian schoolgirl.

But she smelled even better than she looked. She was wearing the same perfume he had noticed the first time he met her—roses and jasmine and something else that reminded him of the smell of walking in the woods after a rain shower on a summer afternoon.

"You won't be embarrassed to go out with me in this outfit? Not like the harem pants?"

"The harem pants were very nice, too, Penny. Just a little, uh, just a little liberal for my taste."

"I know. You're really sweet, Andy, the way you worry about what will happen to me on the street."

"You can't be too careful," he replied seriously. "A

beautiful girl like you—there's always someone who'll take advantage of a defenseless woman." He realized, to his surprise, that he would be extremely upset if anything happened to Penny.

"I'm not defenseless," she told him quickly. "I know karate."

"You *do*?"

"Well, I don't know if I really know karate or not. Janie and I took a course in karate when we first came to New York, but I've never had an opportunity to try out what I know."

"Some opportunity," he said. "Pray you never have to find out."

"You're right. Do you want to go? Or shall we have a drink here first?"

"Let's have a glass of wine first," he answered. He wanted to be alone with her before he was forced to meet a room full of strangers. "Shall I open the bottle?" He held up the heavy gallon of chilled wine which was still in his arms and which was perspiring through a brown bag which had wrinkled in the humidity.

"No, save it for later," she said, taking the bottle from him and setting it down carefully on the work table. "I bought some wine today; I hope you'll like it."

He sat on the Hollywood bed since there was nowhere else to sit except for one stool that had been pushed into a corner, and he looked around the studio. The place had been neatened up so much that he barely recognized it as the same apartment he had first seen early in the week. Of course, the room was still a working studio, but the easel with the Degas painting had been removed, the coffee cans were gone, and even the windows appeared to have been washed from the inside.

"Here," said Penny returning to where he sat with two

mismatched glasses in her hands. "Try this and tell me what you think. The man in the liquor store told me that a wine connoisseur would like this wine. It's called, uh, just a second. I'll have to go out to the kitchen and check the bottle."

"No, wait," said Andy, putting out his hand to take the glass and changing his mind, wrapped his fingers around her wrist instead. The skin of her wrist was soft and silky, just as he had known it would be. The wrist itself was so small that he imagined he could have wrapped his hand around it twice, if he had been so inclined. He gently pulled her toward himself. "Sit down, Penny. Let's just enjoy the wine."

She sat on the bed next to him, her slight weight hardly making a dent in the mattress. He wanted to lean closer to her, drawn in by the elusive fragrance of her perfume, but he stopped himself. Carefully she handed him one of the glasses, a jelly jar with red pineapple decals affixed in a circle half an inch below the rim.

"I haven't seen a glass like this since I was a kid," he said pleasantly, not even irritated that she was serving him what purported to be a fine wine from a jelly jar.

"I know. It's an antique—flea market style. I have a whole collection of them. I think they're kind of funky, don't you?"

"Yes, funky," he agreed, never before having had occasion to use the word, although suddenly very aware of its meaning. The whole situation was funky—the nightgown, the wine which he immediately recognized as a white Chianti, and the eccentric apartment Penny lived in half-a-story below the streets of Greenwich Village.

The apartment seemed suddenly hot to Andy. He raised a hand to his collar, thinking automatically of the Chinese man who did his shirts, but his collar wasn't tight nor starched; it wasn't even buttoned. He glanced over at the air conditioner, certain that it was not functioning, but he clearly heard the hum of its efficient motor in the room.

"I tried to call you at the office yesterday," Penny said, "but no one was there. You get out early on Fridays."

"Yes, in the summer. Everyone was leaving early anyway, to go to the beach and such, so the brass gave in and voted for early closing." But Dieter was going to change all that, thought Andy; Dieter was planning to whip the entire department into unparalleled efficiency with the early closing one of the first perquisites to go. Thinking of Dieter reminded Andy of the telephone call he had received from his boss that morning. If he had left just five minutes earlier for his softball game, his entire morning and afternoon would not have been ruined. On the other hand, a softball game was a small price to pay to stay on Dieter's good side.

"The warehouse was broken into last night," he said before Penny could explain why she had telephoned him. "The paintings were rifled."

"The crates? Whatever for?" She took a sip of the Chianti and put her glass down on a table next to the bed.

"Nothing was stolen."

"Of course not. There's nothing worth stealing, like I told you before."

"But every crate was pried open, and the backs of all the paintings were slashed," he said. "They cut right through the wall of our storeroom with wire cutters."

"Andy, if the pictures are slashed, I can't repair them," Penny exclaimed, disappointment evident in her voice. "You'll have to get new photographs from wherever they came from. It's one thing to fix a tear in a canvas, and quite another to tape a photograph back together. Rats! I knew this job was too good to be true. Do I get to keep the retainer anyway? I hope so, since it's nearly all gone already." Penny stood and walked over to a radio which sat on the book shelf, turning it on and adjusting the dial until some rock music that Andy didn't care for filled the room.

"Don't worry; the job goes on as usual. Dieter, that's my boss, and I went through them all. Only the paper backing is slashed. The front of the paintings are in good shape."

"Alleluia!" she said happily, returning to his side. He watched a frown settle over her profile. "That's the weirdest thing I ever heard of. Who cares about a bunch of repros? First, they're hijacked, then someone cuts them up. What's going on, anyway?"

"I can't imagine," he said. "We're moving them to a more secure storeroom, of course, and I—"

"First hijacked, then—are you certain none was stolen?"

"No, they're all accounted for between what you have here and what's left in the warehouse." He looked over at the crate of Modiglianis which rested against the wall as Penny went to the kitchen and returned with the bottle of white Chianti, filling Andy's glass nearly to the rim of the jelly jar.

"What's that big frown on your face for?" she asked him.

"Nothing," he answered, not wanting to bother her with business, and with his worries that Dieter might find his handling of the case inadequate. Such a simple case, too—only a hundred thousand dollar claim—and yet the headaches were piling up faster than a snowdrift in Vermont.

"There's nothing to worry about, Andy. It's just a fluke. The thieves probably broke into lots of the cages in the warehouse."

"No, only ours. And, don't forget, there was the hijacking of the entire shipment from Kennedy Airport."

"Not the only hijacking from Kennedy, I'm certain. Lord, sending a shipment through JFK is like pouring it through a colander. Everything gets hijacked there. That was just a coincidence. I'm certain you'll find the thieves broke into your shipment by accident. The repros have no value, Andy. Take it from me."

"I suppose," he said doubtfully. He drank some Chianti. "This is fine wine," he said distractedly. "Lots of body for a white wine."

"I'm glad you like it." Penny flushed happily. "Ready to go?"

He followed Penny up the stairs. They had taken a taxi to an address on East Fifth Street that she gave the driver, and Andy had watched aghast as the neighborhood changed from the colorful jumble of Greenwich Village to an area that looked like Dresden after the Allies bombed its streets. Broken glass and burned-out cars littered their path. It worried him that she frequented neighborhoods like the one through which they drove. He told her so.

"What do you expect, Andy?" she had said. "Apartments are expensive, and the people who live here are struggling artists. They don't want to leave the city, but they can't afford anything better until they make it big."

Generations of tenants had eroded the marble steps of the tenement building they entered, until the center of each one was worn in a deep groove on which it was difficult for Andy to keep his balance. Andy prayed the party wasn't taking place on the top floor, whatever floor that was, since he was already out of breath and they had just passed the third. . .or was it only the second landing? The floors were numbered European style, with what he thought of as the second, being marked as the first. He watched Penny's trim ankles and calves as she went up the staircase ahead of him. For a girl who drank only Coke for breakfast, she was in remarkably good shape. And shaped remarkably, he added silently.

"Here!" she said at last. "Shall we rest?"

"No, I feel terrific," he lied. He shifted the gallon of wine, now as heavy as five gallons, to his left arm. He tried to keep his breathing normal, although he longed to take big gulps of the hot, humid air of the dark hallway.

"Why don't you take off your jacket?" she suggested. He looked at her closely, but her face was innocent of guile. He wasn't able to decide if the jacket embarrassed her, or if she was only concerned with his reaction to the long, five-story climb.

Penny opened the scarred door of the apartment, letting escape the full force of a beating drum the thick, reinforced wood had barely contained, and the sweetly-sick smell of what he took to be some exotic incense that rolled toward them in a cloud of wispy smoke.

Andy followed her through a narrow corridor and into a room whose walls were painted florescent orange, and whose woodwork was a contrasting florescent green. He blinked at the flash of a strobe light mounted on an easel in one corner. The bursts of light kept time with the music that came from an intricate stereo system against the window wall. Other than the strobe, the room was dark, although summer night had not yet fallen outside, and the windows were covered with black paper.

He knew he should have invited Penny out to dinner in a restaurant.

"Meet your hostess, Andy," said Penny, leading him toward a woman in a black caftan who appeared to have pink hair. He could have sworn the hair was pink, although it was difficult to tell in the intermittent light. Not only pink, he decided, but combed so it stood straight up from her head. He missed the name Penny shouted in his ear.

She took him around and introduced him to the eight or ten other guests in the room, all of whom lounged on low couches or mattresses which lay on the floor. He didn't hear anyone's name. Finally, she stopped to talk to someone, and he broke away from Penny and carried the gallon of wine to a kitchen that opened off the narrow entrance hall of the apartment. The room was quieter than the main room, although the strident wails of a woman singer still blared from the stereo speakers.

Andy had no desire to spend an evening in the apartment with people to whom he couldn't talk because of the weird noises that passed for music, eating food that was probably not up to his standards of hygiene. He looked doubtfully around the cramped kitchen, discovering that what looked like a counter was in reality a wooden palette on hinges that fell down from the wall to cover the top of an ancient bathtub.

"Are you opening the wine, Andy?" asked Penny from the doorway.

"Umm, er, yes," he answered, his back to her, making a show of breaking the plastic seal on the bottle.

"Anything wrong?" She came into the room and around him so she could see his face.

"No, no. Everything's fine, Penny."

"You're fibbing," she answered. "You hate it here."

"No, it. . .it's very interesting."

"Let's go," she said. "Let's get out of here."

"But your friends, what will they think?" he asked, trying not to sound as relieved as he felt. "We can't just leave. What about dinner?"

"They were just going to order a couple of pizzas, I think. They won't even know we're gone. C'mon," she urged him, pulling him by the arm. "I made a mistake bringing you here. I'm sorry."

"We could take a ride on the Staten Island Ferry," Penny suggested. "Have you ever?"

"No, never," he admitted. He signaled their waitress for the check.

"It's a terrific thing to do on a nice night. There's a wonderful view of Manhattan."

"You're a very romantic person, Penny," Andy said in a quiet voice. His blue eyes had a faraway look in them that seemed almost out of place on his serious face.

"Do you think so?" She looked directly into his eyes. He wasn't as shy as when she had first met him, she realized, because it was Penny who lowered her gaze first, assaulted by an unfamiliar ripple somewhere in the middle of her breast.

"You don't belong with people like that," he said, not bothering to explain to where his thoughts had jumped. It didn't matter anyway; she knew whom he meant.

"They're very nice, really," she defended, but only half heartedly. "They're trying to recapture a little of the flavor of the sixties, I think. You know, like the Woodstock Generation."

"No, what's that?"

"The Woodstock Generation? Nothing important." She had felt guilty all evening, ever since she had realized how out of place Andy must have felt at the party. Bringing him there had been a spur of the moment decision which she had begun to regret almost as soon as the invitation was out of her mouth. Not that she hadn't wanted to see him on Saturday night, but at the time she extended the invitation, she had wanted to prick the balloon of his stuffiness. He was too young and too attractive to be such a serious person. He reminded her too much of the boys she had left behind in Wilmette. She wondered if he ever did anything spontaneous like run down the street just to feel the wind in his hair. It didn't count if there was a bus on the corner you wanted to catch.

Andy had been so sweet to her when he arrived at her apartment. She knew he had been shocked by the thought that she would go to a party in a nightgown, although there was nothing immodest about the cut of the neckline or the density of the cotton of which it was made. In fact her nightgown, which shortened she preferred to think of as a midi-dress, was uncannily similar to the white, lace-bedecked dresses of the romantically garbed women who waited on the linened garden table where they sat. Shocked or not, Andy had been gracious and even complimentary about her toilette.

And then, at her friends' apartment, she had known immediately from the quickly covered look on his face what a mistake she had made in bringing him there. She also realized that he would have stayed as long as she liked, making polite conversation whenever he had to, showing himself to be a gentleman to the tips of his fingers, and she had decided right then that she had been horrid to bring him to a place where he would look foolish. She still felt a little sick from guilt when she thought of what she had done.

She looked around Barbetta, the restaurant in the West Forties Andy had chosen for dinner. She had to admit he had really fine taste in restaurants, in food, and in the wine he had ordered to accompany the cold whole trout, marinated until it was tart, that he had ordered for her. What a change to have a man take care of her! And surprisingly pleasant.

Andy had ordered duckling for himself. He had even offered her a bite of the rich meat, its strong flavor cut by a pungent, clean-tasting lemon sauce, and she had discovered yet another side to him when he admitted shyly that he was a cook himself, duckling being one of his specialties.

For dessert they shared a chocolate mousse. The waitress had not remembered to bring an extra plate and spoon as requested, and they had laughingly eaten the thick, dark, bittersweet mousse from the same spoon. Carefully Andy had removed a fallen puff of whipped cream from Penny's chin with the spoon, and to her surprise, he ate the cream and pronounced it the most delicious part of dinner.

"I haven't been on the Staten Island Ferry," he said, "but I'd rather take a walk after this meal. May I walk you home? Is that too far for you to walk?" Andy signed the check which, although she tried not to look, Penny saw was substantial. He added a tip which equaled fifteen percent exactly.

"No," she assured him. "I love to walk in New York." She stood and smoothed the front of her white gown. "May I have a penny? I want to make a wish." He followed her gaze to the round fountain in the middle of the back yard courtyard of Barbetta. Four fat angels carved of stone perched on the edge of the fountain standing guard.

"Sure," he agreed, digging into his pocket.

She turned her back and tossed the penny he gave her over her left shoulder toward the turquoise water, where it landed and sank with a delicate splash.

"Is it bad luck to tell your wish?"

"I wished to come back here again," she answered. *With you,* she added silently, looking into his eyes. "If it works at the Trevi Fountain in Rome, maybe it'll work here, too. Why don't you try a coin, too?"

Andy, slightly embarrassed, pulled a quarter from his

pocket. Acutely aware of what the sophisticated diners on the gracious patio would think, he tossed the coin over his shoulder. The quarter missed the fountain and rolled away from them, slipping underneath the table of two elderly matrons who smiled indulgently at the couple.

Penny took his arm as they left the courtyard and returned toward the street door, passing through the elegant restaurant on their way.

"It doesn't matter that your coin missed; it's the wish that counts," she said.

"Do you think so?"

"Of course." She gave his arm a squeeze.

They walked directly across town to Fifth Avenue before turning south and window shopping along the thoroughfare above and below Forty-second Street, which divided Manhattan's atmosphere with its invisible line. Above Forty-second Street was all that was new and chic and trendy. Below stood the established, the fashionably genteel, if passé shops. They crossed Fifth Avenue again and again in order to look in the window of whatever shop intrigued them, so that by the time they reached MacDougal Street in the Village they were footsore and giddy from the walk.

"Your shoes will be ruined," Andy told her.

"I know," Penny giggled. She bent over and took off her shoes, carrying them in her hand for half a block. At the corner she pitched them, one at a time, into a trash basket. "Now we won't have to worry about them anymore!"

"But your stockings..."

"I'll take them off, too," she began.

"No, no, that's all right," he told her quickly.

"Stuffy man," she laughed, taking his arm and walking close to him. She had entertained no intention of taking off her stockings. Did he think she was crazy? She'd never walk barefoot on MacDougal Street. She had just wanted to see what he would say to her suggestion, and he had not disappointed her.

They climbed the steps to her apartment building hand in hand. The entrance door, as usual, was unlocked. Penny was so accustomed to finding the door ajar that she thought nothing of it, although the tenants had complained again and again to the superintendent of the danger of an unlocked foyer. Inside the building they descended the steps that led down the half-story to the entrance of her apartment studio. She handed her key chain to Andy so he could unlock the door for her.

She wanted him to kiss her, but she doubted that he would. He was so reserved and quiet that she imagined she would have to go out three or four times with him before he dared kiss her, although she knew he was attracted to her. There was something in his eyes that told her he was.

He took the keys from her hand, but he turned his back to the door and looked at Penny instead. She tilted up her chin to see him in the dim light of the hallway. The blue, blue shade of his eyes—Copenhagen blue, she confirmed again—seemed to deepen dramatically in the light, and she tried to see the tiny gold flecks that marked the irises, but the hallway was too dark to make them out. His eyes were coming closer to hers. She liked those eyes; she liked the way they were serious at times and she liked the way they relaxed into a smile at other times. There were tiny wrinkles made from the sun at the edge of each eye, wrinkles that bespoke time spent outdoors, and just a shade of evening beard had begun to grow on his cheeks. She reached up and, with two fingers, brushed the suggestion of rough stubble on his firm jaw.

At her fingers' touch she felt a thrill shoot through her

body, almost a shock of electricity that shook her to her stocking-covered toes. She blinked her eyes in surprise. She had touched him before. She had regularly taken his arm since they had met, had allowed him to grasp her elbow and guide her. She had even pinched his cheek before, but nothing like the lightning bolt that had shaken her just then, had happened those times.

Very carefully she touched his face again. She shut her eyes quickly. The shock had been no mistake.

Penny swayed slightly as her knees weakened and threatened to buckle beneath the weight of her body. She held her breath as she felt Andy's hands encircle her waist and pull her gently but insistently toward him. She raised herself up on her toes and tilted her head farther back without opening her eyes. His face was coming nearer to hers; she could feel the warmth of his skin as he lowered his lips to her waiting mouth; she could even smell the faintly sweet whispers of the wine they had drunk with dinner as his lips came closer. There was another smell of him, too, the smell of crisp, clean laundry dried in the summer sun.

But, oh, so slowly he approached her! She longed to throw her arms around his neck and crush his mouth to hers, but she held back in deference to him. He was shy; he was reserved. If he wanted to take his time kissing her, she had no intention of spoiling the kiss.

At last, very tentatively, his lips brushed against hers. She imagined those gentle lips on her breasts, and a shiver went through her. She felt her body open to him, and she slowly let her arms crawl up his lapels to slip around his neck. His lips found hers again.

The kiss was long, soft at first, and then more insistent. She felt her lower lip caught up in his teeth. He nibbled her lip, and as he did, she touched his teeth with the tip of her tongue until his tongue sought hers, tentatively and then demandingly, forcing her mouth to open farther under the pressure of his and then, more urgently, searching out the delicate, tingly places of her mouth.

She inhaled his breath; and he hers. There was just enough air for two to share as if they were one person. Penny fit her body to his; felt his chest against the softness of her breasts, felt her nipples harden under the smooth cotton of the white dress, felt a series of tiny pulses burst into life all over her body.

She pulled her head back a fraction of an inch. Air, she needed air. She took a quick, shaky breath before his head followed hers, and she returned his kiss instead of remembering to breathe. Dizziness assaulted her, and she leaned against Andy's firm body, pushing against him as he pulled her small body even more tightly to his.

Suddenly, there was no Andy.

"Damn!" he yelled from the floor.

"What happened?" She grasped the door jamb for support. All the blood seemed to have left her head, to have flown away when his lips were wrenched from hers.

"The damn door was open!" he swore. Penny looked down to where he sprawled on the floor of her apartment, just inside the front door.

"Are you all right? Did you hurt yourself?" She knelt at his side.

"I'm fine. Penny, the door was open. Don't you understand? There's been a break-in here."

"No, Andy. I probably forgot to lock the door. I do that sometimes."

"I locked the door," he said. "I know I did."

Chapter Five

Andy pushed her roughly out of his way and scrambled to his feet. He found the light switch by the dim illumination that came from the bulb in the hall and turned it on with a flick of his hand.

"You stay here," he ordered Penny gruffly. "And don't come in until I call you. That's an order."

"But—"

"Do as I say, I tell you."

"All right," she answered meekly. He certainly was an alarmist, she told herself with assurance, positive he was one of those New Yorkers who had paranoia honed to a fine art, who looked for muggers and burglars under every street lamp. She was sure that nothing had happened to cause worry. The building was not secure, yes, but despite everything, she had never heard of a robbery taking place in the brownstone since she had lived there.

Nevertheless she obeyed him complacently, happy to let Andy take charge, and she leaned against the plaster wall outside in the corridor while willing her breath to return to normal. For a somber, serious insurance man, he certainly knew how to kiss! She longed to splash some cold water on her face which burned in the aftermath of their prolonged embrace.

"You can come in now," Andy shouted from within the apartment. "But don't touch anything."

"What happen—" Penny took one or two steps into the studio and stopped right within the door to survey the apartment, her eyes wide open in shock. "It looks like a tornado went through here!" she cried.

Clothes and canvases lay strewn across the floor. The jars of solvent and coffee cans which she had lined up neatly on a shelf, now lay on their side, their liquid contents spilled at random wherever they had fallen. The warehouse crate was tipped crazily back against the wall, and every picture had been pulled from inside. Three Modigliani nudes lay on the Hollywood bed. Others were propped here and there throughout the square room, their brown paper backing hanging in tattered ribbons and shreds on the floor.

"I'm calling the police," Andy said as Penny climbed over one frame and approached her dresser which stood at right angles to the bookcase in the far corner. She tugged at a reluctant drawer, the one at the top left of the maple dresser.

"My jewelry—such as it is—all of it's right here," she said. She held up a glass box trimmed with brass which had rested inside the drawer. "I don't have much good stuff, but even my watch is here." She stuck a hand into the drawer and felt around the back. "Even my money. I always hide a little under the lining of this drawer for emergencies. They didn't even touch my money. Maybe we scared them away?" she asked in a quiet voice.

She cleared a space for herself on the bed and sat, stunned, while Andy called the police. A vision of walking into her apartment and catching a drug-crazed burglar in the act of ransacking her dresser filled her head, and made her legs tremble with fear. There was no telling what might have happened if they had come home ten minutes earlier—if she had come home alone...

"We didn't scare them away," Andy said, hanging up the telephone. "There's only one way out of here, right? You have bars on all the windows."

Penny nodded.

"So they came in and out the door. They were gone long before we got here." He crossed the room and went to the front door. He was gone only seconds before returning. Penny watched the scowl that darkened his face, as he picked his way across the debris that littered the floor. He sat down next to her and put one arm around her shoulder. The madras cotton of his jacket was soft where it touched the skin of her neck. She leaned against his strong arm, wanting the strength of his calmness to flow into her limbs.

"You're trembling," he said gently, tightening his hold on her. "There's nothing to worry about, the police are on their way, but you can't stay here tonight. The lock has been broken...forced open."

"What does anyone want with me?" she asked with eyes wide open. "Only some of my equipment is worth the trouble and look—the camera's still there, the light box, everything portable. Why would anyone—?" Her voice was high with nervousness. The thought of what might have happened haunted her imagination, and made her hands shake with the delayed adrenaline of fear.

Andy took her chin in his hand and turned her face toward him so she was able to look into his blue eyes, and take comfort from the strength she saw in their serious depths.

"You'll come home with me tonight," he said. "Tomorrow I'll call a locksmith and have the locks replaced."

"But—"

"And I don't want you to worry about money. I'll fix it

so that NAIU pays for everything. I'm certain this break-in is related to the trouble at the warehouse."

"But—" She was going to remind him that she had keys to Winnie's upstairs apartment, that she would be perfectly safe two stories above where they sat, but Andy interrupted her again before she could speak.

"No buts. Penny, you're not safe here. I'd never be able to forgive myself if anything happened to you," he said earnestly.

"Well,—"

"I'll be a perfect gentleman, if that's what's worrying you," he cajoled. Between his eyebrows two lines of concern furrowed the skin. He was so earnest, so solicitous that her heart melted.

That's what's worrying me, she thought. *A perfect gentleman is not what I want you to be.*

"Maybe you're right," she gave in.

Andy gave the report to the two uniformed police officers who arrived within twenty minutes of his call to the emergency number. Their polite concern surprised Penny who had heard nothing but stories of police indifference and cruelty ever since she had lived in New York, but who had never before had occasion to deal with "New York's Finest" as they were commonly called by the citizenry of the five boroughs that comprised the city.

"There's nothing we can do," said one, the tallest and stoutest of the pair. "We'll file the report, but since you say nothing was stolen, there won't be any action, I'm afraid. You tenants have to lean on the landlord to fix the street door."

"I know," answered Penny.

"And get a good lock for your door," he continued. "One of the new combination jobs is best. That way you won't need a key to get inside. Sometimes speed is important.''

Penny, who stood leaning against her worktable, envisioned herself running from a mugger, being followed into the building, punching out a combination that would open the door to her safe haven, but forgetting the correct numbers to her own combination. She shivered again.

Seeing her tremble, Andy crossed the room and put his arm around her shoulder once more. She leaned against him for comfort.

When the police had gone, they turned off the lights and left the apartment in darkness, pulling the door closed behind them as best they could, and hoping that lightning wouldn't strike twice in the same spot. After all the excitement, Penny mused, a second burglary would not surprise her that much.

They took a taxi uptown to Andy's apartment which was located in one of the anonymous and enormous modern buildings faced with white brick in the East Eighties, hugging the shores of the East River. A uniformed doorman greeted Andy, but not by name. Andy led Penny to one of three separate banks of elevators that flanked the marble-floored lobby which was decorated with coordinating couches of taupe-colored leather and with low, square tables of glass and chrome.

''Big place,'' said Penny as they waited for a car to descend to the lobby. She had counted six separate closed-circuit television screens as they passed the doorman's alcove.

She knew Andy's apartment would be as austere and neat as the lobby. As late as it was, Andy still looked as if he had just stepped out of the shower. His shirt was still crisp, and even the madras jacket he wore was unwrinkled and neat.

Inside his apartment he turned on two lamps and went to the built-in air conditioning unit that ran beneath the windows to adjust the controls while Penny looked around at the band-box neatness of the living room. All the furniture was modern and sleek—a nubby wool couch, a streamlined teak coffee table with a neat stack of magazines topped by *Fortune*, and modular bookshelves the length of one wall. Television, stereo, video cassette recorder—Andy owned all the most up-to-date amenities, but everything was in quiet good taste, as befit his personality.

"I'll sleep on the couch," he said. "You can have my bed."

"I couldn't do that," Penny said. "I'm shorter than you are. Can I borrow a T-shirt or something?" She had put on another pair of shoes at her apartment, but she hadn't wanted to spend time changing her clothes, anxious as she was to leave the place.

She sat on the couch and ran her hand across the pebbly wool which irritated her hand pleasantly. "Could I have a drink or something? I'm—I'm...in great need of sedation after all the excitement tonight." *Not liquid sedation, either,* she said silently.

"Sure, of course, how thoughtless of me not to offer you a drink." She knew from his voice that he was nervous, as nervous as she. The kiss at the door to her apartment had been one isolated incident. Now she sat in his living room, on his couch, about to take off her clothes and don one of his shirts—an entirely different situation. She wondered how shy he actually was, and she had no idea how to approach him.

Penny followed him to the long, narrow kitchen which was outfitted with a dishwasher, a microwave oven, and a stove and refrigerator, so sleek and modern they made the appliances in her studio look like flea market antiques.

Down the center of the ceiling, a large stainless steel rack had been installed, and from its hooks hung a set of matte black aluminum pans, a copper colander, a large fish steamer, and various specialized pots whose function she did not recognize.

He really was a gourmet cook, she realized, noticing a magnetized wooden strip on the wall above the counter which held razor sharp carbon knives from Germany, the same brand of knives her father gave a boring little speech about each time he prepared steaks for his ritualized barbecues down by the swimming pool in the back garden.

Andy handed her a balloon glass of brandy, poured one for himself, and led her back to the couch where they sat an awkward eight inches from each other. The memory of his kiss weighed heavily on Penny's mind, so heavily, she was having trouble breathing in a regular pattern. She watched his hand, the way the long fingers wrapped around the clear glass, warming the brandy within, the way his grip seemed to tighten on the fragile crystal until she thought it might break in his capable palm.

"Andy . . ." She blinked the fringe around her eyes.

"Mmm."

"Would you kiss me again?" she asked in a quiet voice.

He sat the glass down atop *Fortune* magazine and took Penny's from her hand to do the same, sliding the eight inches toward her as the glasses clicked together on the table. She kept her eyes open as he neared her, watching the light in the deep blue irises that illuminated his face come closer, wondering at the sudden, crazy, paradoxical attraction that had drawn her so undeniably to this man who represented every conservative aspect of her upbringing which she had gone out of her way to reject since she had been on her own.

They moved toward each other without a smile, without

a word, the only sound in the room the soft, monotonous hum of the central air conditioning's fan under the window. Even his arms did not move as he leaned his face down, so their lips could touch. He did not touch her with his hands. Only their lips met, and with his gentle touch, Penny felt the flame of desire light within her, as if his mouth were a match he had touched to the dried kindling of her lips. Penny's efforts to sit still made her even more keenly aware of every nuance of his kiss, and she feared that he would hurry, because she wanted to enjoy the touch of his lips on hers.

His tongue was teasing the sensitive skin on the outer edge of her upper lip, gently probing the smooth area where it met her lower lip. She opened her mouth a mere fraction of an inch, and his tongue sought its entry, inserting itself until it met the tip of hers. Only a touch, a gentle touch, to soothe and cool the fever that had begun to rise in her body and reflect its erotic light in her open eyes.

She felt his arms slip around her waist and draw her body toward him. Willingly she ran her hands across his jacket, and then underneath, her palms sliding on the starched surface of his cotton shirt. She pressed her fingers against the firm, hard muscles beneath the cotton, the muscles of a strong man who valued the shape of his body. Her hands slipped up around his neck and pulled his head closer to hers, impelling his mouth more tautly against her own lips. His tongue was far-reaching, like an explorer in a new land, seeking out the secret places that opened before him, stirring the nerves there.

She felt his hand on her leg and she inhaled unevenly as he slowly pushed the full, lacy skirt away and ran his fingers up the white stockings, first one leg, then the other, so slowly that she thought he would never find the pale blue garters which held the stockings to her thighs.

But he did, and she leaned back against the pebbly wool of the couch, her lips still glued to his, as he rolled the stocking that covered the left leg down over her ankle and off her foot. Then he began with the right garter, rolling and rolling as if his hand were part of a slow-motion dream in an underwater fantasy. The cool air that blew from the fans tickled and chilled the exposed skin of her thighs, covering them with goose bumps. She shivered almost imperceptibly, until his palm returned to warm and caress the silky skin of her legs, rekindling the fever that lurked just beneath the skin awaiting the soft and gentle touch of his fingers.

She held his head like a cup between her hands to drink long gulps of his sweet breath which smelled more of him than of the brandy they had sipped. His breath smelled of him, yes, but a new smell, one of desire that hung on his lips like musky flowers in a sun-dappled forest.

Then Andy broke away from her and took off his jacket. He began to open his shirt, his fingers in his hurry fumbling with the tiny buttons.

"Let me," she whispered, and her words were so hoarse that she barely recognized her own voice.

"You don't want to sleep on the couch," he whispered in return as she opened the buttons, his mouth next to her ear, his head buried in the fluffy curls of her hair. She shook the curls gently.

"Not unless you'll be there, too," she answered softly. On unsteady legs she stood and pulled her dress over her head, leaning forward to finish tugging it off, exposing, as she did so, the line of her back underneath a loose, satin teddy trimmed with lace that covered her breasts and skimmed across the outward curve of her hips to end high on her thighs.

She turned to face him at the sound of his quick intake

of breath. He had already removed his shirt and his slacks, and he stood staring at the richly shining platinum colored satin with the light of desire dancing in his eyes. His lips were slightly parted, and she could see the tip of his tongue as it touched the bottom of his teeth.

She had been wrong about his shorts, she thought inanely; they were white with a thin dark-red stripe running through them, but Penny had no time to consider her error because he was already kneeling in front of her, his head buried in her thighs as his palms caressed the smooth fabric that covered her hips. He mumbled something into the sensitive skin, and the warmth of his breath sent shivers up her legs, through her womb, and along her torso to kiss the nipples of her breasts which hardened immediately beneath the silvery satin underwear she wore.

"Your tattoo," he was saying. "Where is your tattoo?"

She laughed, a high musical note that lingered in the quiet room. "I was only teasing you," she said, running her fingers through his hair. "Only teasing," she whispered.

Andy stood.

"I'm disappointed," he confessed, but his eyes didn't seem to be unhappy. On the contrary, he looked more alive, more vital than Penny had ever seen him, and a new fullness softened the sometimes angular lines of his face.

In one motion, he lifted her quickly and easily and carried her into the darkened bedroom, where he gently put her down on the bed. He straightened and pulled off his shorts, and then he lay next to her, his body extended the entire length of hers on the maroon coverlet. He wrapped a foot around one of her ankles, as if he feared that she would change her mind and leave his bed.

"I knew this was going to happen, didn't you?" she asked him quietly.

"No. But I'm happy it has," he replied in a low voice. "How does this thing come off?" he asked, referring to the satin teddy. His voice quivered, but she decided it was not insecurity that had changed its timbre. Already he was a strong and enticing lover, more forceful and sensuous than the Andy she had known before. She had never imagined such a seductive person lurked beneath his serious exterior.

"I'll do it," she offered.

"No, please. Allow me."

"Little snaps," she explained. She indicated the closure between her legs where her thighs, slender and white, gleamed in the light that streamed in from the living room.

He eased her thighs apart, raising one leg so that the knee was bent and her heel rested on the bed, and he touched the closure. Penny gasped. She shuddered in response to his fingers as he slowly opened the snaps. She heard the minute, sharp click of all three in the stillness of the bedroom. He lowered his head until his lips were directly above her, and she felt the heat of his breath hover over her intimately, imagining with the touch of his exhalations on her sensitive skin that he already had entered her. His lips brushed against her, bringing with them a thrill, almost a shock of humming electricity, that bolted through her limbs and kissed every finger and toe.

"Andy, Andy," she whispered.

He slid his body up along the bed until his face was near hers. In the dusky light she knew he was smiling, and she traced one finger down the side of his face, feeling for the angular bone of his cheek and the upturned edge of his lips.

One of his hands tugged at the satin teddy, pulling it gently away from her skin, rolling it up so first her abdomen, then her two small, but rounded breasts were exposed to his gaze. The satin fell to the floor with only a whisper, and his lips were on her breasts, his tongue delineating a path from one hardened nipple to the other, the light beard on his chin at times scraping roughly, but not unpleasantly, on the valley between her breasts. She felt the soft inner skin of his mouth close over her left breast at the same time that his hand stroked the bare skin of her abdomen leaving a trail of fire in its wake, and she felt the air cool and kiss the path his tongue had by then abandoned between her breasts.

"Penny, I want you so much. I've never wanted anyone like I want you," he said in a low, hoarse voice.

She put one hand on his back and drew him to her until their torsos were pressed together, and she felt his desire rub against her—hard against her.

"So do I, so do I," she repeated.

He covered her with his body and entered her finally. As if in a dream, she raised up to meet him. They moved together, and it seemed they had made love a hundred...a thousand times before in the voluptuous darkness of the room where they lay. He wrapped his arms tightly around her, and she did the same, offering him the deepest recesses of her body, running her hands up and down the muscles of his back, pulling him hard against her breasts and her throat and her hips, as if she could never get enough of him in her.

She wanted to swallow the essence of him within her, wanted him to do the same with her, wanted to become as one with him. His breath was warm on her face, on her mouth. They inhaled the same air, sharing its oxygen, breathing the same murmurs of passion and endearment that said nothing and meant much more, intoning the words at the same moments.

She discovered what made him groan, and he, what made her cry out with delight. It was as if they had always known those secrets about each other.

And then, suddenly, she cried out in the darkness as he transported her higher and higher to new levels of an ecstasy she had never before thought possible. Behind her closed eyes there were tiny red pinwheels of light which grew ever brighter until each one burst in a series of explosive sensations that shook her body as he carried her up and over the peak of the mountain they had scaled together.

Penny lay still beneath him as the waves ebbed away slowly with only their muted echoes returning now and then, lapping at her to send a delicious shiver through her limbs. Andy still rested atop her body, but his weight was not heavy. Instead his body felt warm and protective and loving.

She felt vaguely on the edge of consciousness when Andy rolled off her and lay at her side, one arm beneath her body, the other free to caress the side of her face with a gentle hand. She was hardly aware when he slid off the bed and pulled the spread and blanket from under her, rearranged the sheet to cover her body, and returned to her side. He nestled his head in the crook between her neck and her shoulder, and she listened to his breathing become more regular, matching the rhythm that had returned to hers.

If he was quiet, Penny thought nothing of it, because she wanted the security of his arm thrown protectively over her just as it was, and there was no need for words. If there was a tiny little frown between his brows when she opened her eyes for one last look at his face, she rubbed it away with a gentle finger. She turned slightly toward him in the darkness and slept.

Chapter Six

Andrew Keller always went out early on Sunday morning to buy fresh croissants and a copy of the *New York Times*. When he awoke as usual at seven, even before he opened his eyes, he felt silky soft curls tickling his nose, he smelled the essence of roses and jasmine, and the events of the previous night came back to him in a rush which filled him with renewed desire.

Penny was curled up in a compact ball, sleeping with her head on his shoulder, her body nearly sideways on the double bed, and her tiny hands relaxed in a half-open position. He turned his head to look at her. Flat morning light filled the room, yet it still cast the shadows of her incredible eyelashes on her full cheeks. Her mouth, naturally pink, was open slightly, and her breathing was deep and regular.

Slowly he extricated his shoulder and raised his body, lowering his feet to the floor, and sitting for a moment, head in hands, to assess the situation. She moaned quietly as he moved and turned on her left side. He reached across with one hand to arrange the sheet over her shoulders.

He didn't know how they had ended up in bed together so quickly. It wasn't that he had forgotten a single detail of the previous night. He remembered everything, all right; his memory was working perfectly, so perfectly that his body was alive with a throbbing desire that grew stronger the more he thought of her, the more he looked at her asleep in his own bedroom. He remembered the way she had looked at him with those enormous hazel eyes, a desire that matched his written in the depths of her pupils. The way she smelled when he kissed her—the evocative mixture of lipstick, of brandy, of roses and jasmine, and of a certain other essence of desire—on her soft lips. He remembered the silky smoothness of her skin, the inward curve of her upper arm, the bone just above her knee on the inside of her leg, the contrast in texture between the satin of her hip and the satin of the flimsy little something she had worn under her dress. He remembered removing the insignificant scrap of fabric that covered the mysteries of her body, slowly rolling it up to reveal the gentle swell of her abdomen, the little mole on her upper stomach, the round fullness of her small and perfect breasts. He remembered kissing the little mole that had fascinated him from the day they had first met.

Her chemise lay on the floor at his feet. He picked it up and crushed it between his hands. The satin released the fragrance of Penny, which floated up to his nostrils and renewed the utter drunkenness he had felt when he parted her legs. . . .

Andy buried his head in the satin.

He thought of how she looked that morning. She seemed so small, so vulnerable, in the middle of the double bed. The light that came through the east window silhouetted the seductive line of her hip. He stood, barefoot and naked, and walked to the window that overlooked the East River, Riker's Island on the other side, Queens even farther away across the Triboro Bridge. The day was overcast with the gray haze that accompanied some very hot, very humid August days on the East Coast. He looked at his expensive view, but he saw nothing. Two lines wrinkled the brow between his eyes.

Andrew Keller had always been a faithful man. Never married, true, but not the kind of man who was able to go out with one woman and carry on a love affair with another—or another and another, as some of his friends did. He had eschewed the singles scene, the awkward meetings of the "in" places, many of which were located in his own neighborhood, the East Eighties where fashionable singles lived and congregated in singly-directed groves. He had always been faithful to Caroline, although he and Caroline had not yet come to a formal arrangement, and he was certain Caroline was faithful to him.

He couldn't imagine that Caroline had ever deceived him. Unlike many men who sought their pleasure where they could, but whose egos would never allow them to believe that their wives and girlfriends were capable of the same desire for variety, Andrew knew that Caroline was faithful because she was basically disinterested in sex. Not frigid, not cold and unyielding, not prudish, but at heart not a sensual woman, not a woman who gave herself over to the transporting, magical, almost mystical experience that sex with someone you loved could be.

Loved. Someone you loved. He whispered the words aloud in the quiet bedroom. Love was the problem, after all.

He looked over his shoulder at Penny once more. Her bare arm was extended on the bed, the tiny hand hanging over the side almost to touch the clock radio on the bedside table. The fingers were curved, so that from where he stood at the window he could see the one flaw in her soft and yielding and incredibly receptive body, the ragged fingernails.

How could he love her? He hardly knew her; they had

met only a week before. She wasn't his type, nor he hers. She was too carefree, too liberal, too uninhibited for him to ever be comfortable with her. Her friends, her apartment, her personal habits left much to be desired. She would drive him right up the wall in forty-eight hours if he let her into his life.

The meticulous Caroline, on the other hand, represented every pathway he sought for his future. He and Caroline had everything in common except perhaps their backgrounds. They liked the same people, the same restaurants, the same game of paddle tennis in the winter where she beat him as often as not. Caroline meant a proper position in a proper firm and, when the workday was over, a proper home to come back to.

With Caroline he could look forward to raising two point three proper children—boys, of course—seeing them through the correct preparatory schools, and matriculating them at his alma mater, the Wharton School of the University of Pennsylvania. Andrew, their proud father, would pay every single penny of the tuition. No scholarships for need, no after-class jobs at the local dry cleaners, pizzeria, or pool maintenance company. His boys would not have to work their way through school as he had. His boys would not be outsiders in a world of insiders, the poor boys on the block, the sons of the landscape gardener who cut and groomed the lawns of the rich Pennsylvanians who inhabited Bryn Mawr, Gladwyn, and the other elegant towns on the Main Line. His boys would hire the gardener.

Yes, Caroline.

Andrew Keller went to a Danish rosewood dresser on one wall and opened a top drawer, extracted a pair of shorts from the neat pile that lay there next to his fourteen pairs of identical black ribbed socks, and began to dress. He pulled on a pair of the black socks, chino slacks, and a striped rugby shirt. He slipped his feet into loafers and went out the door of the apartment quietly, allowing the door to click shut behind him.

On the other hand, he thought as he walked to the corner bakery that baked fresh croissants for the Sunday singles crowd, if one of the two point three children should happen to be a girl, he would hope she looked just like the rosy-cheeked gamine who lay breathing quietly in his bedroom high above Eighty-third Street.

"Breakfast is ready," Andy called from the door of the bedroom.

Penny had been awake for some time, although she lay on the bed listening to the busy noises and smelling the delectable aromas that came from the kitchen while her thoughts turned over the events of the previous night.

She sat up in the bed and ran her fingers through the disheveled curls on her head. She yawned and stretched, allowing the sheet to fall to her waist. Andy still stood at the door watching her. Covertly she watched his eyes in an effort to determine his mood. The Copenhagen blue eyes that regarded her so thoughtfully were soft with the memory of their lovemaking the night before. She recognized the look; she felt the same way. She smiled.

"Do I have time to get dressed?"

"No, it's on the table," he smiled.

"I have to eat naked?"

"Well...." The bell of a timer in the kitchen rang, and Andy left the doorway. On a chair near the door lay the shirt and slacks Andy had worn the night before. She put on the shirt, went to the bathroom to splash some cold water on her face, and came out into the living room barefoot.

Andy held a chair for her at the table which sat in an

alcove in the L-shaped room. She glanced at the table which was set with a sunny yellow cloth, a basket of croissants, and two glasses of freshly-squeezed orange juice. He removed a cover from the plate at her place setting to reveal two perfectly poached eggs under a velvety smooth hollandaise sauce.

"A girl could get spoiled," she said.

"Even a girl who prefers Coke for breakfast?"

"Even that kind of girl." She began to eat with relish. "You made this sauce yourself? Delicious." Andy nodded in confirmation, his mouth full.

"I see you have sailing magazines," Penny said, tilting her head toward the coffee table. "Do you sail?"

He nodded again.

"Where?"

"Wherever I can. I've taken courses. I've been to the Caribbean with some friends. We chartered a boat a few years ago and sailed around the islands. Have you ever been sailing?"

"No, but it sounds like fun. Scary, but exciting. I'd like to try sometime. You aren't what I expected you'd be, Andy, although I should have guessed from the red suspenders."

"In what way?"

"You're more...more adventuresome than you look, I guess I'd say. And sexier," she added mischievously to see if he would blush for her.

He did.

Penny found his feet under the table with her own. He looked up into her eyes and, at his look, her heart melted and a feeling of warmth shot through her with such force that her legs went weak. There was just the beginning of a smile around his lips.

They ate in silence. She figured he was thinking the same

thoughts as she, running the memories of the previous night through his head.

"What are your fantasies, Andy?" she asked suddenly. His eyes opened wide and he choked on a sip of orange juice. At the look on his face she hastened to explain, "Not *that* kind of fantasy. I mean, what would you do if you won the lottery? If someone handed you a million dollars? What would you do if you didn't have to work?"

"I'd buy a boat and sail around the Caribbean," he said without hesitation. "Around the world maybe."

"Really! Oh, I love it! I never thought you'd say that," she exclaimed, although she hadn't decided what she expected him to say.

"Why not?" The blue eyes seemed slightly offended, as if he had revealed a part of him that he wished to keep secret from her, but that he needed to defend once he had made public its existence. "I even had a savings account earmarked just to buy a boat."

"Had? What happened? Don't you have the account anymore?"

"Yes, I do, but that dream will never work. You get so involved in adult life sometimes you just have to let your dreams go for a while. Maybe someday..."

"When? When you're seventy? Andy, you should do what you want to do, and to hell with responsibilities."

"Penny, you're hopelessly romantic. That's what I love—" He cleared his throat. "That's one of the things that makes you so attractive."

"I'm glad you think so," Penny smiled, fluttering her eyelashes in response to what he had almost said. "Why did you stop saving for a boat?"

"I'd never have enough," he answered.

"You don't need a lot to buy a boat. A little down,

promise the bank your soul for the rest of your life. Just like a house, isn't it?''

"Sure, but you need a job to get a loan. And if you have a job you can't sail around the Caribbean. Catch twenty-two, right?'' He was buttering a plump croissant. He had slipped off his loafers and was playing with her feet underneath the table.

"Wrong. You could charter out the boat in the winter season and sail around doing your own thing the rest of the year. I can see you now—Captain Keller on the poop deck. What's a poop deck, anyway? Such a weird word.''

"The quarter deck. In the stern,'' he added at her befuddled look. "In the back of the boat, Penny,'' he said finally.

"Why don't you do it? Go out and buy yourself a boat?''

Andy laughed. "I'm not much of a risk taker, I guess. I usually go for the sure thing.''

"But insurance is nothing if not taking risks,'' she argued. "What about the insurance business?''

"Calculated risks,'' he corrected. "Nothing safer.''

"And sailing all alone in the ocean?''

"Well. . . a little more dangerous,'' he admitted. "But if you know what you're doing, it's fairly safe.''

"Like most things,'' said Penny. "There must be ways to make a lot of money fast in the insurance business.''

"Certainly,'' he answered. "All illegal.''

"And you were never tempted? Come on, Andy, you can tell me. You told me your fantasy, one of your fantasies anyway, although I'm certain there are more.'' She cast him a significant glance and wiggled the toes of her right foot which he had taken into his lap as they talked and was massaging gently with his left hand.

"You don't know me very well, Penny, or you would

understand that I'm not that type of person. I believe in fair pay for a fair day's work, in loyalty to the company, in doing unto others, et cetera. I don't have any desire to cheat NAIU, or anyone else for that matter.''

''You give back the difference if someone hands you too much change at the store?''

He nodded.

''And you wouldn't buy a hot Cartier watch for forty-nine dollars, even if you were positive it wasn't a fake?''

''That's different,'' he said.

''In what way?''

''To knowingly cheat a clerk at a counter is to steal from an individual who is working to keep his belly full just like you. A hot Cartier watch... Do you think Cartier would miss one watch?''

''There are so many hot tank watches around my personal opinion is that Cartier themselves are selling them, but I see your point,'' she answered. ''However NAIU is a big company, isn't it? What difference would a little chicanery make?''

''Penny! I'm a loyal employee of NAIU. I would never—''

''I know, Andy. I was just trying to help you find a way to buy your boat. I know this will sound neurotic, and I don't want you to misunderstand me, but you remind me of my father in many ways.''

''How so?''

''He's a lawyer, but he hates practicing law. He's on the board of directors of his country club, but he doesn't like to play golf. He drives a Mercedes Benz sedan because my mother thinks it's the right car for him, but all the time he's eyeing Datsun 280 Z's and old Corvettes. You know what I mean?''

''Why does he do what he doesn't want to do? He

sounds like a man who could afford to buy and do about anything he'd like. Why does he make himself unhappy?''

"It's sad, isn't it? He thinks it's too late for him to get off the merry-go-round, and he's probably right. I can't imagine what my mother would do without her gold American Express Card or her fur coats.''

"And you? You don't live like your mother. What are your fantasies? I mean your aspirations for the future.''

"I only know what I *don't* want to be,'' she said firmly. Both her feet were in his lap now, and he was running his hands up and down her calves. Little shivers of delight followed his fingers. "I don't want to be in the Wilmette Historical Society, the Junior League, and the League of Women Voters. I don't want to take Junior to the orthodontist in my Mercedes station wagon and meet my sister, Helene, later for tennis and lunch at the club. I don't want—well, you get the picture. I don't want to settle down in Wilmette and spend the next thirty years trying to drive my husband into an early grave with my lifestyle.''

"Don't you want to get married?''

"Not on *their* terms,'' she answered.

"What are their terms? Who are they?''

"My mother, my father. What I just told you—shopping at Bonwit's and hitting the hairdresser every Friday at three. The Greenbriar in the summer and Palm Beach in the winter. A diamond and sapphire engagement ring from Peacock's.''

"What's Peacock's?''

"A jewelry store in Chicago.''

"Oh, like Bailey, Banks and Biddle in Philadelphia.''

"I don't know; I never heard of them.''

"They don't advertise. They don't have to.''

"Yes, like that.''

"So that's why you're here, living in the Village in that dive you call your studio,'' he said.

"It's hardly a dive," Penny objected, slightly offended. "I'm lucky to have all the space I do, and in such a central location."

"It's a dive," he repeated. "What's more, it's an unsafe dive."

"Maybe you're right. I'm going back to Chicago—back to Wilmette in the fall, Andy. I can't make it on my own without Janie. Even together we weren't making ends meet. If it weren't for NAIU's job, I'd already be packing."

"I know, Penny."

"I knew you had my whole situation figured out," Penny sighed. "You were a gentleman, though. If somewhat of a tough bargainer."

"I don't want you to leave," Andy said. "I don't want you to go back to the Midwest. We've only just met."

"I don't want to leave, either," she answered in a voice as quiet as his.

"I've called the locksmith already, but we don't have to be back at your apartment until two-thirty. Would you like to—" He glanced at the open door to the bedroom.

"Andrew Keller, I can't believe you would think of such a pastime while dirty dishes are still sitting on the table!" she exclaimed with a gleam in her eye that matched the light in his. Penny would bet that morning was one of the few times in his life that Andy ever left a dish unwashed.

"Screw the dishes."

Andy lay facedown on the bed. Penny straddled his thighs, her knees on either side of his hips, rubbing his back with long, sweeping caresses, each one of which made him groan in appreciation. She inclined her head and kissed the back of his neck, nuzzling her nose in the short hairs at the base of his scalp. At the same time, she slipped her hands under his arms and suddenly tickled him.

Swiftly he turned over and pinned her to the bed with his strong legs. She looked up into his eyes and smiled as he took her head between his hands, burying his fingers in the cloud of curls.

"You're wonderful, Penny," he said in a low, serious voice. "You're everything—"

The telephone rang at the side of the bed.

"Don't answer," she whispered.

The small frown that had made the two permanent crease lines between Andy's eyebrows reappeared as the telephone shrilled for the third time.

"I have to," he said with another groan. "It's probably Dieter."

"Who's that?"

"My boss."

He rolled away from Penny and, lying on his back, reached out for the beige telephone which rested on the table next to the bed. She followed him, rolling toward him to rest her head on his chest, high enough that her hair tickled his nose, and close enough to his face that she heard the voice of a woman come from the receiver, although she was unable to understand the caller's words. She stiffened slightly and held her breath. Under her hands which lay on Andy's chest, she felt him stiffen, too.

"Early this morning," he was saying in a tone of voice she did not recognize. "A very early flight."

The woman responded.

"It was too early to call you," he said defensively.

Penny didn't want to hear more. She scooted to the opposite side of the bed and reached for Andy's abandoned shirt which lay on the floor in a forgotten heap. Slipping it on without bothering to do up the buttons, she went to the bathroom and closed the door behind her just as he said, "I'm sorry about last night, too.... I can't. I have to see a client this afternoon.'' She tried not to listen, but the door was thin, and she heard him respond. ''At two-thirty.''

Penny turned on the shower full force. She stepped inside and let the water play on her hair and her shoulders.

He doesn't owe me anything, she tried to tell herself. *Anything at all.* She poured shampoo into her palm and began to wash her hair vigorously.

Why shouldn't a man like Andrew Keller—a good catch, as her mother would say—have another woman in his life? Why shouldn't he have ten other women in his life? Without doubt they were lined up around the block to see him. No wonder he carried his precious little black book which probably served to keep all the women at his beck and call straight. She tried to be reasonable and logical and modern, as she knew she should, but there was a new and unfamiliar ache in her breast while she adjusted the chrome shower head, so that the spray would sing out in forceful, needle-like jets that stung her skin and washed away the traces of shampoo that lingered in her dark hair.

''Penny, I'm sorry,'' he said as she came out of the bathroom wrapped in a sable brown bath sheet, another smaller towel around her head to keep her hair from dripping. He lay on the bed with both hands behind his head and the frown between his brows. A sheet covered his body.

''About what?'' she said with false gaiety. ''What's to be sorry about? I never thought you were a priest. Anyone who makes love like you do hasn't spent a lifetime celibate.''

''Let me explain—''

''And, believe me, I should know,'' she went on perversely, wanting to wound him, wanting to make him think he was no more than just another man in a series of lovers. Two could play the same game. ''Oh, yes, I should know.''

She turned her back on him and made a show of looking for her handbag, so he would be unable to see the tears that made her hazel eyes bright. She was furious with herself for what had happened to her: She had let herself fall for the earnest, serious man in the bed beside her, allowed her heart and her body to open to him.

And she had misread him totally, much to her own dismay. He had seemed so sincere, so utterly taken with her; he had seemed as hopelessly attracted to her as she was to him. The way he made love to her, the sweet endearments he whispered in her ear, had been so honest and sincere that she never had the slightest idea another woman lurked in the background. And not just any woman: a woman to whom he owed explanations. A woman to whom he felt compelled to lie about his Saturday night activities.

"Have you a comb to lend me? I can't find mine."

"On the dresser."

She went to the dresser and found the comb. Throwing the damp towel she had wrapped around her hair on the floor at her feet, she began to yank the teeth through her wet hair. As she combed she let the bath sheet fall to the floor at her ankles, but she ignored her nakedness and concentrated her gaze on her own reflection in the mirror that hung above the dresser.

Andy, also naked, left the bed. She stared at his tall, trim body as he came up behind her to slip his arms around her waist. At his touch Penny ceased combing her hair, her arms raised so that her breasts stood out high and lovely, and she trembled inwardly when he lifted his arms, crossing them in front of her so the hands cupped her breasts. Their eyes met in the mirror.

"I don't believe you," he said quietly. "You're only saying those words because you're angry and hurt. I don't believe that the beautiful lovemaking we've just shared is nothing but a one-night stand to you.''

''A lot you know!'' she answered. ''What an ego! You're a generation out of whack, Andrew Keller.'' She began to comb her hair again.

His deep blue eyes in the mirror clouded opaquely with hurt, and she had to tear hers away to avoid the sadness she read there as his skepticism changed to acceptance. Penny put the back of her hand to her mouth, wanting to retract the untrue, offensive words which lay between them, but his features had tightened, had grown cold, and the grim, tight smile she had seen before when they bargained in the warehouse over the price of her services, forced down the corners of his lips.

His hands dropped away, and he turned his back on her. Wordlessly he went into the bathroom and closed the door quietly behind him. She heard the shower start again.

She slipped the wrinkled Laura Ashley nightgown over her head. In the living room she found her handbag, the lacy blue garters, and the white stockings, the soles of which were dirtied from her ill-advised, carefree walk on the sidewalk of MacDougal Street the night before. She threw the garters behind an areca palm that sat in one corner of the living room and the stockings in the trash. She stuffed the platinum teddy into the tiny handbag, although the clasp wouldn't close. Paging unseeingly through the photographs in a sailing magazine she had found on the coffee table, she was ready to leave when he came out of the bedroom with his hair slicked down ten minutes later.

''Where were you on Friday?'' she attacked Mercurio when she opened the door of her studio and studied his innocent-looking face at eleven o'clock on Monday morning. She had been in a foul mood since the day before, since Andy had left with the locksmith after she had curtly turned down his awkward offer to stay and help her clean up the mess in her apartment. Even Winnie's cat had kept its distance when she went upstairs to feed him Sunday and again on Monday morning.

"Me? Was I supposed to be somewhere?"

"Don't play games with me, Mercurio. You were supposed to be here at two o'clock Friday. I waited around all afternoon for you. I have better things to do with my time."

"There must be some mistake, Miss Greenaway. I don't know anything about a Friday delivery."

"I asked Mr. Keller to have you deliver one of the crates to me on Friday. Didn't he tell you?"

"No, but he's a busy man," smiled Mercurio. "He probably forgot. You really got a nice place here, Miss Greenaway." He smiled flirtatiously with Penny, who wasn't buying the seduction of his liquid, black eyes nor his change of topic.

"He didn't forget. *You* forgot, didn't you? You were over in Jersey City visiting the Madonna of First Avenue, no doubt. He's upset enough right now about the whole job."

Mercurio looked worried at the thought that Penny might tell Keller he hadn't shown up on Friday. "I swear I wasn't in New Jersey! I swear!"

"With some other woman, then," she persisted. Penny had no intention of being victimized by Mercurio's erratic schedule for the entire duration of the job. She had to show him who was boss right from the beginning or she would be stuck in her apartment all day every time he was scheduled to make a delivery.

"Caramba," he said softly. "You got me, I guess. But I wasn't with a woman, not like you think. Well, maybe a woman had something to do with it. . . ."

"Women are going to be your downfall, Mercurio."

"Yes, I know. They already are. Please forgive me," he said. "I swear on the heart of the Virgin it will never happen again. I swear on—"

"Okay, okay," she laughed finally. He was impossible to stay angry with, and she could see how those flashing black eyes attracted the girl from Jersey City and anyone else for whom he turned on his considerable charm. "Get the crate in here. No, wait—you'd better take it upstairs. I don't have room for it yet; I have to do more work on these ten first. My place was broken into over the weekend, and the thief made a mess of the pictures." Penny had already begun to put new backing on the Modigliani reproductions, but she had finished with only two of them that morning.

She led Mercurio upstairs to Winnie's apartment where he rested the wooden crate against the wall in the front hall.

"What really happened to you?" she asked him on the way down the stairs. "Did you meet Marilyn Monroe on the street?"

"I should tell you yes," he laughed. "My reputation as a Latin forces me to agree with you. However, the truth is not so romantic, Miss Greenaway. I did pick up the crate for you on Friday, but on the way here I had to go to the bathroom. It's not so easy when you drive a van all day, you know. I bet you never thought of that."

"Correct," she agreed. "I never thought of it."

"There's a coffee shop on Houston Street where my brother-in-law works—"

"With a gorgeous waitress to flirt with, too, I'm sure."

"Yeah, you're right," he agreed with an embarrassed smile. "Her name is Petra. Anyway, I usually stop in if I'm in the neighborhood, and leave the van out front. My brother-in-law, he keeps an eye on the van for me. But Friday, when I came out, the van was gone.''

''Stolen?'' Penny's eyes were wide with surprise. If the van had been stolen from Mercurio, there were suddenly too many coincidences. The hijacking, the break-in at the warehouse, at her apartment... ''Something big is going on, Mercurio,'' she exclaimed with excitement. ''Somebody wants these pictures you've been hauling around awfully badly.''

''No, nothing like that. Of course, the first thing to pop into my head was what was stolen—and with the new crate of pictures in the back, too. But the cops had it. They towed it to the pier in the West Thirties where they take the illegally parked cars. I been down there all morning trying to bail it out.''

''Does Mr. Keller know? He's worried about the shipment. There've been problems at the warehouse,'' she said.

''No, nobody knows. Please don't tell him, either. The pictures are okay; the crate wasn't touched. I been towed twice before, and they said if it happened again I'm out of a job.''

''What about the van? Are you allowed to take it home for the weekend? What happened when you didn't turn it in on Friday night?''

''The dispatcher's a friend of mine. He owed me one, so he signed the van in for me, even though I couldn't go down to pay the fine and the towing fee until this morning.''

''You had to pay the fee yourself? Isn't that expensive?''

''Better than losing my job, I figure. Are you going to tell Mr. Keller?''

''I can't believe Mr. Keller would fire you just because the van got towed, Mercurio—even for the third time. He's not like that.'' Hadn't Andy said he would return an over-payment to a counter clerk rather than stick a lowly employee with a shortage? He would never sack Mercurio for a parking ticket. Well, maybe he would. What did she know? She barely knew Andrew Keller, she realized, despite the intimacy they had shared on Saturday night and part of Sunday.

''Not him, but Dieter, the big boss. Promise you won't say anything? I'll never be late again with your deliveries, I swear.''

''I know what it is to be out of work, Mercurio. I'll keep your secret, I promise.''

''Thanks, Miss Greenaway. Well, see you next time.''

''Hey, Mercurio—'' she called after him as he went out the door to MacDougal Street. He stopped in the brilliant sunshine and turned to face her. ''Are you certain the traffic police took the van from where you were parked? No one else?''

''Sure, I'm sure.''

''How long were you inside the coffee shop?''

''Fifteen, twenty minutes,'' he answered. ''The traffic police are fast, but just try to find a regular cop when you need one. Why do you ask?''

''Nothing, just wondering. It's all so strange. All this interest in a bunch of photographs.''

Chapter Seven

Mercurio was as good as his word. Even better, Penny discovered when he arrived two days later to pick up the Modiglianis and brought another crate from the warehouse.

"But I already have a crate upstairs, the one you brought on Monday," she told him. "I told Mr. Keller I wanted only a pickup."

It occurred to her that Andy might have misunderstood her request. She had spoken rapidly to Andy late the previous afternoon, hurrying through the words of instruction, rushing to finish the conversation so she wouldn't have to hear his voice longer than was necessary. And then she had hung up, pretending the conversation was finished, when she knew that Andy was about to say something personal to her. She didn't want to hear his excuses. She hadn't even wanted to talk to him. She had tried to leave a message with the switchboard operator, but was put through to Andy before half a dozen words were out of her mouth. The conversation, businesslike as it was, had made her breast ache because it reminded her of the feeling of deception she had experienced the previous Sunday.

"So what can I do? Take it back to the warehouse?" asked Mercurio. "It's past five already. The warehouse will be closed."

"No, put it over there against the wall," sighed Penny. "Oh, I suppose it doesn't make any difference which crate I get to first. We'll leave the other crate upstairs until this one is finished." Winnie would not return to her apartment for weeks yet. There was plenty of time.

Mercurio lowered the crate to the floor. As before, he took a crowbar and pried off one side. Idly Penny slid out a picture.

"Cézanne," she said, staring at the reproduction of a still life.

"Looks like a monkey painted it to me," said Mercurio.

"A lot you know," she said. "If it isn't a girl, you aren't interested."

"Now, you're talking. So long." Mercurio left, closing the apartment's door behind him.

The Cézannes were only a little worse than the Modiglianis had been. Two of the frames were slightly warped, so she removed their pictures and locked the frames into wood presses to straighten them out. While they were drying, she spent the next three days reaffixing the reproductions to the museum board where they had come loose at various points at the bottom of the illustrations in places that the paper had touched the damp frames. She put new backing on all the pictures because the paper had been uniformly slashed by unseen hands.

The more she thought of the break-in at the warehouse, the more convinced she was that it had something to do with the break-in at her apartment the previous weekend. Several times she went to the frames in the wood press and ran her hands over their edges, wondering what secrets they held. The pictures were worth nothing. The answer had to be in the frames.

While the Modigliani reproductions were still in her apartment, she had gone over every one of the frames, tapping them with a small tack hammer, shaking them, even weighing each one of the ten pictures on her bathroom scale to see if the weight varied from one to another.

In frustration she had taken one of the frames apart, but she found only that its construction was common. The wood was truly wood, not some valuable metal painted to resemble wood. The wood was not hollow, and did not offer any hidden recesses in which to hide a small, but valuable contraband.

The frames had yielded no secrets, no secrets at all, and yet Penny was certain that the mystery lay within her grasp. A hijacking and two break-ins were too much activity to be merely coincidence. Anyway, Penny didn't believe in coincidence. The only concession she was willing to give to fate was that Mercurio's van had been towed by the traffic police, and even that event worried her when she thought about it enough.

As she worked she tried to listen to the radio, but her thoughts wavered between the mystery of the frames and the previous weekend with Andy, although she tried to push memories of him from her mind, finding it painful to compare the ecstasy they had shared with the sick, heavy feeling that now lay in her stomach.

When it came to Andy, she believed in coincidence. Coincidence that she had met him just as she had resigned herself to leaving New York. Coincidence that he had given her a job which enabled her to stay a bit longer, get to know him a bit better. Coincidence that she had seen the same look in his eyes that she knew glowed in hers.

And then, like a dash of water in the face, coincidence that the woman—whoever she was—had called Andy while Penny was lying in his arms.

She wanted to be angry with him for seducing her under false pretenses, but she had to smile and chuckle out loud as she thought back on the sequence of events of that Saturday evening the week before. He had not seduced her. *She*, knowingly, had seduced him—not that he had been unwilling. And what a surprise he had been when he took off his Ivy League clothes. What a delightful, stimulating, wonderful, sensual, surprising man lurked behind his serious façade! She thought how deceiving appearances sometimes were in a world where people judged others by their clothes, their jewelry, and the hood ornament on the cars they drove.

Perhaps, Penny mused, she had been too severe in her response. Perhaps she should have given him an opportunity to explain who it was that called him on Sunday afternoons demanding explanations for his absence.

But, no, she shook her curls. Andy had been all too willing to accept Penny's harsh words, all too willing to believe that she fell into bed with the man of the hour, of the day, of the week. If he was used to seeing—and bedding—women like that, Penny was not the woman for him. Inexperienced she was not—she was twenty-seven years old, after all. She'd been on her own for many years. She'd had her limited share of love affairs that turned sour, but she didn't jump from bed to bed, nor did she knowingly go with men who did.

"I'll call you tomorrow," he had said instead of goodbye, and he hadn't met her eyes when he spoke. She knew what he meant. *Every* single girl knew that phrase. She knew she would never hear from him again on a personal basis. Things turned out the way they were supposed to turn out, she told herself, not too convincingly. She was slated to go back to Chicago, and Andy to the arms of the other woman. *Fate, ships passing in the night, any port in a storm,* she whispered the clichéd words as she worked. But too bad.

Penny switched off the hot press with which she was sealing the loose paper of one of the Cézanne reproductions, and stood erect, her hands on the small of her aching back. She knew there was nothing interesting in her refrigerator for dinner, so she decided to go out to the coffee shop on the corner and eat. She hadn't spoken to anyone in two days. Even a ten-word conversation with the Greek man who worked behind the counter at the coffee shop was better than the heavy silence of her apartment. From the sublime cuisine of Barbetta to the sometimes unidentifiable entrees of the greasy spoon of MacDougal Street was a stunning leap in one short week, she mused.

She took off her blue jeans and workshirt, and left them on the floor. After a quick shower, she stepped into a sleeveless, waistless, full-skirted summer dress festooned with tiny navy-blue forget-me-nots on a pale blue background. The dress was gathered at the bottom of its yoke, resembling a child's smock and, in it, she knew she looked about fifteen years old, if not younger, but it was the coolest dress she owned, and she knew the coffee shop would be steamy and close. Slipping her feet into sandals, she went out the door and walked to the corner swinging her cotton purse as she went along.

Above her, the sky was heavy with dark and swollen clouds, and in the distance she heard the rumble of far-off thunder over the Palisades in New Jersey across the Hudson River from Manhattan, but the air did not yet smell of rain, and she was certain she could eat and be back in the studio before the skies opened.

"One Number Seven Special and an iced tea," she said, closing the plastic laminated menu and laying it on the counter. "And a Bromo-selzer," she added under her breath. The usual counter man was not in the restaurant. In his place stood a finely featured young woman, whose dark eyes and fussily arranged hair had an old-world beauty. Penny decided that the waitress was probably another one of the endless supply of newly-arrived cousins, nieces, and godchildren with which the owner staffed the restaurant. As soon as the girl's English was good enough, she would leave MacDougal Street as all the others who preceded her had done. Off to start her own coffee shop, Penny assumed, like the rest of the family.

"What's your name?" Penny asked her.

"Maria." Her accent was heavy and her dark eyes enormous. Her legs, ending in sensible white shoes with crepe soles, were voluptuous and highly visible beneath the short, black dress she wore. *Have I got a guy for you,* said Penny to herself, thinking of the ever watchful Mercurio.

Maria put the iced tea on the counter in front of Penny and went to the other end to wait on a heavyset man in a shiny suit who had just come into the coffee shop and taken the last stool at the counter. Maria was back in a few minutes with a chipped white china plate containing a small Salisbury steak and a dollop of mashed potatoes, all swimming in greasy brown gravy on the thick oval.

Penny took a paperback book from her purse, laid it on the counter, and began to read as she tasted the potatoes and gravy. Sometimes it was better if she couldn't see what she was eating at the Parthenon Palace.

The rain began to fall in thick drops as Penny wiped her mouth with a paper napkin and laid a dollar on the counter for Maria's tip. She went to the door of the coffee shop and assessed her chances of getting back to her building before the drops turned into a deluge. The sky was nearly black now, and although true darkness would not fall for another hour, it seemed to be night already. Summer evening strollers had taken shelter from the rain, and the block was empty. The burly man, who had been the only

other customer at the counter, stepped around Penny and
held the door politely for her. Vaguely she noticed a
smashed, oft-broken nose and the stub of a dead cigar
clamped between his teeth as he passed close to her. He
made up her mind for her; she would make a run for her
own doorway, half a block away.

She stepped down to the sidewalk and took two quick
steps toward the curb just as a dark gray Cadillac with
heavily tinted windows pulled up, blocking her way with a
screech of tires. Annoyed, and already wet from the plump
rain scented with cordite that was splashing on the concrete
sidewalk, Penny turned to her left to sprint around the
long car.

"No, you don't," rumbled a gruff voice at her ear. A
strong arm went around her neck and another around her
waist. Without hesitation, with only the cold stab of fear
that the man's rough hold gave birth to, she thought of her
karate class. She leaned forward quickly and tried to throw
him over her head, just as the teacher had demonstrated
again and again, proving that a small woman was more
than a match for a strong, heavy man caught off guard.
But his left arm crushed her ribs.

So much for theory, she thought inanely as the two of
them went down on the sidewalk together in a tangled
heap. He was supposed to have sailed over her head while
she ran screaming down the block. Penny heard the sicken-
ing thud of bone against concrete, but she knew it wasn't
her bone, or at least she felt nothing but the heavy weight
of her assailant on her back. With a groan, she rolled away
from him, gasping for the breath which had been knocked
from her lungs by the force of the fall, and catching a
quick glimpse of the pockmarked face of the man who had
held the door for her in the coffee shop.

She crawled on all fours in an effort to get away from his

arms which had loosened their grip as they fell, but he lay on her skirt, one hand closed around the bunched fabric. She turned and grabbed at the cotton which tore away from the bodice, and finally the skirt came free from his grasp with a suddenness that nearly made her lose her balance again. She jumped to her feet. Her sandals were gone, and so was her purse, lying too far away in the rain-soaked gutter to reach, its contents scattered and rolling crazily about the street, but she was intact. The car still blocked her escape, and one of its rear doors opened just as she stood upright to gain her balance and run for her life. She crashed into the door of the Cadillac.

"Inside," said another voice.

She knew she should scream, but she was frozen. Unable to believe she was being abducted from her own familiar corner, her mind was a blank.

Wide-eyed, she opened her mouth to scream. No sound came from her throat. A strong arm reached out and pulled her toward the dark recesses of the car. The man on the sidewalk was up now, and he pushed her body roughly from behind. Penny fell onto the gray carpeted floor of the car. The opposite door opened and her assailant got in as the car took off down the street with an enormous lurch.

He put a gritty shoe on the back of her neck and held her head to the floor.

"You can't get away with this!" she screamed, her voice muffled by the abrasive loops of the carpet. Someone must have seen what happened. Someone—the waitress, the strollers on MacDougal Street. Someone had seen and copied down the license plate number, someone had called the police already. In seconds she would hear the wail of a police siren behind them. She strained her ears to listen.

"Shut up!" said the gruff voice. "You bitch, you broke my wrist."

"We're not going to hurt you, Miss Greenaway." A second voice was low—almost a whisper—with an odd, mechanical hoarseness that vibrated with a tinny echo. "We only want to talk to you."

"So call me on the phone. I'm in the book," she said with false bravado. "You know my name already." Her mind was working frantically. They weren't going to rape her, which had been her first fear. They knew her name, they knew where she was eating dinner. The heavy man had been waiting for her, watching her in the coffee shop. Maybe what the weird whisperer had said was true. Maybe they wouldn't hurt her. She began to pray—short quick prayers to Jesus that came back from her Sunday school days, simple, childish words of entreaty she didn't even know she remembered.

The car stopped. Penny tried to raise her head, but the shoe came down hard on her neck.

"Stay where you are," ordered the owner of the foot.

The car started up again, smoothly this time, and she realized they had stopped only for a traffic light. She tried to tell herself she was safe as long as the car was moving. No one would want a spreading bloodstain in the back of his Cadillac. What would they do with her body? Would anyone even know she was missing? She thought of her mother, so far away in Illinois, saying to her father, *I told you no good would come of her going to New York*. She thought of Andy. . .

"You don't want to see us," whispered the hoarse voice which she could barely hear over the hum of the engine of the Cadillac. "That's very important to you. Do you understand?"

"Yes." She had already seen the hefty man who jumped her on the street, seen his scarred face, seen his broken nose. She would see him again in her dreams, for a long time to come, if they let her live and dream. "I. . . I haven't seen anyone's face," she whispered. "I won't look, I promise." *Oh, Lord, get me out of this. I'll do anything You want. I'll go back to Wilmette, I'll join the Peace Corps, I'll become a doctor and work in the jungle. Anything You want.*

She tried to relax the screaming muscles in her neck by turning her face toward the front seat and resting her cheek on the gray loops of the carpet. In reward, the heavy shoe lifted slightly, but it still lay on the back of her neck waiting for a false move. She heard a heavy sigh, the scrape of a match, and she wrinkled her nose as the scent of cigar smoke reached her, making her want to cough. She struggled to quiet the unsteady rhythm of her breathing. She took two, gasping breaths of the frigid, air-conditioned air in the Cadillac, and the smoke-tainted oxygen in her lungs calmed her enough to accept the fact that she was their prisoner. With that thought, her body relaxed visibly, and her brain began to function.

"That's better," said the whisperer in his odd, sibilant tone. *A laryngectomy,* she said to herself. *He's had a laryngectomy.*

"Wh. . . what do you want?" Her voice quivered with fear, and one of her legs began to shake uncontrollably. She willed the muscles of her thigh to still, suddenly more afraid of her own fear than of any other threat. If she allowed panic to rule her, she would not be able to think, to react, to save herself. There must have been three of them: a driver, the man with the humming whisper, and the man in the coffee shop. They were too strong for her. She was in their car, at their mercy. She had no choice but to cooperate with whatever they wanted.

"We're just going to have a little chat about your work, and then we'll let you go," hummed the ingratiating whisper. "Rocco, take your foot off the little lady."

"The little lady broke my wrist," complained Rocco peevishly. But the foot slid off her neck and rested on the floor at the top of her head. Penny sensed the tension of the foot, ready to pounce on her if she moved her head an inch.

"The wrist is not broken, only bruised," croaked the whisperer as if he were a bored doctor doing triage in a hospital. "And Rocco, put out that damned cigar."

"Yessir," grumbled Rocco.

"What do you want?" mumbled Penny again.

"The Seurats," whispered the man. "I want the Seurats."

"I don't know what you're talking about."

"I think you do," he said, leaning so close to her that she could smell the sandalwood cologne he wore, and what he had eaten for dinner, as well.

She tensed at the menace in his voice.

"You have ten Seurat reproductions in your possession," he went on. "I want them."

"No, you're wrong. I have ten Cézannes. I don't know anything about Seurats. I've never seen any Seurats. All the other pictures are in a warehouse somewhere."

"Where?"

"I...I don't know. They used to be on Christopher Street, but I think they moved them somewhere else. I don't know anything." She began to cry softly. If she couldn't tell them what they wanted to know, perhaps they would kill her after all. "I swear!" she shouted through her tears. She had to make the evil whisperer believe her. "I swear I've never seen any Seurats!"

There was a terrible silence in the car, broken only by the monotonous thump of windshield wipers. They seemed to be driving on a long stretch of road without traffic lights then, the tires humming, almost singing under the carriage of the heavy car. Penny held her breath in the stillness, hoping and praying that she had said the right words, not knowing what the right words were, but feeling the truth was her only way out of the dangerous moment. She had never seen any Seurats; she hadn't seen the entire shipment. How would she know what was in the crates? Andy had told her some: Monets, Cézannes... She couldn't remember everything he had said about the shipment.

"But you will," the whisperer, still close to her ear, finally predicted ominously. "You will. And when you do, I want to know about it, do you understand? I want to know when you have the Seurats."

"Sure, of course," she answered quickly, exhaling all the stored up air in a long rush. "How can I tell you? How can I get hold of you to tell you?" They were going to let her go, after all. He needed her for some reason. She was going to live. For now.

"We will find you," he said. "We will be watching. And we will know if the police are involved. You wouldn't be so foolish as to contact the police. Would you, Miss Greenaway? I know you are too intelligent to do something as thoughtless and risky as that."

"N-no. No police," Penny confirmed. "Of course not."

"Good. You will be safe if you do as I tell you."

She heard the whisperer slide back on the ample seat. "I'm done with her, now. Put her out."

"Yes, boss." The foot at her head moved as its owner leaned forward and told the driver in a harsh voice to pull over. She felt the car change lanes, slow slightly, change lanes again, and roll to a stop amidst the noise of heavy traffic. "Keep your head down," he ordered her, "and back out of the car."

Penny obeyed the command willingly. She saw his

shoes, and she saw the shiny, black shoes of the whisperer in the dim light that came into the car from a street lamp somewhere above the car as she crawled backward on her knees which burned from abrasions she hadn't even realized she had. The whisperer wore sheer, gray-and-black ribbed socks that hugged his bony ankles. Never was she tempted to lift her head, never was she tempted to see the faces of her captors. All she thought of was the glorious surprise that they were actually letting her go.

She felt her bare feet touch cinders on the side of the road. The hard, pebbled surface felt like the clouds of heaven to her feet, like feathers, like a bath of scented oils. Then both her feet were on the wet ground, both her hands covered her eyes willingly, and she heard the steady fall of rain all around her as she stood blindly at the side of the car. She heard the door slam shut, and the roar of a motor as the Cadillac pulled away from where she stood, its tires hissing on the wet pavement.

She looked toward the sound and saw the rear end of a gray Cadillac with New Jersey plates merging back into streaming traffic, but already the car was too far ahead of where she stood to read the letters and numbers on the plate. The night was misty from rain, but far up ahead she could make out the glow of lights from the Triboro Bridge, and behind her she heard the rush of the East River. To her left, and not far away, lay the Fifty-ninth Street Bridge and the tram to Roosevelt Island.

She realized immediately that she was on the Franklin D. Roosevelt Drive, the highway that guarded the East Side of Manhattan, and that the men had left her on a narrow lay-by, off the northbound lanes of the heavily-traveled artery.

She lifted her skirt to look at her knees which were raw and bleeding from the fall on MacDougal Street. As she saw the abrasions for the first time, her knees began to ache. Before that moment, there had been no pain.

A car went by honking, male voices shouting at her in Spanish, and she jumped back, startled, from the edge of the road. The first priority was to cross the FDR Drive. With only the river at her back, there was no way to walk in either direction; she had to cross to get off the road in order to be safe.

Safe! Penny had thought she would never be safe again. She had thought she would never leave the Cadillac alive. Her knees went weak beneath her, threatened to buckle with the aftermath of the fear she had felt in the car. She was safe for the moment, yes; but she knew she might not be safe from the three men in the future. They knew who she was. They knew her name. They even knew where she lived, she realized with another cold assault of fear, and how to get into her apartment. It was they who had broken in the previous weekend. She was as certain as if they had told her themselves.

She saw a lull in the traffic. She raced to the median strip amid a cacophony of cars' horns and vulgar shouts from drivers. Climbing over the barrier, she waited for another lull to appear in the southbound lane. Broken glass sparkled wetly in the light cast by the rhodium lamps above her head. She stepped carefully to avoid cutting her bare feet, and when she thought there was time, she sprinted across the oily, wet pavement to safety on the other side. Once there, she found she could cross to a short ramp which slanted off the FDR Drive and onto an access road, and she discovered that she was not as far uptown as she had imagined. According to an orange and black street sign, she was only as far north as the East Seventies. She ran uphill on the street, heading for York Avenue, where she was certain she would find a police car in short order.

She passed the open door of a parking garage. Perhaps she should stop and call the police from there, she thought. The open doors beckoned her inside. But the threat implied by the words of the man with the whispering voice echoed in her head, and she knew that calling the police was the last thing she wanted to do. She was safe if the police weren't involved. Isn't that what he had told her? She would have to watch the streets carefully to be certain the police didn't stop *her*. She must look a sight.

She passed the door and kept walking toward York, watching her step to avoid glass on the sidewalk. It was one thing to walk down MacDougal on a lark and toss her shoes in a trash can in a grand gesture aimed at making a man think she was a madcap, and quite another to be forced to walk barefoot in a strange neighborhood in the pouring rain. As she walked she began to get angry.

By the time she reached York Avenue and stood on the corner near the showroom of Sotheby Parke Bernet, she was cold and wet and furious. *Why is this happening to me?* she asked herself over and over again, standing in the rain and trying futilely to make up her mind what to do. *All I want is a chance to do business without going broke.*

A taxi pulled up to the corner where Penny stood, certain that the driver had purposely aimed for the deep water in the gutter in front of her. She jumped back as the oily water splashed across the front of her dress.

The door opened and a well-dressed couple got out, leaving the door gaping as they left the cab.

"Another druggie," muttered the woman, brushing past her, but careful not to come in physical contact with the creature on the corner. The couple hurried off up York. Penny looked down at herself in surprise. Barefoot, soaking, her dress torn and soiled, she could imagine the state of her hair, plastered flat against her head. She probably looked like a drowned weasel. Just like what the woman had assumed—a panhandling druggie.

Andrew Keller got her into this mess; he'd damn well get her out of it, she said to herself.

"Are you free?" she asked the cabbie.

"Where to?"

"Eighty-third and York," she said, getting into the taxi.

"Just a minute, kid. You got any money?"

Money. No, she had no money. In her mind she saw her purse lying outside the coffee shop on MacDougal Street, a tube of lipstick and a pair of tokens spilling out to roll crazily in the gutter. "No, but when I get where I'm going, someone will pay you," she answered with an assurance she certainly did not feel, sinking back on the lumpy torn leather of the seat. She prayed Andy would be home, prayed the driver would let her stay in the back of the taxi and ride the ten short blocks to his apartment building. Short blocks in a taxi, she thought; long blocks to walk barefoot in the rain. If Andy wasn't there, she'd have the driver take her home, have him wait outside, and then she'd write him a check for the fare, doubling the amount in appreciation for his kindness.

"Yeah, I heard that already. Out," he said. "Out you go."

"Please—"

"Out!" he shouted in a menacing tone, turning to face her, the shadows cast by the light of the dashboard menacingly heavy on his dark, thick mustache and the roll of his beard-shadowed jowls.

Meekly she got out of the taxi, letting the door fall shut behind her. She turned uptown and began to walk, watching carefully for the blue-and-white patrol cars that cruised the streets, planning to jump into a darkened doorway if she saw one, and praying that none would spot her first. It was too far to walk to the Village, especially barefoot, so the plan to go to Andy's was still uppermost in her mind, but she resented every step that took her closer to his fancy building. The doorman would never let her in, she knew with certainty. Never in a million, trillion years, not looking the way she did. She stopped when she caught her reflection in a dry cleaner's window, and winced when she saw what she looked like, even worse than she had imagined.

Penny approached Andy's building on the wrong side of the street, purposely reconnoitering the situation. There was no doorman visible, but she knew he was inside in his electronic cubicle, watching one of the six television screens that flickered there. She stood across the street, half-hidden behind an illegally parked van for almost ten minutes, until finally she saw him come outside with a whistle in his mouth, his visored cap hidden underneath the protection of an over-sized umbrella. He started toward the corner, whistling for a cab for the couple that stood underneath the white awning, and as soon as he turned away, Penny sprinted across the street, into the warm yellow light of the lobby, and through the just-closing doors of an elevator.

She wasn't certain she remembered Andy's apartment number, but she was certain of the floor on which it was located and the direction in which the apartment faced. She thought she could pick out the right door without too much trouble.

Luckily, the tenants' names were on the doors, just under the black doorbell button. She put her ear to the door to listen for a moment, and a great surge of relief went through her as she heard music coming from the stereo inside.

Andy was home! And was he going to get a piece of her mind, she said to herself.

She rang the bell, three short angry bursts.

"Would you get that, Caroline?" she heard his voice call from the kitchen which was to the right of the door if she remembered correctly.

So, Caroline was it? She'd spoil his Sunday night date, his Sunday night seduction. She didn't care if ten Carolines were there inside the apartment with him. He owed her something for all the trouble he'd caused her, and she wasn't afraid to tell him so.

The door opened, and Penny found herself looking up into the placid brown eyes of a neatly dressed blonde six inches taller than she was. The woman stared at Penny as if she had seen something highly disagreeable. Her slightly aquiline nose wrinkled in distaste.

"What is this, trick or treat?" she asked.

"I want to see Keller," said Penny distinctly. "Tell him his client is here."

Chapter Eight

"Who's there at the door, Caroline?" Andy closed the door of the oven into which he had just placed a chocolate soufflé, and he walked toward the front hall of his apartment. Tonight was one of the rare Sunday evenings they spent together. Because Andy had felt guilty about lying to Caroline the previous weekend, he had invited her to his apartment for dinner in expiation for his deceit, and he had chosen the menu carefully, knowing that she liked showy dishes—desserts that flamed, meat wrapped in pastry, salads in fussy, decorated aspics.

When he cooked for company, his own preference was for Chinese food, quickly stir-fried in his weathered wok, but Caroline was lukewarm about his Szechwan and Hunan specialties, so he had deferred to her taste for the occasion, certain that eventually he would convert her to the glories of Chinese cuisine. She had enjoyed the meal he cooked, and they were waiting now for their dessert.

"Lord only knows," whispered Caroline, appearing at the kitchen door. "It's a young girl, and she looks like she swam to get here. She says she's a client," she added doubtfully.

Andy, habitual frown between his brows, slipped around Caroline, but as he did, Penny appeared right behind her.

"It's me," she said. Although making an obvious struggle for control, she burst into tears when she saw Andy.

"My God, Penny! What's wrong? Are you all right? What happened to you?" He threw his arms around her and, forgetting Caroline at his elbow, held her tightly. She sobbed against his chest. "It's all right, it's all right," he said softly, running a soothing hand over her sopping hair. "Who did this to you? I'll kill the son of a bitch," he muttered in a low voice, already imagining the worst. "What did he look like?"

"Andrew, who is this girl? What's going on?"

He felt Penny stiffen in his arms and draw away. Awkwardly, he dropped his arms.

He tried to introduce them, not knowing what to say. She had told Caroline she was a client, and the word stuck in his mind, so he repeated it to Caroline, but her brown eyes narrowed with skepticism, and there was a growing thundercloud on her face. He knew he would have some questions to answer later.

"I'm sorry," Penny was saying at the same time. "Can I borrow your handkerchief? I had to come here. I have no money, I lost my purse—"

"Just tell me you're all right," Andy said, turning away from the cold look on Caroline's features and handing Penny a white handkerchief he took from the back pocket of his slacks. "Come in and sit down. Let me get you a drink."

"I'm all right," said Penny before she burst into fresh tears.

"An-drew," said Caroline ominously, drawing out the syllables of his name.

He knew that tone; it meant trouble brewing, and he had to admit Penny's presence was awkward, to say the least. But he couldn't just ask Penny to leave. She looked terrible—pale and shaky, her dress soiled and torn, her face streaked with grime. Livid, red bruises on her upper arms were already turning blue. Blood on one of her legs. The dress gaped at the tear in the bodice, exposing the top of one perfectly rounded breast. Automatically, Andy pulled the fabric up to cover the skin. Penny gave him a grateful look.

"How did you get into the building?" asked Caroline.

"Just a minute, Caroline. Can't you see she's been hurt?" He took Penny by the hand and led her into the living room, settling her on the couch and sitting on its arm next to her. As she sat he saw the abrasions on her knees.

"Caroline, get her a brandy," Andy ordered. Caroline went to the kitchen without a word as Andy turned to Penny, bending close to her ear. "Tell me what happened. Do you have to go to the hospital? Do you need an examination or anything?" he asked in a low voice, knowing the police would want medical proof of what happened, but torn because he wanted to spare Penny all the degrading agonies that awaited her in the hospital and later at the police station. She looked so young and so wounded. She looked about twelve years old, and he couldn't imagine what kind of pervert would attack—

"No, no, it's not what you're thinking. Three men grabbed me, took me into their car. I thought they were going to kill me, but all they wanted was—" Penny hesitated. She blew her nose into the handkerchief and shook her head at the same time.

"All they wanted was what?" prompted Caroline, setting a glass of brandy down on the coffee table with a thump. She sat in a chair opposite the couch and settled in to hear Penny's explanation.

Andy held the glass of brandy to Penny's lips. Somehow he found his arm was around her shoulder, and he felt her body still quivering from the ordeal in the car as he touched her.

Penny sipped the amber liquid gratefully. "I don't know what they wanted," she said. Then, brightly, she added, "Isn't it silly? They took me for a ride up the FDR and left me at Seventy-second Street, just threw me out of the car."

"What did they do? What did they say? What the hell happened?" he asked frantically. "What did they look like?"

"Call the police, Andrew," said Caroline with an air of finality. "Let the police handle her."

"No, don't," said Penny quickly. "I'm all right, really I am. They didn't hurt me. I never saw their faces or their car. What could I tell the police?" She took another sip of the brandy he offered her and pushed away his hand. "Look, I'm really sorry to have burst in on you like this, Andy. Could you lend me ten dollars? I don't have any money to get home."

"They stole her purse," said Caroline. "That's enough reason to call the police."

"No, I lost my purse and shoes when they grabbed me on MacDougal Street. I don't want to see the police," said Penny. "They'll come to my studio again, they'll be all over the place, and then..." A look of fear crossed her face, but it passed quickly. "Well, I just don't want that to happen." She blew her hair out of her eyes, touched her hand to her head as if surprised to find her hair was wet, and said, "I must look a sight. God, I was so scared! Please, I just want to go home."

"I'll take you home," Andy offered, the words out of his mouth before he had a chance to think about what he had said.

"And what am I supposed to do while you're gone?" asked Caroline. "Eat the dessert soufflé all by myself?"

Andy had never heard the petulant, querulous side of Caroline before, and he had to admit it was as surprising as it was unattractive. Caroline had always seemed so serene and unruffled by any person, place or thing.

"Come into the kitchen for a moment, Caroline," he said. She stood, and he let her precede him, looking at her with new eyes, appraising the sleek, blond hair and the raspberry-colored linen shift she wore, its simple lines hinting at its extravagant price tag. Her lips were pressed together in a thin, white line, and she looked uncannily like her mother. Suddenly he had a vision of what Caroline would look like thirty years hence.

In the kitchen Andy began to talk to Caroline in a low voice, leaning toward her so that his words did not carry around the corner to the living room where Penny sat. "Caroline, I know you have a really good head on your shoulders. You've always understood what's what when it comes to business. Miss Greenaway may look like a child, but she's actively involved in the art restoration case I'm working on, and her good will is most important to the outcome of the case. Now, I've explained to you what kind of trouble Dieter has been stirring up at the office, haven't I?"

Caroline nodded her head.

"And you're aware of what a thorn in my side he's been." She nodded again.

"I'm certain there have been times that your father's had to do things for clients that are inconvenient for the family. Isn't that true?" Andy didn't want to go as far as mentioning that his job was on the line if he blew the case, but he would say so if he had to.

"Why don't we take her home together?" asked Caroline. The question was reasonable, but Andy didn't entertain it for a minute. Penny was liable to say or do anything without thought. Besides, for no reason he could fathom, he suddenly wanted to be alone with Penny.

"I'll take you home first, Caroline," he said decisively.

"Otherwise you'll have to spend hours while I straighten out everything. I really think she ought to go to the hospital. There's more to her story than what she's told us, don't you think?" He watched Caroline's eyes carefully. He saw skepticism, but he also saw a hesitation that led him to believe Caroline would capitulate to his desires because he couldn't imagine Caroline volunteering to spend hours and hours in a Manhattan emergency room as a kindness to some stranger. "You have to get up so early in the morning," he exaggerated. "I really regret this inconvenience."

"All right," she said at last. "I suppose you're right, Andrew."

Andy smiled and went to the bedroom for his sport jacket, returning before Caroline changed her mind.

"Come on, let's go," he said impatiently. "You just rest, Penny. I'll pick up some antiseptic and some bandages at the drug store, and I'll be back in twenty or thirty minutes."

Caroline stood at the entrance to the living room, her chin raised regally. "A pleasure to meet you, Miss Greenaway," she said stiffly.

"Mmm," said Penny from the couch. Andy looked back as he went out the door. Was that a tiny smile he saw on Penny's face?

Penny was in the bathroom when he returned half an hour later. She was sitting on the edge of the tub with the water running from the tap, soaping her feet, which were grimy and stained from her walk up York Avenue. She had drunk the brandy Caroline had poured and helped herself to another which sat precariously balanced on the edge of the tub next to her. Gingerly she moved the skirt of her torn dress so that the fabric would not touch her knees. She had tried to clean the cuts, but she had lost her nerve, deciding to wait for Andy to return.

"I'm back," he said.

"In the bathroom," she called, happy to hear his voice. She had been as angry as a boil when she arrived at his door, and even angrier when the glacial Caroline opened it, but one look at Andy's face had made her realize how relieved she was to see him. His eyes told her all she needed to know, that he would take care of everything. He'd soothe her nerves, fix her wounds, and make certain she was safe. He was a man upon whom she could rely. Instinctively she knew that about him, despite his black book, despite the presence of Caroline, despite everything.

He came to the door in his shirt sleeves holding a navy blue box with a bright red cross on its side. "You should have waited for me," he said with a gentle rebuke in his voice, as he rolled up the sleeves of his shirt. "I'll take care of your knees for you."

"I know you will. I did wait for you." He knelt on the floor at her side and took the bar of soap, turning it over and over in his wet hands to make a good lather.

"This may hurt, Penny."

"You won't hurt me," she said softly. "I know how gentle your hands are."

He looked up at her and their eyes locked, for a long moment looking at each other without moving. She saw his pupils flicker and grow dark, and then she saw the glow of feeling begin to grow there, and she leaned over and rested her head on his hair. "Those things I said to you last weekend, Andy. They weren't true. I was hurt and angry when I heard what you said on the telephone."

"I know. I was angry, too. I didn't call you because I thought you didn't want to see me again. But Penny! When you came here tonight, I wanted to kill someone. You looked so lost and hurt. If you'd been...if anything had happened to you, I would have found the man and—"

"I'm all right. Really, I am." She rubbed her cheek

against his hair as he soaped her knees with gentle hands, scooping up water from the tap, rinsing, and soaping again. His hands were soft and gentle on her skin, touching her as if she were fashioned of the finest and thinnest of crystal.

"Was there a scene?" she asked after awhile.

"With Caroline, you mean? Caroline doesn't make scenes."

"No, she doesn't seem like the type. Now, *me*. I make scenes. You ought to know that beforehand."

"Before what?" he teased.

"Just before. You know what I mean," she answered.

"I'll keep that in mind. Ne'er the rose without the thorn, eh?"

"Are you. . . are you and Caroline serious?"

"I. . . I don't know. We were before. . ." He reached over to turn off the tap. The frown on his brow deepened.

"Before what?" asked Penny hesitantly.

"Before I met you," he answered quietly.

Penny relaxed and put one arm around his neck as he worked, a contented glow burning somewhere in her breast. She picked up the glass of brandy at her side and was just about to take a small sip when she wrinkled her nose with curiosity.

"What's that weird smell, Andy?" The room was filling with acrid fumes that stung Penny's nose.

"Oh, lord!" He jumped to his feet and ran out of the bathroom. "The soufflé is burning!" she heard him call as he ran to the kitchen.

While he was gone, she stripped off the torn, ruined dress and stood, dressed only in the briefest of bikini panties, adjusting the shower. Her skin was cold from the rain that had pelted her, her arms and legs covered with goose bumps despite the warming effect of the brandy, and her hair was plastered to her head. Stepping out of her panties, she jumped under the spray, being careful to keep her back to the shower head so the water would not fall on her knees. While she soaped her arms she discovered the bruises the burly man had left on the tender flesh. She shuddered to recall the incident.

The men would return, she knew. As long as they did not possess what they wanted, they would return. She knew she was in danger, and yet she did not have the answer they sought. Perhaps she should have called the police despite their threats, but what would she have told them? A dark car, three men, one who spoke in an eerie whisper, another named Rocco with an injured wrist. She should brush up on her karate—she had intended to break Rocco's head, not his wrist. She hadn't even broken his wrist, she thought ruefully.

Penny went into the bedroom, wrapped carefully in a big towel. As she sat on the bed and dabbed at her knees to dry them, wincing at every touch, she thought of the ten crates of pictures. The answer was in the crates—that was it! In the crates themselves, and not in the frames. A false bottom, an extra panel... She would have Andy take her back to the warehouse; she would examine the construction of the crates, the one that contained the Seurats in particular.

She halted her train of thought. Suddenly she realized she couldn't confide in Andy at all. Andy might be different from the man she had first suspected he was—more sensuous, more caring of her than she had thought possible—but she had no illusions about his character. He fancied himself a protector of women, some sort of old-fashioned Galahad. Just look at the way he had stood up to Caroline when he thought Penny was injured! But to tell him what the men wanted of her would make him aware that the assignment he had given her was a dangerous one. And if he thought Penny was in danger, he'd cancel the commission, without which she'd go under immediately and have to close up shop, not at all what she wanted to do. He would never let Penny continue with the restoring job if he thought her safety was at stake, and she had to continue, if she wanted to salvage her business.

She had almost blurted out what the men had really wanted from her when Andy and Caroline had probed. Almost, but not quite. No, not Andy for her accomplice. Andy was the only person who had the power to remove her from the job. And now that her curiosity was so peaked, now that she had actually paid with her own blood—albeit just a bit of blood—for the knowledge, she would not let him interfere.

Mercurio. She would ask Mercurio for help. He owed her a favor, after all. She had kept her mouth shut about the time the NAIU van had been towed, and now she would call in the favor.

Andy came back into the room and took the edge of the towel from her hands, kneeling in front of her and dabbing at the tender skin. He eased her back on the bed and made her lie down.

"How's the soufflé?" she asked him as he finished drying her knees.

"Ruined. The dish, too. It broke when I put it in the sink."

"I hate soufflés anyway," she answered.

"Me, too." He went to the bathroom for the bandages and a pair of scissors, returning in a few seconds. "Move over," he said. "The doctor needs operating space."

Penny obeyed him, scooting over so he could sit on the edge of the bed. "Every time I come over here I take off my clothes. Do you think there's something in the air?"

"Whatever it is, I'm becoming addicted to it," he answered. "If I'd known the emergency room was like this," he said, unwrapping the towel around her legs and exposing her thighs, "I would have become a doctor long ago."

"I don't want to go home tonight, Andy. I'm afraid," said Penny who was staring up at the ceiling in an attempt to ignore his attentions to her knees. She had seen a bottle of hydrogen peroxide on the table, and she knew he would pour it on the cuts.

"You'll stay here," he said. It was a statement, not a request. "You haven't told me everything, have you," he said suddenly, standing at the side of the bed with the bottle of hydrogen peroxide in his hand.

"What do you mean?" she asked, alarmed. "Of course, I've told you everything! It's just that...just that"—her mind raced—"just that it was such an unsettling experience I don't want to be alone tonight."

"Penny, things are getting dangerous. All these crimes—break-ins, hijackings, even kidnapping—have to be related somehow. I want you to withdraw from the job tomorrow. I'd never forgive myself if anything happened to you."

She sighed. "I knew you'd say that! What do you think I am made of—china? I have a job to do, I need the money, and I'm going to do my job. You had the new lock installed in my apartment, and the locksmith said it's the best device on the market, didn't he? No one can get in. I'll be safe," she assured him.

"But what did those men want of you?" he asked.

"They mistook me for someone else," she assured him. "They had no idea who I was, they kept insisting my name was...was Maria or something," she said quickly, remembering the waitress in the Parthenon Palace. "I convinced them they were wrong, and they let me go."

"You were so lucky, so lucky..." He sat on the bed once more, laid a sterile gauze atop each knee, and poured the hydrogen peroxide over the gauze. Penny winced and gritted her teeth. "Does it hurt much?" he asked.

"I love pain," she said with a small laugh.

"I'll make it better for you," he said in a low voice.

"I know you will."

He bandaged her knees using too much fresh gauze and too much adhesive tape, acting as if she had been subjected to major surgery, and she knew she was right in not confiding her secret to him. He never would have let her proceed with her plan. Later, later when she made her discovery—for she was very certain there was an earthshaking discovery to be made—then she would tell him.

When he had finished, he put aside the bandages and scissors, and took off his shirt. She gazed at his chest, at the hair that grew in a triangle over the muscles there, and then up into his blue, blue eyes.

"I want to make love to you," he said. "But I don't want to hurt you."

She nodded at him, her eyes wide as they looked at each other. *And what about Caroline?* she said to herself, but he was unwrapping the towel that covered the rest of her body and touching her midriff with his gentle fingers, running his hands lightly up and down the taut skin of her stomach, over her breasts, and back to her abdomen.

Yet he had sent Caroline away so he could care for her, hadn't he?

Andy's lips followed his fingers and she felt his warm breath when he lowered his mouth to kiss the tiny mole on her stomach, and when he rested his head there for a long moment. She heard him sigh.

Then he was stroking her calves and her thighs almost in slow motion, while underneath her skin tiny nerves were bursting into existence and making her twitch her legs in impatience for him.

As his hands slowly traveled up the inside of her legs avoiding her knees, and resting lightly on the skin of her thighs, she forgot Caroline and the men in the Cadillac and her plans to talk to Mercurio and everything that had danced in her thoughts only moments before, giving herself over only to the sensations that his fingers engendered. He stood and took her by the feet to slide her willing body down to the foot of the bed until her legs dangled off the side, and he knelt between her knees.

"What . . . what are you going to do?" she asked quietly, little flutters of fear or embarrassment tingling in her breast.

"Shh. Just relax." He buried his head between her thighs and began to touch the soft and sensitive skin there with his lips. Instead of reaching right for the center of her body, he ran his tongue along the thighs, one at a time, so slowly she thought she would cry out in an agony of frustration, and his touch enveloped her in a cloud of new feeling that rippled subtly through her limbs. Something in the studied slowness of his caresses did not seek fulfillment for himself, but rather prolongation of her pleasure.

Penny closed her eyes, reaching for the coverlet with both hands, and bunching it between her fists in an effort to keep her body as still as a statue, in order to more fully enjoy the ruffles of pleasure that radiated from the touch of his tongue on her bare legs.

His hands searched her body, his open palms flat against her skin, as if he were feeling for the places where her flesh would respond most to his caresses—the flat of her stomach, the slight protuberance of her hipbones, knowing from the slightest tremor when he had reached those areas sensitized to his touch.

And tremble she did, but her diffused feelings were gathering, were concentrating themselves strongly in one part of her body, as if all her strength and blood had met there to greet the loving assault of his tongue which by then had neared its desired object.

"I've never done this before," she whispered.

"Neither have I," he mumbled against her. "I've never wanted to, before."

She felt his words against her as well as heard them, and his warm, moist breath sent shivers of desire racing through her limbs. His confession of inexperience endeared him to her, and she put one hand on his head to caress the hair.

His palms were warm as he slipped them under her hips and drew her up to meet his mouth. Now Penny buried her face in a pillow she had dragged down from above her head to muffle her strangled cries of joy, and she was burning and dancing beneath him, beneath his tongue which fueled the flames within her and made all the sensations she was feeling melt together.

She strained up to meet him, suddenly unaware of her body, of the bed on which she lay, of the four walls of the subdued bedroom, only suspended in a raging sea of ardor and heat, only conscious of the tremors that grew to explosions within her, one after another, ever greater, ever more powerful, each seizure making her call out a sound into the pillow. She meant to mouth his name, but she did not recognize the garbled words that escaped from her throat in low, incoherent moans.

After an indeterminable moment that seemed like a blissful eternity, but was actually only as long as she could tolerate the sweet extremes of pleasure he gave her, she shuddered and was still.

Slowly she opened her eyes and became aware of her own labored breathing in the quiet room.

"Am I still alive?" she said in a tiny voice that quivered as she spoke.

"Mmm," he answered. His head was resting on her stomach, and his arms were wrapped tightly around her thighs. "Am I hurting your knees?"

"What knees?"

He sat back on his heels and looked at her with a shy smile on his face. "You're a beautiful woman, Penny. Everywhere, in every way. I don't know what comes over me when I'm around you."

"Come up here, next to me," she said.

He obeyed immediately. As she scooted backward so she could lie flat on the bed, he lay next to her, his face very close to hers. In his eyes she saw a new and glowing intimacy that warmed her in the way his gentle caresses had done.

"You smell of me," she said uncertainly.

"I know. A beautiful smell, like sea shells." He buried his face in her neck.

"I haven't really been around that much, Andy. I never knew about . . . about that," she said, referring to the way he had just made love to her. She had heard of it, of course. Read of it. But she had never known what extremes of pleasure and intimacy a man and woman were capable of sharing.

"Penny, I can't believe you. You don't have to tell me stories, you know. I love you just the way you are."

He had misunderstood her. She hastened to explain what she meant, but she stopped suddenly, realizing the import of the words he had just spoken. "You love me?"

"Yes, I love you."

"I think I love you, too," she said softly. "Isn't that funny?"

"What's funny about it?" Andy drew his head back to peer into her face, the look in his blue eyes serious, a touch of hurt clouding their depths.

"Not funny. I don't mean funny, as in jokes and laughing. I only mean—it's so strange how we met, how you seemed so stiff and straight, everything I've always tried to avoid and now I find that I love you. . . . I've been selfish," she said with a little laugh. "You brought me so much pleasure, and I haven't even thought about you."

"Are you thinking about me now?"

"Yes."

"Show me, then," he said.

She had not lied to him about her ignorance, but some natural facility that was born in love gave her a woman's innate expertise which helped her to bring him to the pleasure he had given to her. She watched him when he closed his eyes, listened to the irregular intake of his breath when he gasped at her touches which grew bolder the more he responded, and she smiled. Remembering how slowly he had led her to the joys he unfolded for her, she took her time bringing him to his. She knew he was with her when his fingers dug into her hair and twisted it almost painfully, but she ignored the touch to concentrate on Andy, and thus she brought him to his gasping happiness.

"I suppose you never did that before, either," he said.

"No, never," she assured him, snuggling close to him after he had turned off the lights and come back to her side. "I don't expect you to believe me, but it's the truth."

"Why shouldn't I believe you?" he asked quietly.

"You *should*," she said. But in the darkness there was a tiny frown between Penny's brows. They had just declared their love for each other, declared it in both word and deed, declared it in a way that had brought them as close as a man and a woman could be, and yet she was going to deceive him as soon as she was able, and already she felt the guilt of her plans hanging heavily between them.

Chapter Nine

On Monday morning Andy was up early, showered, dressed, and just finishing breakfast by the time Penny opened her eyes and realized where she was. She went into the living room dressed in his bathrobe and found him reading the business section of the *New York Times*, a cup of coffee in front of him. From the dishes on the table, she realized he had juice, cereal, and fresh fruit for breakfast.

"I didn't want to wake you," he said. "You were sleeping so peacefully. Are you hungry?"

"No. Got any Coke?"

"No! You should eat a good breakfast, Penny. You—"

"You sound just like my mother," she said. She came around the table to kiss him, and as she bent down she saw the black leather notebook sticking out of the pocket of his suit jacket which hung over the back of one chair. Mercurio's telephone number was in the book, and she needed the number to contact him without Andy's becoming suspicious.

"Well, maybe just a cup of coffee," she said. As Andy went to the kitchen for her coffee she slipped the book from the inside pocket of the jacket and dropped it into a pocket of the bathrobe, hoping he would not miss the book before he left for work.

He put the coffee down in front of her. "I've been thinking, Penny. You should stay here today. I'll take you home later."

"Not go home? How can I not go home? I have work to do, Andy."

"No. Anything's liable to happen to you if you go out in the clothes you have—torn, ripped. You have no shoes. Walking around like that could be dangerous. You stay here, and after work I'll go to your apartment and get you some fresh clothes to wear, and then I'll take you home. I insist you stay here."

Penny's heart sank. What he said was true. She had no clothes, only the soiled, torn dress in which she had arrived, and she had no shoes. What's more, she had no money to get home. And, although Andy had no idea how close he had come to the truth, it might well be dangerous to go home.

On the other hand, she thought, *where there's a will, there's a way.* And as soon as he left for work she would find the way. If she were quick—and careful—she could be home, talk to Mercurio, get to the warehouse, and be back at Andy's before he returned from the office. There was no reason for Andy to know she had even left the apartment.

"All right, Andy. I know you're right. What time do you get home?" she asked.

"Usually before six, but I'll try to leave the office early this afternoon. Make me a list of the items you need from your apartment." He reached for the black book in his jacket pocket.

Her heart leapt. "I'll be here. Shouldn't you leave me a key?" she asked quickly to divert his attention.

"Whatever for? You won't go out, will you?"

"No. I just thought. . ."

"There's an extra key in one of the kitchen drawers," he

said. "But Penny, I don't want you to take any chances, do you understand? I know how your mind works, and you're likely to do something foolhardy. I want you to stay here all day." He was patting the various pockets in his suit in search of the black book.

Penny put her hand in the bathrobe's pocket and closed her fingers around the small leather folder. He had no monopoly on how a person's mind worked; she knew he would never leave for work without his all-important book.

"What's the matter?" she asked him.

"My black book. I was certain it was in the pocket. I must have left it in the bedroom." He stood and left the room. While he was gone she whipped the book out of her pocket and paged to the G's, finding Mercurio's name immediately.

"I'll look in the kitchen," she called. Next to a wall phone she found a pencil, but no paper. She scribbled Mercurio's number beneath the formica counter on the raw wood of its frame, and raced back to the dining alcove.

"Here it is," she called him. "Right here on the floor under the table."

"Thanks," he said. She told him the few things she needed from the apartment, and he wrote them down with a thin, silver Mark Cross pencil she was certain was a gift from Caroline. "I have to leave right away," he said. "If not, I'll be late for work."

Penny stood up from the table and walked with him to the door. She'd bet he was never late for work, never absent, never tardy returning from lunch. He put his arms around her in the hall and spoke to her quietly. "Please don't do anything foolish," he said. "I would never forgive myself if anything happened to you."

"You said that before," she answered. "What could happen to me here? I'll watch the soap operas and eat all day. I won't even take off your bathrobe. A totally non-productive day.''

''That's all right. It's better than being kidnapped, isn't it?''

''But not as exciting.''

''I'll try to make it up to you when I come home,'' he murmured, his lips nibbling at one of her earlobes. He kissed her, and his mouth tasted of honey. Penny returned his kiss with a growing passion that made her knees weak, almost as if her legs had turned to rubber beneath her. Now his lips were nuzzling her neck, sending pleasant shivers through her.

''Why don't you stay home today?'' she whispered. The words surprised her, coming as they did when she was most anxious for him to leave, so she could start her sleuthing, but when Andy touched her she tended to forget all her other plans. His touch, his kiss made her heedless of everything else. She began to loosen the knot in his tie.

''I'd love to, but I can't,'' he said, opening the lapels of the bathrobe and kissing the cleavage between her breasts. ''Too many things happening at the office. All Dieter needs is a good excuse to get rid of me.''

She could hardly talk now, her breath was coming so quickly. And Andy's matched hers. ''If you really promise to make it up to me tonight, I'll be good,'' she said, with no intention of complying.

''That's a promise.''

Twenty minutes later she was on the downtown Lexington Avenue IRT dressed in a sweat shirt and a pair of Andy's warm-up pants that were held up by a piece of rope she had found in a cabinet beneath one of the kitchen counters. On her feet, she wore a pair of rubber beach sandals. She had located a neat stack of subway tokens in the top drawer of his desk next to an unopened roll of quarters in a dark orange bank wrapper, to which she had helped herself, as well. The precise order of the drawer of Andy's desk had both shocked and amused her. If he could see her dresser drawers, he'd probably never speak to her again.

There was plenty of room for Penny on the subway car because the rush hour had peaked, and the quickly averted stares of the later riders told her that she looked like a young, albeit freshly-washed bag lady, the type of passenger a native New Yorker would not choose to stand next to, for fear of being drawn into a surrealistic conversation, or worse. She thought she looked more like a clown from the circus, Andy's clothes being so big on her that she practically tripped every time she walked, and she wished she had chosen something much cooler than the fleecy gray sweat shirt fabric, but there had been so little time, and so much else to think about. She stood, holding onto a pole in the middle of the rocking car as the hot, stuffy local rumbled downtown.

Penny smiled to herself. Her day wasn't going as planned, but she still had other options to explore. Mercurio, for instance, had left for work long before she had a frustrating telephone conversation with his mother, so there was no way to contact him until later. On the other hand, there was a crate upstairs in Winnie's apartment, a crate that no one had yet seen. The crate had been in the van when the police towed it from its illegal space on Houston Street. And while the van was in police custody, the warehouse had been broken into. No one but Penny and Mercurio knew there was a crate of reproductions in Winnie's apartment.

She got off the subway at Bleecker Street and walked west in the direction of her apartment, but when she neared her own block, she took a parallel street and walked past, circling around to the Parthenon Palace, and avoiding her own building. She went into the coffee shop and sat in a booth near the window. That way she was able to study her own block while she drank a Coke, and assure herself that no one was watching for her. When she finished the Coke, she paid with some of the purloined quarters and ran across the street and into the vestibule. She watched through the panes for a moment and, certain no one had followed her, she ran up to Winnie's floor, taking the stairs two at a time. But she had forgotten the keys and had to race back to her own apartment to find them.

Everything was as she had left it the evening before. Her jeans and shirt were on the floor in a heap, and the air conditioner whirred efficiently. She almost turned it off, but then she thought that if the man called Rocco was watching her apartment, he might notice from outside, so she left the machine as it was.

"You poor cat," she said distractedly as she let herself into Winnie's sunny rooms. She wanted to tear into the wooden crate immediately, but the cat rubbed against her and put himself under every step she took, so she gave up and fed him immediately.

At last she approached the crate. One side gaped open where Mercurio had pried it off with the crow bar. Kicking off the rubber sandals, she slid out the first picture.

Seurat! Just as she had expected. The picture was a well-known work, *Bathing at Asnières*, and she recognized it immediately, although the copy was much smaller than the original. Seurat had painted large canvases in the pointillist style, a series of multicolored dots that, seen as a whole, created a recognizable pattern of picnickers or park visitors, or like the one before Penny, of swimmers in which the landscape background had nearly as much importance as the people depicted.

She pulled the mesh screen out as far as it would go, removed the first framed reproduction, and rested it against the wall. She took out the other nine and laid them wherever there was space—against the couch, against a wall dominated by a fake fireplace, at the door leading to the kitchen. Then she dragged the crate to a window in the living room and peered inside with the aid of the sunlight that came through the window.

Without a flashlight she could barely see its construction, but what she saw seemed ordinary enough. On the other hand, she had nothing with which to compare the crate. Downstairs in her apartment lay the box that held the Cézannes. She could always go down and look it over, she thought, but right then she was impatient to examine the empty wooden container before her.

She found a table knife in a kitchen drawer and used it to tap the crate on every side. She didn't know what she was seeking, but she thought that perhaps a hollow sound would expose a secret hiding place in the box.

Then she found a measuring tape and checked the inside and outside dimensions of the crate, but the construction was even on all sides of the box.

Penny sat back on her heels. Short of taking the crate apart panel by panel, there was nothing else she could do to see if there were something amiss in its construction.

"I can't be wrong," she said out loud. "There's something here, something a lot of people want." The cat came up to her and rubbed himself against her thigh.

She stood and walked to the first reproduction. She ran her hand over its frame which was identical in construction to the other twenty she had already checked during the previous week. She ran her fingertips down the photograph which was smooth to her touch, although the photograph itself was so clear that every brush stroke and shadow showed clearly and created a three-dimensional effect in the picture. She laid the frame face down on the floor and gazed at its brown paper backing.

In the warehouse break-in, all the backings had been slashed apart. The same thing had happened to the reproductions in her apartment. In the back of her mind, there was a tiny tingle of excitement, and she was conscious of an unexplained feeling that she should hurry. "What the hell," she whispered. "I'll have to replace them all anyway." With the knife, she slit the paper around the edges and peeled it away from the frame. She had to cut away the backing of six more pictures until she found what she sought.

The back of the seventh picture was not the drab museum board of all the rest; the back of the seventh picture was canvas. Her heart leapt, and a thin line of perspiration burst out on her forehead. "Photo on the front," she whispered, "but canvas on the back. Mmm."

With a rush of excitement, she cleared a space in the middle of the floor and removed the Seurat reproduction from its frame. Slipping the knife under the lower right edge of the picture, she peeled three inches of the photograph away from its backing to reveal what lay below, but the surface of the picture was opaque. She ran her fingers over the varnished rice paper that covered the canvas.

Penny immediately recognized what process had been used; she had seen it demonstrated often enough in the restoration classes she had taken from Henry Ostrov, although she had never had occasion to use the technique in her own work. Someone very experienced had covered a canvas, probably a painted canvas, with gelatin and chalk, laid rice paper over that, and varnished the entire concoction. After the varnish dried, the unknown restorer had affixed the photograph of *Bathing at Asnières* atop, and framed it to match the other works.

Why? Such skill . . . Such cunning . . . Such care . . .

Her mind leapt to the obvious. Below the opaque paper was a work of art so valuable that men would steal and kidnap to find its location. "For money, of course," she said to the cat who sat on a windowsill licking the underside of one paw.

Penny was dying to rip the photograph from the canvas, but she needed the tools and chemicals downstairs in her studio to do an adequate job. She had to soften the varnish, peel off the rice paper, remove the gelatin. There were scores of tricks to doing the job correctly, and she was more than willing to try. But first, she needed to get the art work downstairs and, with it in hand, consult some of the textbooks she owned.

Quickly she replaced all the backless works in the crate. In case more than one painting was hidden, she cut the brown paper from the rest of the Seurat reproductions, but she found they were plain museum board like the rest. The cat was playing with the kraft paper that now littered the floor, but Penny found two pieces intact and wrapped them around the canvas.

She went to the door which led to the hall and opened it quietly. She heard nothing but the familiar daytime noises of her building. No one was in the hall or on the creaking staircase. There seemed to be no one stirring in the corridors at all. Barefoot, she stepped outside with the canvas under her arm, and she tiptoed down the stairs to her own door.

She punched out the numbers on the push-button lock and tried to turn the knob, but she was so excited she must have pressed the wrong numbers. She would have to calm down, think the combination through one more time, just take it easy, for once. But her mind was racing with the possibility that she would find a famous, stolen Rembrandt or Titian beneath the rice paper. She could just imagine what the publicity would do for her failing business! She punched out another combination to no avail.

"Damn!" she said outloud, stepping back, her plan being to lay the canvas carefully against the wall. All alone in the dark, deserted hall, her shoulder touched something hard and warm at her back. She screamed and dropped the painting on her bare foot. She tried to scoop up the painting and run, but a pair of strong arms grabbed her from behind.

"Penny, for God's sake, it's just me."

"Andy!" She leaned against the wall, her knees weak with fright. She laughed in a high note of fear and relief. "What are you doing here?"

"What are *you* doing here? Dammit, I told you to stay home!"

Penny was hopping on one foot now, holding the bruised toes in her hands. "Oh, my toe! I had to work, Andy," she lied quickly. "I couldn't stay cooped up all day. Lord, is it five o'clock already? I can't believe the whole day has gone by." Had she really been poking around in the crate for an entire day? She was so excited by her find, she had lost track of time, and hunger, and the fact that Andy would be coming to her apartment for her clothes.

"No, it's only twelve thirty."

"What are you doing here?" Eyeing the paper-wrapped painting at her feet, she stopped hopping long enough to straighten the canvas and lean it against the wall so it would not be damaged.

"I came by for your clothes on my lunch hour, so I could get home earlier tonight, but I see you've already changed," he said with obvious disapproval. "What the hell are you wearing?"

"Your clothes."

"I can see that."

"I'm sorry. I borrowed some money, too; I hope you don't mind."

"Penny, all I care about is that you're safe, and I can see you are. C'mon, let's go inside."

"I can't get the door open. I can't seem to remember the combination."

He gave her a funny look. "The combination is your birthday, you nitwit. You chose the numbers yourself. How could you forget your own birthday? Are you all right?"

"Right, of course. How silly of me!" She would have to be cooler. He could see right through her, and he was far from stupid.

Andy picked up the painting and opened the door on the first try. She had been on the verge of objecting, but she said nothing as he carried the canvas inside.

"Where do you want this?" he asked.

"Er, on my worktable. It's new canvas I just picked up at Sam Flax." As if he knew what Sam Flax was, as if he cared, she thought, reminding herself not to overelaborate again.

"Are you going to paint something? Finished with the Degas already?" he asked politely, but she could tell he had something else on his mind. There was a tone of preoccupation in his voice that she was unaccustomed to hearing. He took off his jacket and threw it on the Hollywood bed, and then he took off his tie as well, and rolled up the sleeves of his shirt. He lay on the bed and looked up at the ceiling, not even aware that his head was on the jacket and would wrinkle it. He looked worried, and she imagined something terrible had happened at his office.

"Is something the matter at work?" Penny asked.

"No, everything's fine," he replied. "Better than ever, in fact. The boss is away for the week."

"Then what's the matter?"

"Nothing. Do I act like there's something wrong?"

"You seem preoccupied," replied Penny. "You can tell me."

He sat up quickly, realized his jacket was wrinkled, and shook it out. He went to her closet and hung the jacket carefully. "I've got a few things on my mind," he said lightly. "But nothing I can't take care of easily enough."

"Would you like to have lunch here, Andy?"

"Sure. What's to eat?" he asked.

"Nothing worth writing home about, but I'll fix us something," said Penny. "What time do you have to be back at the office?"

"I'm in no hurry. Dieter's out of town until Monday, and I'm supposed to be uptown on a call to a client, but my appointment isn't actually until three o'clock. As for lunch, I'd rather cook it myself, if it's all the same to you. You aren't offended, are you?"

"Not at all. Help yourself to whatever there is in the kitchen," she said. "Or one of us could run out to the deli..." She knew there was nothing worth eating in the kitchen, and that Andy would have to go out. She was anxious to get to work on the painting, and had no intention of stopping to eat anyway. She didn't know how else she would get rid of him if he didn't intend to leave soon, but he would be gone before three, so she figured it didn't matter.

Andy went out in search of a deli to buy cold meats for lunch. While he was gone, she heated the surface of the Seurat photograph and carefully peeled it away from the painting. She rolled the Seurat and slipped it into a cardboard tube, placing it in the midst of a stack of empty mailing tubes on the book shelf. Then she applied a solvent to soften the varnish over the hidden painting. When Andy returned forty-five minutes later with two large grocery bags, she was in the bathroom combing her hair, acting as if she had done nothing in his absence but change from his clothes into blue jeans and a cotton shirt, and apply her makeup.

"I thought you were just going to the deli," she said.

"You don't have anything worth eating around here, so I stopped at the grocery store. You really need someone to take care of you, did you know that?"

"The thought had occurred to me," she said, taking one bag from his arms and carrying it to the kitchen where she began to unpack its contents. "There's enough food here for weeks! What are you going to do, move in with me?"

"The thought had occurred to me," he answered, and he slipped his arms around her waist and nuzzled his nose in her neck.

"You could never stand the mess I make," she said.

"You'll improve."

While Andy made sandwiches for lunch, Penny decided to work on the canvas right in front of him, explaining nothing, and hoping he would not ask. She ate quickly, and returned to work, leaving the clean-up to him. With the painting on her work table, and the solvent properly gummy, she consulted her textbooks and scraped off the rice paper which had turned soft beneath the melted varnish. She began at the lower right hand side, listening to Andy chatter about his job and the boss whom he hated. She nodded at all the appropriate places and clucked sympathetically, but her mind was on the painting before her.

He lay on the Hollywood bed, his arms behind his head, and talked for a full hour without stopping, and she had the idea that he was a lonely man, one who seldom confided in others. She asked him about his parents, and he told her that they were both dead, but that his father had been a landscape gardener and his mother a clerk in the town hall of Bryn Mawr, and that they had pushed him to make something of himself since he was young. He had put himself through school, done his stint in the Marines, and then gone into the insurance business, working for NAIU ever since. He told her long, complicated stories about Dieter and the intricacies of working for NAIU, and she asked him how he could tolerate an atmosphere in which politics meant more than merit, but he defended the company, blaming all his troubles on his boss.

After awhile he went into the kitchen, and she heard him straightening the cupboards and rummaging through the refrigerator. He was much more organized than she, she realized, and the fact that he had taken over in the kitchen bothered her not at all. In addition, it kept him out of the room as she began to uncover the first part of the painting. She saw heavy pigment and what appeared to be the bluish green background of a landscape. Slowly and carefully she nudged the old varnish and rice paper away with a spatula, being exceedingly careful not to damage the painting beneath.

Penny gasped. Beneath the spatula in her hand was a signature and a date.

"What is it? What's the matter?" Andy called from the kitchen door.

"Nothing," she replied with false calm. "Nothing at all." Her heart was thumping wildly, and it took all her control not to shout to him, "I've found a Gauguin, a Gauguin right here on MacDougal Street!"

She looked again at the signature. "P. Gauguin," it read in a loose, but readable script. And beneath, in tiny numbers, two nines. At first she did not believe the painting could be genuine. She suspected that she would uncover the rest and find a painted copy of a famous Gauguin work, something like *The Spirit of the Dead Watches*, or *The Yellow Christ*. But then she remembered all the trouble that had surrounded the shipment of reproductions, and she knew—she *knew*—she had a genuine Gauguin in her hands.

"I can't see you for dinner tonight," said Andy at her elbow.

"That's all right," she answered. "I've got too much to do anyway," she said vaguely without raising her head. "I'd be lousy company."

"I had no idea you were such a worker," he said, quickly changing the subject. Penny was aware of his relief that she hadn't questioned him about his plans for the evening, but she let the moment pass, happy to be left alone with the painting, although she enjoyed Andy's presence and would miss him under any other circumstance. "You've been at work all afternoon," he went on. "You need a break."

"I'll take a break later. I always work like this. Compulsive, I guess," she said, blowing her hair out of her eyes. Her back and her neck ached from the muscular tension of leaning over the painting.

"Did you paint that?" he asked, peering over her shoulder. Half the picture was exposed now, and he saw the brown midriff and full breasts of a dark-skinned woman in a loosely-wrapped sarong.

"Me?"

"It's a Gauguin copy, I see. What are you doing to it?"

"Yes. Yes, I painted it," she said quickly, grasping at the handy explanation he had offered. "And afterward I didn't like what I'd done, so I painted it out to use the canvas again. But now I've decided to remove the covering after all. You know us women: We're always changing our minds." She laughed, but inside she winced. She hated to lie to him. "You've learned a lot about art, Andy."

"Not really, but I was intrigued with your stories about the copies. I read a book or two after our lunch that day.

How much will your decorator friend pay you for this one?''

Penny turned to him, anxious to change the subject. "Did you really read up on fakes? Why?"

"Because I was so taken with you," he answered shyly. "Penny, I know we haven't known each other very long, but I have to tell you how important you've become to me in such a short time. You're like a breath of fresh air in my life. You're everything I ever dreamed of in a woman, and then you're more, so much more. I can't even explain how I feel. When I try to put it into words, everything goes out of my head."

She peeled off the thin rubber gloves she wore and put her arms around his neck, drawing him close to her. "Who could ask for a better explanation?" she whispered. "I feel the same way about you, but you must know that already. Don't you?"

He nodded, his head resting on her curls. His arms were around her waist, and his hands slipped under her shirt and gently massaged the skin of her back.

"Do you want to make love?" she asked him.

"Oh, I want to," he exclaimed. "I always want to make love with you, but I can't. I'll have to leave now for my three o'clock appointment. It's already after two thirty."

"What about tonight, then? Where are you going?"

"I...I have to pick up my shirts at the laundry. I have a few other errands to run, and then I'll be back later. You have dinner without me."

"Why do you need shirts, Andy? You can pick them up in the morning. Your boss is away: go in when you feel like it. I don't want you to go, but if you come back right after work, I'll forgive you." She began to open the buttons of his shirt, but he put his hand on hers to stop her.

"I want to more than anything in the world, Penny, but

I really have things to do." Something in his tone made her look into his eyes, but they slipped away from hers. His face was so transparent, so honest, she had no trouble deciding he was hiding the truth from her as he spoke. Her first instinct was to confront him with his deceit, but Penny hesitated. After all, she hadn't told him about the Gauguin. Why shouldn't he have a private part of his life, as well?

She wanted to trust him. For a quick moment she was convinced she should tell him about the painting, and about the men in the dark Cadillac, but Andy was so protective of her, she knew he would make her leave the studio and call the police. There was so much more to do before letting anyone else in on her discovery of the Gauguin, and if he didn't come back until late, she would have privacy in which to work.

Penny decided to let Andy go without further questions. But there was a flutter of disappointment in her breast, and a sadness, as well. Here they were, two people newly in love, and both telling lies.

"All right," she said with a gentle sigh. "I'll see you later."

He kissed the tip of her nose. "Don't forget to eat something while I'm gone. You've had your head in your work all day. Don't you ever take a break?"

"Sure. Sure, I do," she said with distraction. She was already thinking of the painting again, already planning her next step, which was to verify that the full-breasted nude had actually been painted by Gauguin. And she was wondering how she would keep its existence a secret—from Andy, but more important, from the man with the whispering voice.

Chapter Ten

Penny sat across the scarred oak table from Henry Ostrov in the cluttered kitchen at the back of his Fifty-seventh Street studio. He held up one of the five Polaroid photographs she had brought for him to study and moved the magnifying glass in his hand slowly across its glossy surface. She watched nervously and sipped the last of her tea which had grown cold in its porcelain cup without handles, the way Henry, a Russian by birth—although a long-term resident of New York—preferred to drink it. She knew she should be hungry, having skipped dinner, but she was too excited to eat, and had rushed uptown as soon as Henry had told her on the telephone that he was able to see her.

"Where did you say these photos came from, Penny?" He had cleared the remains of his sparse dinner from the oak table, and spread the five photographs in front of him. Picking them up one at a time, he examined them again, oblivious when a glowing ash from one of the malodorous crooked, black cigars he loved to smoke at the end of the day, fell, narrowly missing his scraggly, yellowed goatee as it came to rest on the spotted vest he wore, where it burned briefly on the fabric.

Penny reached across the table and brushed at Henry's vest. There was the faint odor of burning wool, and then the coal died, adding one more tiny hole to the confetti of holes that already peppered the thin wool. Henry ignored the entire procedure.

"In a letter," she invented quickly. "There was no return address. The sender asked me if I would be interested in cleaning the painting, and how much I would estimate for the job."

"And who was the sender? Was there a signature?"

"No. He—she—I don't know who, said he would contact me for my prices."

"Was the letter postmarked in South America, by any chance?"

"Gee, Henry, I can't remember. I don't even know if I've saved the envelope."

Where was Ostrov going with his questions? she wondered. She hated to tell lies; they always escalated to unmanageable proportions. She knew if he kept probing that she would admit she had taken the photographs herself with her Omega studio camera, setting up the lights after carefully closing the draperies in her apartment, so no one outside could see what she was doing. She had taken the five shots at various distances, the last one as closely as the camera's lenses allowed. The photo Henry now examined was the final one, the close-up of Gauguin's signature and the date, 1899.

"Well, what do you think, Henry? Does the painting look genuine?"

"How can one tell, honestly tell, from a photograph, Penny?" He sighed and laid the Polaroid snapshot on the table. "More tea?" he asked her. At her nod, he crossed to the stove and began to boil water for a fresh pot of tea. With his back to her at the sink, he poured out the cooled tea that remained in a white china pot they had used, rinsed the pot with hot water, and began to measure out fresh leaves to brew. "I'm not familiar with such a work by Gauguin," he began. "I've never seen it in person or photograph before, but that, of course does not imply the painting is not a Gauguin. There are always unknown works of great artists that turn up now and again. An old lady finds a canvas in her attic, a restorer removes a modern work to disclose a master beneath. You've heard the stories. And, of course, the subject matter—a brown-skinned native woman of such voluptuous proportions— cries out to be labeled Gauguin."

Penny nodded with outward calm, but her heart had leapt guiltily at Ostrov's reference to restorers uncovering masterpieces. He had touched too close to the truth for her comfort, and yet she needed his advice. He had been so many years in the business that his expertise was surpassed by no one.

"How could one tell if the painting were genuine?" she asked him.

"Only in person," he replied. "There are tests. There are chemicals. And then, there is the eye of the expert."

"I've told you a little fib, Henry," she said. "I took those photographs. I have that painting in my possession."

"Oh? You have a Gauguin?" He looked at her skeptically, returning to the table and sitting gently, as if his elderly bones pained him.

"I don't know if it's a Gauguin; that's why I'm here," she answered. "I need to know if the painting is real before I touch it. What if it's stolen? What if it came from a museum? If I clean the painting, am I not then involved in a crime?"

"Where did you get the painting?"

"I can't tell you the answer to that question. At least right now, Henry. The matter is too sensitive."

"Why don't you bring it to me, then, and I'll take a look

at it. Together we can come to some conclusion as to how to proceed.''

"That impossible, I'm afraid. I wouldn't dare leave my place with a Gauguin. Would you—could you come to my studio and take a look at it?''

"Certainly, Penny, but I have to tell you now that if what you have is a stolen piece of art, the best thing you can do is get uninvolved immediately. First of all, if you do have a genuine Gauguin, your life is in danger. The thieves who make a market in stolen art are not people to be trifled with. Secondly, unless you have one whopping good story as to how you came across a Gauguin, we'll be visiting you in some prison when the word gets out.''

"Yes, I know, Henry. I've already been approached by people who suspect I know where the painting is. That's one of the reasons I believe it may be genuine. Can you come with me now?'' she asked. "Is that a terribly inconvenient favor to ask of you?''

"You are giving me an opportunity to touch a Gauguin, and you ask if it's inconvenient! You must not know old Henry too well, my dear Penny. We will bring my infrared camera with us, eh? We will uncover the mysteries of your painting.''

The telephone in her apartment was ringing as Penny opened the door, but she wasn't quick enough to answer before the caller on the other end hung up. Leaving Henry momentarily alone in her studio, she ran up the stairs to Winnie's. The new lock on her studio door was impressive looking, true, but she had not trusted its efficiency enough to leave what might be a Gauguin unguarded while she was uptown at Henry Ostrov's when she knew that the Whisperer, as she now called him, was watching her. Earlier that evening, when Henry agreed to see her immediately, she had not left MacDougal Street before taking the precaution of hiding the painting, and the mailing tube in which she had concealed the Seurat photograph, in Winnie's apartment.

It never occurred to her not to trust Henry, however. He lived as Spartanly as a monk, eschewing such niceties as decent clothing, vacations, and comfortable furniture. He had told Penny once, many years before, that money was not important to him. Compared to his life in the Soviet Union, he said, living in New York was like living in a palace of the tsar, and for what did he need riches? He had no family—no wife, no children. He had enough to eat, and he had his school, which he ran lovingly, if sternly. Even if he confirmed she had found a Gauguin worth millions, he would do nothing to betray Penny's discovery. He would only applaud the celebrity her find promised and congratulate her on keeping her business afloat.

"Here it is," she told him, returning to the studio, her arms laden with the canvas which was again wrapped in the wrinkled brown kraft paper. She propped the painting on the easel, and she turned on the photo lamps which she had left set up when she called Henry.

Henry walked back and forth in front of the easel silently, never taking his eyes from the portrait that sat there. Penny found she was holding her breath as he examined the doe eyes and full lips of the nude girl holding a flat container of red blossoms in her two hands. At last he let out a low whistle and said in a voice that betrayed a trace of the Russian accent he had lost a generation before Penny was even born, "This is very nice. Very nice." He picked up the painting and carried it to the worktable, carefully arranging the padded blocks beneath before resting the work face down. "Very nice, indeed."

She dragged a lamp over to the worktable and shone its

light on the canvas for him as he unsheathed a magnifying glass he had taken from his pocket. In silence he began to examine the canvas inch by inch.

"Be a good girl and set up the ultraviolet for me, eh?" She did as he asked. He turned over the painting and shone the ultraviolet light on its surface. "No repainting under the varnish, I see," he mumbled, talking to himself more than to her. "But something underneath, hum? Yes, something under the top layer of oil." Ostrov took a penknife from his pocket and flicked it open.

"What are you doing?" asked Penny, fascinated.

"I'm going to take a few scrapings of the pigment from the edge here, where the canvas is wrapped around the stretcher. And then I'm going to slice off the smallest piece of canvas—just here." He indicated a ragged edge with the point of the knife. "I'll take those back to my studio and analyze them. Ah, Penny, you have forgotten your lessons in chemical microscopy so soon? We put the paint fragments under the microscope and do spot tests to determine its composition. If the paint is modern, we know immediately. If it is turn-of-the-century..." He left the exciting conclusion of his speculation to Penny's imagination.

He bent down and carefully shaved a minute fragment of paint and varnish from the edge, gently urging it to fall on a sheet of white paper. With concentration he shaved another and another, and then he folded and taped the paper into the shape of an envelope. "Afterward, I will grind down one edge of the pigment and study it further. Sometimes I can tell you the exact type of paint used by the artist. I have paint sections mounted and typed that I use for reference. I haven't been in this business more than fifty years for nothing, young lady."

"Yes, Henry. I know."

"And you see this?" he indicated, laying the edge of the knife on one of four metal contraptions shaped somewhat like keys that held together each edge of the stretcher. "Tell your old teacher what this key signifies." He looked up at Penny with a gleam in his eye, his bushy white eyebrows quivering like antennae above his jet black pupils.

"Today's test, Henry? Punishment for overlooking microscopy?"

"No stalling, Penny. What is your measured opinion?"

"I'm going to fool you, Henry; you see, I remember that lesson. That's a late nineteenth century invention that enables one to adjust the canvas when the stretcher expands and contracts with heat and humidity changes."

"Very good, an A plus for you. So you see," he commented, "you have another piece of evidence indicating the age of your painting."

"Not my painting, Henry."

"Whose, then?"

"I don't know," Penny replied.

"Or you're not telling," he chuckled.

"No, I swear to you, I don't know," she exclaimed. "I literally found the painting in the course of a restoration job. I found it where it should not have been, and until I discover where it belongs, I plan to keep it safe and sound."

"Oh, how I love a mystery," said Henry with a chuckle. "I know how we can discover to whom this painting rightfully belongs."

"How?"

"If my tests prove the painting dates from Gauguin's era," he said, "I'll do the research for you. Let me think: When did he die? 1903? 1904? I'll consult my books. And I'll consult them for the body of his work, where it is located, to whom it belongs. If the answer is not in my library, I'll pay a visit to my friends, the conservators at the Metropolitan Museum of Art. Finally I will resort to the Frick Art Reference Library which houses the largest collection of photographic records of paintings in this country. What they do not know at the Frick Library is not worth knowing, eh?

"Now hand me the infrared camera while I replace the painting on the easel. And go out of the room while I photograph," he admonished. "You are too young for exposure to such harmful effects."

Penny went to the kitchen and waited for Henry's call telling her all was safe from the camera. She fixed a pot of tea, very black the way Henry liked it, and sat on a stool as the leaves steeped in hot water. She was filled with bubbles of excitement. Even without tests, the construction of the stretchers and the keys at its edges indicated that the painting was not a modern one. And Henry had seen evidence of something underneath the painting, as well. That could mean many things: a sketch by the artist, perhaps, or another work painted beneath the surface. She didn't allow her mind to dwell too long on the possibility, knowing she would have to wait days for the results of Henry's photographs and tests.

Absentmindedly she straightened up the kitchen as she thought, wiping up droplets of water and putting away the dishes in the drainer, while waiting impatiently for Henry's call.

"All set, Penny. I've done all I can do here," called Henry, at last, from the next room.

"I've made tea, Henry," she said, returning to the main room with the teapot which she set down on the work table. She found him repacking his camera in the black case he had brought with him. "Won't you stay for awhile?"

"No, Penny. It's already past my bedtime as it is. I'll run along now, and I'll call you in a couple of days with the results of the tests, although I might say—without getting your hopes up too high—that I'm as convinced as you that you're onto something big here." He lowered his voice. "If, in fact, you have come upon a genuine Gauguin, I caution you again—"

"To be careful," she finished. "You and I are the only two people in New York that know the painting is here, Henry."

"You don't have to ask me to be quiet," he said.

"I would never insult you by asking," Penny replied. She kissed Henry on his dry cheek and walked with him to the door. As soon as he had left, she wrapped the painting in brown paper and returned with it to Winnie's apartment. She couldn't be too careful now, she told herself, not with the Whisperer looking for the Gauguin, and his heavies aware of her address. She planned never to let down her guard for a single moment.

Andy left Penny's and went directly to a pay telephone near Washington Square. He dialed Caroline's office number from memory and nervously waited for her to pick up the phone. He had to talk to her, the sooner the better, and that very night seemed as good a time as any to take care of the unpleasant task that lay before him.

Andy was incapable of carrying on two affairs at one time, and he had come to the conclusion that to break off with Caroline was the only honorable course open to him in light of his developing relationship with Penny. He didn't know what had happened to him. It was as if he'd been struck by lightning. Andy was not an impetuous man, and he always thought through his moves, but in the short time he'd known Penny, he'd realized his entire life plan with Caroline had been a horrendous mistake. But it wasn't too late to change his plans; no, nothing irrevocable had yet taken place. He and Caroline were not formally committed to one another. Not yet.

All day he had been preoccupied to distraction with the upcoming confrontation. So preoccupied, in fact, that Penny had commented on his demeanor, but there was no need to explain the onerous duty that lay before him to Penny. He had already implied to Penny that he and Caroline had no arrangement, so what Penny did not know wouldn't hurt her. Better to call it quits with Caroline, and be done with it. He would then be unencumbered when he came back to Penny.

He knew Caroline would not understand what had happened to him; he wasn't even certain himself. He had known Penny only a short time, but during those days he had been forced to reassess the entire course of his future, every year of which had been so carefully planned—first by his parents, then by himself, and then by Caroline and her family when they had entered the scene.

Caroline answered the telephone with the wary, questioning tone she used when she hadn't yet sized up a situation, and she told him to be at her apartment by seven, never mentioning that his request seemed slightly out of the ordinary, although he and Caroline seldom, if ever, saw one another on weeknights, by her choice.

Andy felt from their conversation that it was almost as if she had expected to see him that evening. But the coolness of her Sunday night treatment of him had thawed somewhat, and he suspected from her tone that she had been awaiting a call, and perhaps even an unscheduled visit from her penitent suitor. She would hope to extract an apology from him for having so unceremoniously brought her home the night before, but she was not going to receive one.

He saw his client, and went home early to change his clothes, first picking up his shirts at the Chinese laundry. It was exactly seven o'clock when he arrived at the door of Caroline's Tudor City apartment and stood nervously, still preparing the words he would say. To his surprise, there was a low murmur of voices coming from within the apartment. At his knock, Caroline opened the door and leaned her head forward, allowing Andy to peck her stiffly on the cheek, which he did from long habit.

"I see you remembered Mummy and Daddy are in town for the night," she said coolly. "Frankly, I thought you hadn't heard a single word I said last night, Andrew, and your vague excuses hardly held water. We're just having cocktails before going out to dinner. I'm so glad you decided to join us after all. I tried to call you at the office to give you a chance to reconsider, but they told me you'd left early." There was a grimace of disapproval on Caroline's fine features, which seemed unusually severe because of the way her blond hair was pulled so tightly behind her head and fastened with a dark blue grosgrain bow. And the simple lines of her navy blue silk sheath didn't help warm her appearance, either.

Andy swallowed awkwardly, never having expected such an announcement, but he vaguely remembered Caroline's having mentioned that her parents would be in town that week, and even an invitation to dinner. At the time he had been so concerned about Penny's waiting for him back at the apartment, he'd sloughed off the entire conversation. Her words of the previous night came back to him in a rush.

"I got free unexpectedly," he said. "Caroline, could I talk to you privately?" he asked nervously.

"Where, dear boy, in the bathroom? You know all I have is the one room, and my parents are sitting in there now." She said "one room" with deprecation, as if she lived in a cold-water flat, but in truth, Caroline's one room had cost the price of a small house to decorate, something she rationalized easily since she had the money, and she was also employed in some vague capacity at the showroom of one of the most pre-eminent of Manhattan decorators and was able to buy her furniture and accessories at a substantial discount. "We can't stand all night at the door chatting—it isn't polite to Mummy and Daddy. If it's about last night, I'm willing to forgive and forget as long as you're here now, so come in and join us."

"Uh—"

"*Please*, Andrew. Do you intend to embarrass me in front of my parents as well? I've been patient with you, but enough is enough."

"All right," he capitulated. Penny was not expecting him until after dinner anyway. He would call her from whatever restaurant the Potters had chosen to go to. Afterward, when Caroline's parents had gone back to their hotel, he would tell her what he had planned to say, not that he had decided yet exactly what the words would be, but he was certain he would devise a suitable explanation of his change of heart by then. Words that would maintain Caroline's dignity, as well as his own. Caroline, after all, had done nothing wrong. She couldn't help what she was, any more than Andy could resist the magic that had so unexpectedly taken hold of him when he met Penny.

Mr. Potter stood at his entrance and heartily shook his hand. Andy accepted a drink and sat quietly as the Potters talked about the safari to Africa from which they had recently returned. He remembered that Mr. Potter had a game room decorated with the heads of dead animals, and with paintings of game birds and the dogs used to flush them from their cover, and he felt vindicated in the decision he had made to break off with Caroline. The life in Gladwyn to which he had aspired a few short weeks before suddenly seemed artificial and empty without the right woman with whom to share it.

Quietly he gazed at Caroline as her parents—mostly her father—chatted on and on about their trip. She was a beautiful woman, in the manner of an ice princess, he supposed. She sat on a straight-backed chair with her legs crossed at the ankles as she had been taught, her navy blue dress modestly covering her knees, and she made no eye contact whatsoever with Andy, almost as if he were not in the room. Strictly speaking, that was not true. She had brought him a drink and a tiny embroidered white napkin on which to rest it, and she included him politely in the conversation, so she was aware of his presence, but her posture indicated that his presence was only to be expected, like. . . like electric light at the flip of a switch, hot water from the left tap, and sunset each evening. There was no current between Andy and Caroline, no electricity. Unlike what he felt when he was around Penny.

When he was with Penny, he was aware of every nuance of her. He listened to her breathing, heard every little gasp of surprise or pleasure, heard every sigh of frustration or fatigue. He was aware of the sweet smell she had, not just the perfume of roses she used, but another enticing, but more primitive aroma: the seductive smell of Penny herself. He saw every change in the green of her eyes, from hazel to jade to a murky, pale brown when something was troubling her.

He had known she was distracted that afternoon, more absorbed in her work than he had dreamed possible, although he had realized from the first she was dedicated to her calling. He hadn't taken her distraction as disinterest in him. On the contrary, he had ascribed it to the trauma of her kidnapping two days previously. Andy figured she purposely lost herself in whatever job she was doing in order to forget the ugly events of Saturday, and he approved of her methods. They far surpassed the use of alcohol or barbiturates, not that he supposed Penny was interested in sedative drugs.

"Peacock Alley it is, then," said Mr. Potter, and everyone but Andy stood to leave. Andy awoke from his reverie and followed Caroline's parents to the door while Caroline went around switching off the table lamps in her fussily-decorated apartment.

"We always eat at Peacock Alley when we stay at the Waldorf," said Mrs. Potter.

"And we always stay at the Waldorf," added her husband.

Under the guise of visiting the men's room, he left the Potters' choice table in the subdued and elegant Peacock Alley and dialed the number of Penny's studio, letting the telephone ring twelve times before he hung up with a frown between his brows. At first he thought she would worry when he did not come back as promised, but then he found himself worrying about her. She had said nothing about going out, and he knew there was food for dinner because he had bought it himself. Andy had never met a woman more prone to trouble than Penny. It was almost as if a black cloud followed her around, and he was concerned for her safety. While he was almost certain she had been a victim of coincidence, there were enough unusual occurrences about the shipment of reproductions to make Andy wary. And Penny herself was such a daring madcap; left to her own devices, she might walk into any sort of trouble. This sudden urge to protect Penny surprised him. He had never felt that way about the capable Caroline.

"Here you are!" said Mr. Potter at his side next to the telephone. "The girls are wondering about you."

"Just a business call I had to make," said Andy quickly, grateful now that Penny had not answered the telephone, which would have put him in a position to explain Mr. Potter to her. "Caroline isn't too crazy about business interfering with social occasions, you know." He laughed nervously.

"Just like her mother," said Mr. Potter, clapping him soundly on the back. "When are you and Caroline going to make everything legal, Keller? I've got a spot open right now in my outfit, and I don't want to fill it up with a stranger if I can keep it in the family. How would you like to be a vice president? I can speak to the boys over at NAIU for you. They'll hate to lose you, I'm sure, but I'll make it worth your while. Not just the money, but you get my precious baby as well."

Andy felt himself blush. He hadn't expected such a direct offer from Caroline's father. He had thought this maneuver would wait until after the engagement, but Caroline must have become impatient with Andy's delay in proposing. He was certain Caroline had urged her father to speak up to Andy, forcing his hand in the courtship. A week ago he would have jumped at such an opportunity. Today, however...

"Has Caroline said anything to you and Mrs. Potter?" asked Andy. He couldn't very well tell her father he and Caroline were finished before he told her. "I really should speak to her first."

"Caroline always keeps her mouth shut, that's her nature. But her old Daddy can make her talk. My wife and I are tired of waiting around, to tell you the truth. She wants to plan a big, fancy wedding at the club, and I want to see a couple of grandchildren before I get too old to play with them. You and Caroline are of a cautious generation, my boy. When we were young, we jumped first and then looked around to see where we had landed.''

"And if you landed in quicksand...?" asked Andy.

Mr. Potter gave him a second look, and then laughed. Andy could smell the scotches he'd had, on his breath. "There are always paddles to get out of quicksand. I know what you mean, Keller. Her mother's a bit of a cold fish at times, too, but you can live with it when there are other compensations. Take it from me, you can.''

"I'm certain you're right, Mr. Potter," said Andy, inwardly shrinking away from the man and his distasteful conversation. Mr. Potter went through to the men's room, and Andy back to the table where the women sat waiting. He put the conversation with his would-be father-in-law out of his mind, already worrying about Penny again.

And well he might have worried. At the same moment that Andy resumed his seat at the table with Caroline and Mrs. Potter, Penny returned from Winnie's apartment, stood at her combination lock, and pressed out the dates of her birthday to open the door of her apartment.

She didn't hear the man come up behind her on quiet feet as much as sense his menacing presence. She tensed to run, but one rough hand clamped around her mouth and another squeezed her rib cage in a viselike grip with a suddenness that made her legs dissolve beneath her.

"No noise, missy," whispered a gravelly voice in her ear. "Time for another talk."

She knew it was the man called Rocco. She smelled garlic and the stale, metallic odor of cigars on his breath, and her throat closed, paralyzed with fear. She wouldn't have been able to scream even if he uncovered her mouth. He kicked open the unlatched door before shoving her roughly into the apartment and slamming the door behind them.

"Will you be quiet?"

Penny nodded her head, and he loosened his grip, giving her a push which sent her halfway across the small room.

"W-what do you want?" She stumbled, almost fell, but caught herself in time and stood erect. Turning to look, she backed away from him, arms around her midriff and hands rubbing at her bruised ribs.

"Where've you been?" he asked. "I've been waiting for you." So he didn't know she had just come from Winnie's; he hadn't thought anything of the key ring she clenched innocently in her hand, hadn't realized that she didn't need the keys to enter her own apartment, although, of course, he had seen the new push button lock that was installed after his previous visit.

"I...I've been taking out the garbage," she lied quickly. "Why are you here? What do you want from me?"

"The paintings," he said. "One painting. You know what I mean."

"I don't know anything, and now you've let me see you. I don't want to see you! What are you going to do to me?"

"You saw me before," he answered, leaning up against the door so she couldn't run. "I'm not as dumb as everybody thinks. Don't think that fancy new lock you got will keep me out if I want to come back. You can't stop me!"

Penny backed up against the bookshelves, her eyes wide with fear, her heart pounding so loudly she could barely hear herself think. He began to walk slowly toward her.

"Your boss said he wanted the Seurats, right?" she said quickly. "I don't have any—all I have is Cézannes. Here, take a look!" She went to the crate and pulled out one mesh screen. "Here, look! These are all Cézannes. All of them." She pulled out a second and a third screen. Her throat was dry with fear and threatened to close around her words.

There was a perplexed frown on Rocco's brow. "When do you get your next shipment from the warehouse?" he asked.

"When I'm finished with these. I phone the insurance company and a messenger brings them to me. I'll tell you. I promise I'll tell you! Please, what have I done to you? Please, please leave me alone!"

"If you're lying to me..." He advanced on her and stood so close she could see the craterous pocks in his skin, smell the stale cigar smoke that hung in his clothes, and count the black whiskers he had missed while shaving that morning. She watched a vein pulse at the side of his temple, and she knew he was a man given to violently ungovernable rages.

"What was Ostrov doing here?" he asked. He wrapped a great, hamlike hand around one of her wrists and twisted it slightly, showing her a mere shadow of his strength.

"Ostrov? You know Ostrov?" Now Penny's hazel eyes were wide with surprise, and she became aware of an increased pressure on her arm, although there wasn't much pain. Yet.

"I know everything, missy. I told you I ain't so dumb. I asked you what he was doing here." He cast a significant glance down at her wrist in his hand. His fist didn't move, but Penny imagined the slight effort he would need to exert to make the bone crack beneath his fingers.

And yet, he did not know why Henry had been to her studio. Why would he ask the question if he knew the answer? she reasoned. Why tell him? Henry had been to Penny's studio often, and she to his, but never before had there been any suspicious reasons for their visits to each other. The more threatening the Whisperer and Rocco behaved, the more determined was Penny to protect the secret she had discovered.

"He's a friend of mine, an old teacher," she explained in a rush of words. "He came by for a cup of tea." She looked pointedly at the teapot still sitting on the work-table, and Rocco's eyes followed her gaze, lighting on the flea market find, a bright yellow Fiestaware pot. "I see Ostrov often, and he has nothing to do with this shipment of paintings. If you know him, you know he's a famous restorer, one of the best in the city; he wouldn't touch a photo-reproduction with a ten-foot pole. I didn't even tell him about the job because I was embarrassed." She prayed Rocco and his friends weren't watching her full time and weren't aware that she had gone to Henry's Fifty-seventh Street studio earlier in the evening to seek him out.

"You'll be more than embarrassed if you're lying to me," he threatened, but he need not have bothered. Penny was already so frightened she could barely think, let alone talk, and yet one small compartment of her mind was working efficiently, attempting to size up the hefty Rocco, and screaming at her to change tactics with him. Here was a man used to brute force, her brain was clicking, and yet he worried that everyone thought him stupid. All she had to do was play on the obvious insecurity even a giant like Rocco exuded.

"Why would I lie to you, Rocco? That's your name, isn't it? Rocco, I've got nothing to gain, and everything to lose. You're stronger than I am, and much, much smarter. I'd never try to fool you, Rocco. I'm not quick enough for you."

Rocco smiled, evidently pleased at what she had said about his intelligence. He showed his teeth, his face breaking into an ugly grimace that Penny knew as a smile only because it differed so radically from the scowl that had preceded it. He weighed her reply for another long minute before he loosened his hold on her wrist. Then he went on, evidently deciding she was to be trusted.

"That's right, and don't you forget it! I'll be back," he said. "And I'll be watching you. Don't think you can get away with anything."

"How can I find you to tell you when the Seurats arrive?" asked Penny. As she spoke, she rubbed her lower arm to return the circulation to her wrist once more.

"I'll find you," he said. "I'll be around watching you. Don't you worry; I'll find you when I want to."

He was gone as quickly and silently as he had come, and she knew he meant every word of what he had said.

Chapter Eleven

Penny gave up dialing the number of Andy's apartment at midnight. She had sat on the edge of her bed and just trembled for fifteen minutes after Rocco left her apartment, and then she had roused herself from the crippling fear and began to dial Andy's phone number, but he was not at home. She couldn't imagine where he was at first, until her suspicions began to take hold as her mind calmed down enough to remember that he had been evasive, had even lied to her, before leaving her earlier that afternoon. She thought immediately of Caroline.

Penny felt very alone by midnight. She wanted Andy there to comfort her, wanted him to kiss away the very real goblins that threatened her, and she knew she would have to confide the entire story in him. She had been willing to take the chance after Rocco left her studio, but as the hours wore on and Andy did not answer his telephone, she was torn between anger and distrust, and she did not know what to do.

Finally, she went to bed, but even the slightest noise in the building or on the street outside made her blink open hot, gritty eyes with the tension of fear. Every so often, someone walked by her windows and she looked up through a crack where the draperies did not quite meet, watched the trouser-clad legs hurry down MacDougal Street, and wondered if Rocco would return to threaten her, or worse. She went to the window three times and peered up and down the street, but unable to see far in either direction, she couldn't tell if the Cadillac was parked nearby. Mentally she enumerated the possibilities: There could be no one outside; Rocco could be outside; or another, faceless stranger might be watching. The final possibility scared her more than another meeting with Rocco.

At last she was forced to decide that no one was there, convincing herself that Rocco had delivered his threat and gone home. Only then was she able to drop off into a light and restless sleep.

She called Andy's apartment as soon as she awoke at eight o'clock, but there was no answer. Knowing he might have left for work already, she did not allow herself to assume the worst, but her mind toyed with the possibility that he had spent the night with Caroline, and she felt the fist of sick jealousy close around her heart. At its wretched pain, she forced herself to think of other things. She showered and dressed, leaving the bathroom door open in case Andy called while she was in the shower. She even made herself eat a decent breakfast when she found orange juice and fresh milk in the refrigerator, and a box of cereal in one of the cupboards. At exactly nine o'clock, she called Andy at the office.

She hated to sound like a shrew, but before they had exchanged the minimum of courtesies, she blurted out, "Where were you last night?"

"I had something to do that couldn't be avoided," he answered tightly.

"I needed you, Andy, and you let me down. Something

terrible has happened.'' She hadn't really decided to tell him the entire story immediately, but as soon as she heard his voice, she had been so relieved, she wanted to blurt out about Rocco's visit. Once she told him about Rocco, the rest of the story would have to unfold.

"I'm sorry, Penny," he said. "Some things can't be avoided."

"Your voice sounds funny. Can't you talk?"

"Not easily, but tell me what happened."

"I don't want to tell you on the telephone. Someone might overhear."

"A tapped line? My, Penny, you are dramatic!"

After all she had been through with the thug, Rocco, his skepticism made something snap within Penny. She realized she was extremely angry with Andy for standing her up the night before, and she attacked without thought.

"Forget it, then! You said you were coming back here last night, and you didn't show up. Obviously you don't care what I think, or even what happens to me. All you care about is being with Caroline, so I suppose we have nothing further to discuss."

"How did you know I was with Caroline?" he asked, a note of guilty surprise evident in his voice, but all Penny heard was the confirming words of his question which still echoed between them. The fist that hovered around her heart closed tightly, causing a cold nausea to well up in her stomach. "I tried to call you last night," he was saying, "and I can explain everything, Penny."

"I'm certain you can, but not to me. I don't share my men with other women. Good-bye, Andy. It's been fun." She hung up the telephone which began to ring almost immediately. She snapped the wire from the jack in the wall and went upstairs to feed Winnie's cat.

Andy hung up the telephone after twenty monotonous
rings. Obviously Penny was not going to answer. He had
planned to call her again last night, after he and the Potters
finished dinner at Peacock Alley, but he hadn't been alone
for a minute. Before he knew what was happening, the
four of them were in a taxi and on their way to Studio 54
which Caroline's father wanted to visit, and where Mr.
Potter had talked them past the doorman with a
strategically-placed twenty-dollar bill and a slap on the
back. Caroline had ordered stingers, one after another,
and she was tipsy enough to bring up the subject of the
wedding, much to her mother's glee. Plans had gotten out
of hand, the date had been set, and somehow Andy, who
disliked drinking after dinner and already had consumed
more than an ample share of gin and tonics, found himself
formally engaged and nodding genially when he was told
to report to work at Mr. Potter's insurance company in
Philadelphia on September first.

He had no intention of marrying Caroline, nor of going
to work for her father, but at the time acquiescing seemed
easier than announcing to Caroline in front of her parents
that the engagement was off. Caroline was giggly and silly
from the stingers; the music was too loud; and, frankly, he
did not want to incur Mr. Potter's wrath in the midst of the
Studio 54 dance floor. He planned to tell her tomorrow, or
the next day at the latest. He was sorry arrangements had
progressed to this point but a man had his own life to lead,
and he didn't plan to lead it with Caroline—not when he
had fallen in love with Penelope Greenaway.

He would run up to the Village on his lunch hour and
beg Penny's forgiveness. If she felt half as strongly about
Andy as he felt about her, then she would understand and
make up with him. What did he care if one thing led to
another and he wasn't back in the office on time? He'd

never taken a day off from work before, except for one time when he'd had the flu, and besides, Dieter was out of town and would never know.

At noon Penny was on the steps leading up to Henry Ostrov's studio. She had plugged in her telephone late in the morning, just as Henry dialed her number and tried to blurt out his news. She cut him off, telling him she feared for her privacy, and breathlessly she promised to meet him on Fifty-seventh Street in forty-five minutes. His voice held a contained excitement that made his words heavily accented with his native Russian.

"I've had the infrared photographs developed, Penny," said Henry immediately after he had led her through the door that separated his apartment from the cavernous room in which he conducted the classes in art conservation and restoration.

"So soon, Henry?"

"I could not wait. I analyzed the paint last night, and it was old—definitely turn-of-the-century. I went to a friend to have the photographs developed—I stayed with him in the darkroom the entire time, and there is no chance that he took a copy. As soon as I returned, I called you."

"The painting could still be a forgery."

"The canvas is old, too," he pointed out.

"Still, the painting itself may be new. You taught me yourself that with the right supplies, anything can be duplicated." She enjoyed playing the devil's advocate for Henry. She knew he expected her doubts, as well as she knew from the sparkle in his dark eyes that he was going to prove to her, beyond a doubt, that he had authenticated the painting.

"Ah, but look at my photographs." He spread the glossy prints on the table in front of Penny.

The first was of the neck and head of the native girl. To the left of her head, a faint outline of her face appeared, echoing, but not exactly duplicating the face on the canvas.

"So?" asked Penny. "What does this mean?"

"This photograph shows that the artist first sketched, and later began to paint, the face three inches to the left. Then, deciding to change his composition, he painted out what he had done and began again."

"I see. And this one?" She picked up another photograph which showed the entire face, the faint sketch beneath, and the breasts of the woman.

"That one is not as important as the last, although it, too, shows that the original sketch was conceived to be painted more to the left, and the finished work is more centered. You see?" He ran a finger down the side of the nude's body, pointing out faint, black lines that appeared beneath the background. "Now, Penny, look at the final photograph."

The final picture was of the entire work. Penny held it close to her face and peered carefully. Then, noticing detail at the bottom, she turned the photograph on its side, and she made out the face of another woman at what would have been the lower right of the finished painting, but in the photograph was turned so the face was meant to be seen in the upper right of the canvas.

"There's another portrait here," she whispered.

"A partial portrait," he agreed. "An unfinished head, clearly no more than a detailed sketch, while on the surface is a finished painting of another woman. I *told* you something showed beneath the oil under ultraviolet light," he chuckled. He took an oversized book of Gauguin's works from the table and opened it to a page he had previously marked with an envelope. "Look. Look right here." He indicated a colored plate, a picture of two bare-breasted women, each holding flowers in her hands. "Does this look familiar, Penny?"

"One of the faces in the painting appears on the photograph. What does this mean, Henry?"

"It means that Gauguin began this painting, which is called *Tahitian Women with Mango Blossoms*, on the canvas you have in your possession. Then, deciding to paint his work in another way—in this case, a smaller canvas— he abandoned your canvas and redrew the sketch on another, painting it to completion. *Tahitian Women* is now in the Metropolitan Museum of Art."

"I've seen it there," concurred Penny. "So what do I have, a genuine Gauguin?"

"Another work, one painted later. He painted out the first face, turned the canvas upright, and painted what you now have."

"Conclusively? Henry, how can we be certain?"

"A forger would sketch the original exactly as it is. He would mark off the canvas in grids before copying the work, would he not?"

"Yes, that's what I do when I copy a work."

"Do you see any grids in the infrared photograph? When using a grid, what are your chances of starting your portrait three inches to the left of the original?"

"Zero," she agreed. "But Henry, a forger, a copyist could easily have sketched the face from *Tahitian Woman* on this canvas. Maybe he intended to copy *Tahitian Woman* and changed his mind for some reason. What do you think?"

"I think that no one would go to the trouble of precisely duplicating a work of Gauguin, go to the expense and effort of obtaining an exact match of paint type and canvas, if he wasn't certain beforehand what he intended to paint. Nor is the face in the infrared photograph an exact match of *Tahitian Woman,* I might point out. Had you noticed?''

She studied the photograph more closely, aided by a magnifying glass Henry slipped into her hand. ''You're correct,'' agreed Penny. ''She is facing down and to her right in the Metropolitan's painting, but looking toward the artist in the infrared photograph. Oh, lord, I do believe you're right, Henry. We really have a Gauguin here!

''There's more to my story. I can't find this painting anywhere in my books, Penny. I believe you have a previously unknown work on your hands.''

''You mean it's stolen?''

''No, I don't mean that it hasn't been stolen from someone, somewhere. I'm certain it has been. I only mean that it doesn't come from a museum or from a well-known collection. I must own a dozen books on Gauguin, and the painting you have found appears in none of them, but as you know, many collectors keep their acquisitions secret for tax reasons, or to prevent trouble like robbery.''

''Now what?'' she said, overwhelmed with excitement. Not only finding a Gauguin, but discovering one previously unknown to the world was almost more than Penny could take in at one time.

''Now I visit the Frick to see what I can find about the origins of this painting. I will call you just as soon as I know anything.''

''Be very circumspect on the telephone, Henry. There are people watching me; for all I know, they may even be listening on my phone.''

''I'll come to your place, then. You will make me the tea I did not drink last night. I was in such a hurry to come back here and work on the paint samples—''

"No, don't come to my studio! They know who you are. Let me call you from a pay phone."

"Me? They know Henry Ostrov?" He frowned. "Who is watching you?"

"There's a man called Rocco. Do you know him?" Penny described Rocco in detail, but Henry could not place him. "He seems to be a bodyguard for another man whose name I don't know. They go around in a gray Cadillac with New Jersey license plates. Do you have any idea who they are?"

But Henry didn't know, since Penny had not seen the Whisperer's face, and could describe nothing of him but his shoes and socks, which she did not bother to do. "But there was one thing about the other man, the boss," she added. "He spoke in a whisper, almost as if he had suffered a laryngectomy. Do you know who he is? Rocco knew your name. He recognized you immediately at my apartment."

"No, nothing that you say rings a bell for me," replied Henry before giving Penny a stern lecture about her safety.

"I'm careful," she told him. "Extremely careful. I don't intend to bring the painting back into my studio at all. No one—not even you—know where it is, Henry, and I won't burden you with the knowledge. No one in the world can connect me with the Gauguin."

Thank goodness, she thought happily, there was a safe place for the *Tahitian Maiden*, as she decided to call the painting. A Gauguin! An authentic Gauguin, and only Penny knew that it hung safely out of the cat's reach above the fake fireplace in Winnie's living room. Winnie did not plan to return from Europe until the weekend of Labor Day, which meant there was plenty of time to decide what to do with her treasure, and even if the worst happened, even if Winnie's apartment was burglarized by extreme coincidence, no run-of-the-mill New York burglar would steal a painting from the wall of an ordinary working girl's brownstone walk-up apartment. He would never, ever suspect that an original Paul Gauguin hung on the wall for all the world to see.

"I'll see you after work," said the message from Andy that Penny found slipped under her door when she returned from Henry Ostrov's studio. Clearly Andy had been by during his lunch hour, and had scribbled the note on a page torn from his ubiquitous black book. He had even signed "Love, Andy" in an obvious effort to cajole forgiveness from Penny. She was still angry with him—who would not be, under the circumstances, she asked herself—but the news about the Gauguin had so overwhelmed her with excitement she had trouble remembering to keep her anger burning. In reality she could barely wait to see him and tell him her news. She wanted to share her discovery with someone, and that someone was Andy.

After considerable reflection on her way back to the Village, Penny had concluded the painting was stolen. Whether the Gauguin was well-known or not, paintings did not travel around hidden underneath photographic reproductions unless someone wanted to bring them into the country illegally. Immediately her mind leapt to the possibility that a reward existed for the Gauguin's recovery. There might be fame and money in returning the painting to its rightful owner. She could reasonably expect ten percent of its value, at least, but what *was* the value of a magnificent Gauguin—three million? Five? She shivered with anticipation at the thought, and then wondered where to begin.

"I'm sorry," both Penny and Andy blurted out at the same moment as she opened her door to greet him that evening shortly before six o'clock. He took her in his arms and kissed her soundly. She wrapped her arms around his neck and ran her fingers through his hair while his tongue sought out hers. They stood kissing in a long embrace that left them both breathless.

"I was an awful shrew," she said. "Awful. Can you ever forgive me?"

"I really did try to call you," he explained. "I had a date with Caroline and her family that I couldn't get out of."

"Why didn't you tell me first? I would have understood," she lied, certain that she would have used every possible feminine wile to change his mind if he had implied any such arrangement.

"I'd forgotten myself, but I know you would have understood if I had explained the situation." He held out a bouquet of daisies that he had purchased from a vendor at the top of the stairs leading up from the subway. "The flowers are a bit wilted."

"They're beautiful, Andy. Just beautiful." She recognized the peace offering for what it was. She had seen her father bring home bouquets of flowers—usually roses—again and again, after her parents exchanged angry words behind the closed door of their bedroom suite back home in Wilmette, so she decided to forget her pique with Andy, thrilled to have him dominating the small kitchen with his sturdy presence. Just his being there dissipated the fear she had lived with since Rocco's visit the evening before. As he took off his jacket and tie and laid them in one corner of the counter, she filled an empty mayonnaise jar with water and placed the daisies within, setting the jar on the table.

She poured him a glass of wine, and one for herself,

pulling up a stool to sit facing Andy so that their knees just touched.

"I expected you to be much angrier, Penny," he said seriously.

"I was, but then something happened, something so spectacular, so unbelievable, I couldn't stay angry. Guess what I found! Guess!"

"I can't imagine. Tell me," he urged her, his eyes infected by the dancing excitement he saw in hers.

"A million dollars. Two million, maybe. Maybe even three!" Secretly she believed the painting was worth much, much more.

"Umm." He watched her with an amused expression.

"I've found an authentic Gauguin!" she whispered dramatically.

"Where? In a museum?"

"No, in your shipment of repros." Penny took a sip of her wine and waited for the import of her announcement to sink into Andy's understanding.

"I don't get it," he said, clearly confused.

"Underneath one of the photographs there was a real Gauguin," she explained. "I found it there. No one knows but you and me. Do you get it now?"

Andy still seemed perplexed, so she hurried on, explaining to him the real truth about the men who had kidnapped her, their connection to the break-in at the warehouse and later at her apartment, and finishing with Rocco's visit the previous evening.

"Where is this fabulous painting?" he asked, his expression patient and so condescending that Penny wanted to scream.

"It's hidden away," she said. "Don't worry, the painting is safe."

"Is it here in your apartment?"

"No, it's somewhere else." Andy wasn't reacting in any way as she had expected. She didn't know what she had anticipated from him: great elation like what she felt at the discovery, a worried concern for her safety? Penny frowned.

"What are you going to do now?" he asked.

"I don't know. That's why I was so anxious to see you and discuss the options we have. We could contact the U.S. Customs people, I suppose. Clearly the Gauguin is smuggled, and most probably it's stolen as well. In fact, I'm certain it's stolen. Why else would anyone smuggle it into the country?"

"Options, bah! If there is such a painting, it's under the protection of North American International Underwriters. The reputation of the firm is at stake here, and NAIU is hardly a firm that deals in smuggled merchandise." He narrowed his eyes. "Exactly what crazy scheme are you hatching, Penny?"

"I'll remove the Gauguin from the shipment. The company won't have to be involved," she hastened to add.

"You can't take anything from the shipment," Andy sputtered, shocked. "That wouldn't be right, Penny, and you know it."

"What are you talking about!" she said with disgust. "NAIU doesn't even know the painting exists!" She gulped her wine and refilled the jelly glass.

"It belongs to the consignee, Penny. You would be stealing!"

"I have no intention of stealing the painting. I'm aware the painting belongs to someone else. What do you take me for, anyway—some kind of sneak thief? Don't you understand? The painting is already stolen, and I have found it. I merely want credit for my discovery. If you find a Gauguin, you're on the map, Andy. I'll be someone. My business will get a much-needed shot in the arm, and all my problems will be solved. Don't you see what a fantastic opportunity this discovery is for me? I have it all figured out so that NAIU won't be involved at all.''

Something made Penny hold back her growing hope of receiving a substantial finder's fee. Andy was having enough trouble with the idea that the painting existed in the first place. Besides, he was hopelessly moralistic and had an antiquated concept of company loyalty that was naive, unrealistic, and thankless. If a reward was to be paid, who was more deserving—Penelope Greenaway or North American International Underwriters? Who had discovered the Gauguin in the first place? Did an international firm need a piddling extra income that would be lost among the numbers of its annual report, or did she, a hardworking single girl down on her luck? The question was beyond discussion.

''Why are you telling me all this?''

''Because I need you to fix up the shipping papers so that they show only ninety-nine paintings were sent from Germany. Or perhaps, that only ninety-nine were recovered after the hijacking.''

''You know I can't do that, Penny,'' he said, now genuinely shocked at her suggestion. ''The mere idea is outrageous. The consignee owns the painting. You can't just pluck a painting from a crate that belongs to them.''

''Wake up, mister,'' she spat. ''You're hopeless! The consignee doesn't have any idea the painting is in that shipment. How much did you tell me that load of junk is insured for?''

''A hundred thousand dollars. And you yourself said at the time, that was too much money for a bunch of reproductions. So you see, they were insuring the purported Gauguin, as well.''

''You don't know beans, Andy. Monets, Manets, Cézannes—they regularly fetch a million apiece. Sotheby's sold a Degas pastel for three-and-three-quarters of a million dollars not long ago. A *pastel*. I'm talking about an oil painting by Paul Gauguin. A genuine Gauguin. A major post-Impressionist work by a major artist. I don't think you understand the significance of what I'm trying to tell you, Andy.''

"You're right, I don't understand. Explain to me what you plan to do with your so-called discovery.''

"My so-called discovery! You sound like you don't believe a word of what I'm telling you. Don't you even care that I was kidnapped? Don't you care that a man forced his way into my apartment last night and threatened me? Why should I take all the heat for your crummy shipment?'' She was furious by now, up on her feet, pacing around the kitchen gesturing wildly, her wine slopping over the side of the jelly glass. She looked down at her hand which was damp from the wine, and suddenly she tossed the wine, glass and all, into the sink where the glass broke into fifteen pieces. She sat down hard on the stool and stared at Andy.

"Take it easy, Penny,'' said Andy, never one to encourage a scene. "You're overwrought, and you've allowed your imagination to run away with you. I'm the first to admit the circumstances surrounding this shipment are suspicious, but I can't believe you've come across a piece of art as valuable as you claim. If you had your hands on a painting worth millions, would you let it out of your sight for a moment? Would you ship it in a crate you couldn't follow every step of the way?''

"I admit the story sounds far-fetched, but the painting is out of my sight right now, and I'm not worried in the slightest,'' she told him. "But you! You're driving me crazy! How can I take it easy?'' she shouted. "This is the most incredible opportunity of my life—of yours, too, if you want some glory—and you pooh-pooh the entire matter. What do you want me to do?"

"Just turn everything over to me, and I'll talk to my boss. He can decide the best way to handle the situation," said Andy calmly. "He's out of town until Monday, but I'll ask him then. Will the so-called painting be safe until Monday?"

"And North American International Underwriters get all the publicity for the find," she finished. "No thanks, Andy. I'll take care of the matter myself. Forget I ever mentioned the Gauguin to you."

"C'mon, Penny, it's too late for that," he replied, still calm, which infuriated her even more. "Give me the painting."

"You'd never get off my block with it. There's a man watching my every move."

"Now, Penny," he chuckled. "You're hopelessly dramatic." Casually he topped off the wine in his jelly glass. "Admit it: There is no painting. You painted a copy that you want to foist off on the world as an original. If you were telling the truth, you'd let me turn the matter over to Dieter and be done with it. Now, wouldn't you?"

"I don't care if you believe me or not!" she shouted. "You're hopelessly stuffy! If I were you, I wouldn't give a tinker's damn what that stupid company of yours thinks. I'm talking about a major discovery, Andy, and you'd blow the entire thing by telling your boss. They don't care about you over at NAIU—it's every man for himself. Haven't you told me that already? Lord, you're like a little Bob Cratchit working yourself into an early grave for the greater good of North American International Underwriters to whom you're just another employee number. Where's your sense of adventure? Where's your nerve? I know together we could pull off this little caper, and no one will be hurt, least of all us. I don't want to do anything dishonest. I'm not a thief! All I want is a shot at making a name for myself.''

"I can't be a part of your scheme," he said. "My career would be ruined if any of this ever came out."

"Your career would be ruined," she said, sarcasm dripping from every word. "You pompous ass! Caroline might not want you anymore if your name got sullied, is that it?"

"What does Caroline have to do with this discussion?" asked Andy, genuinely perplexed.

"Nothing. Everything! Where were you last night? You said you'd be here, and instead you went to Caroline. You told me you were finished with her, but the first chance you get you hop from my bed to hers. I needed you last night, Andy, and you let me down."

"I did not go from your bed to hers," he said. "I went to see her to explain about you, to tell her that she and I were finished."

"I hope you didn't speak too soon, you stuffy moron. What makes you think I want to see you again after today? You drive me right up the wall!" She lowered her voice. "What did she say when you told her?" asked Penny, touched, despite her anger, that Andy had spoken so quickly to Caroline, and broken off the arrangement between them, whatever it had been.

"I didn't tell her, after all," he said quietly, discomfort written all over his features.

"Why not?" Penny frowned, disappointment quickly replacing the warm glow she had felt a moment earlier. His story had sounded too good to be true, she realized quickly. Men these days weren't that ethical, not with all the single women available to them.

"We got engaged instead," he admitted reluctantly. "It was just the result of an unfortunate circumstance. But I'm going to fix all that, Penny,'' he hastened to explain. ''As soon as I'm able, I plan to tell her everything.''

''What! You went to break up and got engaged instead? What do you take me for, the biggest fool in New York? You had no intention of breaking up with Caroline. Get out of here, Andrew Keller. I don't want anything to do with you after that shabby admission. I can just imagine when you plan to come clean with Caroline—sometime in the twenty-first century! You must think I'm pretty stupid, huh?''

''I'm telling you the truth, Penny. You mean more to me than a hundred Carolines, a thousand Carolines. She doesn't mean a thing to me anymore, nor does the job offer from her father. I—''

''Her father offered you a job? And you accepted?''

''Yes, but—''

''Last night you accepted a job? You went to break an engagement and you accepted a job. You're certainly a strongly-motivated man, Andrew Keller. A man who truly knows his own mind.''

''Penny, let me explain—''

''Out, Keller. I mean it! You made your choice, so go live with it! I thought you were different; I thought you had some ethics, but I can see I was mistaken. You aren't much of a man anyway. I've known better—in bed and out!''

Penny turned her face away at the look of pain she saw on Andy's features, knowing she had struck blindly and thoughtlessly and hit him squarely where men felt most insecure. No matter that the time with him had been the most fantastic, the most transporting in her life. No matter that she knew she already loved him. Right then, all she wanted was to hurt him as much as he had hurt her with his damning admissions about Caroline and her father, and she saw from the look on his face that she had succeeded beyond expectation. In a low voice, nearly choking on the words, she said,

"Just get out of my studio and out of my life, and don't come back."

There was a moment of heavy silence. Finally Andy raised himself from the stool and stood looking down at her hair. "Just look who's talking about ethics, Miss Greenaway. What about the painting?" he asked with dignity, reaching for his suit jacket which lay at one side of the counter.

"Forget the painting," she told him. "Forget I ever mentioned the painting. I was mistaken. Just a trick of my imagination, as you suggested. My imagination has been working overtime lately." *Starting with the way I thought you cared for me,* she thought. "You'll get your hundred reproductions restored, as agreed."

"You didn't mean what you said, did you, Penny?" he asked in a voice that was rough with emotion.

"I meant every single word of it," she told him. "You're a weak man, a poor lover, and a social climber. You have what you want in Caroline, so why are you hanging around me? Caroline's not only what you want, but she's just what you deserve. I wish you all the success of my father; I can see you're just like him. Good luck, Andy."

"I mean, what you said about bed," he persisted. "You told me a different story before. In bed."

"You're a real masochist, aren't you? Do I have to spell out the alphabet for you? Why did you whisper the sweet nothings you did when all along you were planning to marry that society bitch? Those are just words people say when they're in bed together, Keller. They don't mean a thing. I've been around," she lied cruelly, "and I know what I'm talking about."

There was another long silence.

"I know you're lying to me, Penny. I know I've hurt you, and I'm sorry. You and I aren't cut out for each other, I guess that's obvious. We have different standards and different ideas of what's important in life. If there's one thing important to me, it's honesty, but you tell so many lies you don't know what the truth is.''

"I am not a liar," she said dully.

"Let me rephrase," said Andy. "You're a very charming child-woman. Part of your charm is the different way you look at life, coupled with your lack of inhibition. I suppose those qualities are connected somehow with your artistic abilities. I don't know; I've never met a woman like you before, but the problem is that your imagination is so vivid you don't know reality from wishful thinking. Your story about Gauguins and thugs is very amusing, but hardly the stuff everyday life is made of. Your story about your lovers...well, if it's true, I feel sorry for you. You're terrific just the way you are; you don't need to validate yourself by being promiscuous. There's more to life than running around hopping in and out of beds looking for God knows what. A lot more to life.

"You're off the job first thing in the morning," he said finally, and, as he spoke, she saw the look of strength she had first seen when they negotiated her fee in the warehouse one morning so long ago. One thing about Andy, Penny thought, when it came to NAIU, he was all business, no matter what else was going on around him. "I'll send Mercurio by to pick up everything you have. Everything, do you understand?''

"They won't be ready tomorrow," she told him quickly. "I have to put things back together. Some of the frames are dismantled." She needed much more time to work out a decent plan, but right then she was unable to think clearly. Right then all she felt was the pain of his betrayal with Caroline. She had lied about his love-making, pretending she didn't care when she cared more than anything in the world. Again she had lied about her sexual experience, which was nothing to send to the *Guinness Book of World Records*, purposely leading him to believe he was just another man in a long string of lovers in order to protect herself from more pain from him. But she meant what she told him about his future; one glimpse of Caroline's aristocratic face and she had seen the Wilmette Syndrome all over again. Andy deserved her! *Let me see you take a Mercedes Benz upstairs to bed on a cold winter night,* she thought bitterly, thinking of her poor father and the emotional starvation of his life with her mother.

"Now, what about the painting?"

"What do you mean?" asked Penny, looking at him sharply.

"Are you going to admit you told me a falsehood? Come on, Penny: Own up to the truth, for once." He looked at her sternly. He reminded her of a schoolmaster demanding to know who was responsible for the latest trick. She couldn't believe he was dense enough to believe she'd make up a story so easily proven. All he needed to do was demand to see the Gauguin, and the painting itself— whether he believed it was authentic or fake—would prove that the shipment was tainted by unknown hands. But Andy was stubborn, she realized. Stubborn, and hurt by her accusations. He needed to wrest at least one victory from their confrontation, and she was happy to cede, since she needed time more than her pride.

"You're right," she said with what she hoped seemed like contrition. "I painted the Gauguin. I don't know why I told you such a ridiculous lie. Maybe to get your attention. I was worried about Caroline, I guess. I wanted you all to myself."

"We had a nice time together," he said gently. "I'll never forget you, but Caroline and I have been planning to marry all along. Good luck to you, Penny."

"You, too, Andy." She kept her eyes down.

"All right," said Andy, immediately back to business. "I don't suppose there's any harm leaving the job with you for a while. I'll try to get another restorer so you and I won't have to work together again, but if not, please promise you'll do your best on the job. If you screw up, Dieter will have my head."

She pictured herself dressed as a veiled Salome with Andy's head resting on a platter, an apple in his mouth. *I'd like to have your head,* she said to herself, the pain in her heart burning brightly then, but quickly congealing into a cold anger. She should be happy with her victory, she thought. He had given her what she wanted: He was going to leave the job in her care awhile longer. But instead of elation, she was insulted that the man who had whispered such glorious love words into her ears, the man who had made such tender, thoughtful love to her entire soul, thought so little of her that he'd believe words shouted in the heat of the moment, ignore her discovery, and downplay the dangers she had faced. She realized he thought she was a little crazy. More than a little: He seemed to think she was a compulsive liar.

Penny sighed, mentally thanking the gods that Andy was totally ignorant of the art world. If he had the slightest idea how important her discovery was, he'd be tearing the studio apart to find the Gauguin. She accepted his proposal without showing the slightest bit of gratitude, as if it were the most normal thing in the world to leave a Gauguin lying around unclaimed for a few days. She focused on the painting and what its discovery meant for her future. Anything was better than accepting the import of the statement that he still planned to marry Caroline.

She remained on the stool with her eyes downcast, when he let himself out the front door.

Chapter Twelve

"Penny, how would you like to meet me for dinner?" asked Henry, Friday afternoon on the telephone. "I know it has taken me most of the week, but now I have something for you."

"My pleasure, and my treat, Henry. When and where?" They settled on a small Japanese restaurant on Fifty-seventh Street, not far from his studio. Penny was there exactly on time, but she found Henry already waiting for her at a table in the back. His black eyes literally danced with excitement as she sat down across from him, mentally pleased to see they would not be forced to kneel on the floor, Japanese style. Usually Penny was game for any new experience, but the last few days she felt drugged with lethargy. Ever since Andy and she had parted, she found the slightest movement an effort. Even getting out of bed in the morning took supreme courage. She knew she should be elated about the Gauguin painting, but, strangely, the thought of it safely tucked away in Winnie's apartment brought her no consolation. All she wanted was Andy, as stuffy and stubborn as he was. But she knew it was too late to make up with him. He had walked out of her door—as she had requested—and she hadn't heard from him again.

"You're looking thin and sad, dear Penny. What is your problem? Do you want to try saki, the Japanese wine?"

Penny nodded at Henry's suggestion of wine. "A man, what else?" she answered his query. "But I'll get over him. He was never my type, Henry, and it's much better to extricate yourself from a bad situation early on than to do something foolish—like marry in haste. Not that I was thinking of getting married!" she hurriedly added. "I need a little time to get over him, that's all."

Penny spoke bravely, having spent a solid week telling herself exactly the justifications she had mouthed to Henry, but in truth, she missed Andy desperately. She was aware of the dark smudges beneath her eyes and of the sudden thinness that had appeared below her cheekbones, and she knew that at night she was having trouble sleeping. Before he came into her life, she had always slept like a top. She lay in her bed and thought of her times with Andy, alternately loving him and damning him for his rigidity and moral superiority. She tried not to think of his engagement to Caroline at all because the thought wrenched her heart.

Henry poured two small glasses of warm saki from the white container the waitress brought to their table at his request. Penny looked at the menu in confusion.

"Will you order for me, please? I have no idea what all these things are. *Sushi, sashimi, fukiyose chirashi*... What does all this mean, Henry?"

He explained that *fukiyose chirashi* was a spectacular presentation in a *bento* or lacquered container, like a picnic box lunch. "It consists of shrimp, hard-boiled egg, *sashimi*, and pickled vegetables on a layer of vinegared rice."

"What's *sashimi*?"

"That's raw fish," he explained. "I can ask what is fresh today. You would like the red snapper, or perhaps the tuna—"

"I've heard they eat shark and mackerel, too. No—no raw fish for me, Henry. Order me something normal like fried shrimp, please."

"It's not like you to be such a stick-in-the-mud," he observed. "You've always been the first to try something new, Penny."

"I know, Henry. I'm not myself these days. But I'll get better." She smiled, an effort which cost her considerable energy. She didn't want to worry Henry who could be sternly paternalistic toward his students, present and former, when the spirit moved him.

"I have some exciting news for you," said Henry, after he ordered the *fukiyose chirashi* for himself, having determined that the specialty fish was *toro*, or fatty tuna, one of his favorites. He ordered a basket of tempura, which was fried shrimp, for Penny. "I know who owns the painting."

"Tell me everything!" She bit into the tempura, found it thoroughly cooked and delicious as well, and she began to eat with relish for the first time that week.

"The Count von Rombauer, formerly of Bavaria, but now a resident of Asuncíon, Paraguay. Have you heard of him, Penny?"

"No, never. But he sounds like a Nazi if he's living in Paraguay."

"You are an intelligent young lady. Yes, he was a colonel in the S.S. who fled to Paraguay after the Second World War. He is still alive, although quite elderly by now, and he has a small, but impressive art collection."

"In Paraguay? I've never heard of an important collection there, have you?"

"No, his art is stored secretly in Germany. Many have searched for the collection, but no one has yet located it. You may well imagine, many have looked for the count, as well, but he is wealthy; he pays royally for his protection;

and the government of Paraguay is apparently willing to overlook his unsavory past and allow him to live out what is left of his life in peace. Such a privilege is frightfully expensive, as well, so periodically the count sells off a piece from his collection to raise money. He always sells privately, and although no one knows for certain, it is assumed that the works go for far below their fair market value because the count is in no position to hold a public auction.''

"So the painting is stolen, after all. He took it from a museum during the war. Or, probably, he put its rightful owner in a concentration camp. Someone—someone's survivors, that is—are going to be very surprised to suddenly inherit a genuine Gauguin. I hope they'll be willing to give me a finder's fee.''

"The painting is not stolen, *cherie*. There is no record of a painting such as yours having been stolen,'' said Henry.

"Mine!'' she exclaimed. "I wish it *were* mine. I'm just a very frightened baby-sitter.

"Nevertheless in the absence of other claims, the Gauguin apparently belongs to the count, although he, like many others of the Third Reich, amassed his share of art from the unfortunate victims of Hitler's rampage. When the war was drawing to a close and it became evident that the Allies were to be the victors, Count von Rombauer disappeared. He took what art he could—what he owned before the war and what he fancied—but he left some works behind, left them hanging on the walls of his ancestral castle. Those paintings were repatriated to their owners—to their rightful countries, at least—to museums and governments. Some went eventually to the State of Israel, in absence of surviving claimants. Some, as you probably know, are in the Hermitage in Leningrad, part of war reparations paid to the Russians. But, I am getting off the subject.

"There was a man after the war, a Rumanian, I believe, who made his living repatriating works of art—naturally, for a fee. At the time, he was called Steve Crescu or something of the sort. I met him in the course of my work in those days—authenticating paintings, things like that. Crescu made a lot of money back then, not very nice money. It was a shady occupation. First of all, how does one know where to find a lost Rembrandt, for example? How can one deal with a hidden Nazi who is sought by many governments for his crimes, and still not reveal the whereabouts of such a monster? But Crescu made himself a fortune by doing exactly that, and then he changed his name to Stephen Crespin and came to New York where he opened a gallery on Madison Avenue. Even as Crespin, I dealt with him now and again years ago, a few small jobs, nothing illegal at all. Tightening a canvas on its stretcher, cleaning off the grime of years. The little jobs we all take to survive."

Penny nodded. "Why are you telling me about Crespin, Henry?" They had finished the container of warm saki by then, and Penny was pouring tea.

"Because you know him already, dear Penny," he said in a voice fraught with meaning.

"I don't think so," she said with a frown of doubt.

"Oh, yes. He has had his larynx removed due to cancer. Now do you know who I mean?"

"The Whisperer!" Penny felt a shiver snake up her spine and down her arms, making the hair that grew there stand up in fear.

"Your Whisperer is known to take care of business for the Count von Rombauer. When you first mentioned him to me, I made no connection. But later, when all the signs in my research pointed to Paraguay, I realized it was Crespin who came to you that night. You do not want to be involved with this man, Penny. Take my word for it, he is a dangerous adversary."

"But I'm involved already. He knows who I am, where I live. He knows everything about me!" She pushed away the basket of shrimp, having lost her appetite completely.

"But he does not know you have the Gauguin, or you would not be here to have dinner with me."

"No, he doesn't know I have the painting. Not yet."

"How did you get the Gauguin in the first place?"

Penny explained her involvement with the painting, beginning with the NAIU shipment, going through the hijacking at the airport, her subsequent hiring to repair water damage to the frames, the break-in at the warehouse, and finishing with her discovery of the Gauguin beneath the photographic reproduction. Henry sat listening to the entire account, trying to fit the pieces together.

"The hijacking was unrelated," he said at last. "Something is always stolen and ransomed from those cargo buildings at JFK. It's a regular hotbed of crime out there."

"Yes, that's exactly what An... that's exactly what the insurance agent told me," she replied, finding it too painful to use Andy's name, and afraid Henry would ask her to explain who Andy was.

"The break-in clearly was staged by Crespin," said Henry. "Somehow he used the cover of the shipment to secretly bring the painting into the country, never expecting that von Rombauer's Gauguin would be hijacked. When it was, he broke into the warehouse to steal the painting entrusted to him, knowing that any restorer who went through the pictures was capable of finding the authentic painting. Why didn't he find the Gauguin in the warehouse?"

"Because the crate hiding the Gauguin was already in transit to my studio, but hadn't arrived by the time they broke into my place looking for it," she explained. "They slashed open everything I had on hand to see if the canvas was there."

"They've been in your studio?" Henry paled visibly.

"But they didn't find the painting, Henry. It's safely hidden away now. No one but me knows where it is."

"Penny, you have no idea how much danger you're in! Crespin is ruthless, and we're talking about millions of dollars. Millions!"

"Yes, I know, Henry. But even if this Count von what's-his-name owns the Gauguin legally, why should I hand it back to him? It's the same as putting a million dollars into his blood-stained, Nazi-murderer hands. Why can't I just make public that I've found a Gauguin? What can he do then? Can he come up from Paraguay and claim the painting is his? I doubt it, Henry."

"Forget your crazy scheme!" Henry exploded. "Put everything back the way you found it, give Crespin the crate of paintings, and then just forget about this Gauguin. You are playing with your life, Penny. I assure you."

"But a Gauguin belongs to the world!" she insisted. "It's already been hidden away for a generation. This... this count has a debt to pay to humanity, and I hardly think putting the painting back in his hands is a good start, Henry. It's like endorsing the Holocaust, or on the most insignificant level, it's rewarding von what's-his-name for his cunning and his ability to terrorize innocent people like you and me. Besides, you know what will happen: He'll squirrel the Gauguin back into hiding until things cool off, and then he'll try to sell it again, this time successfully. The Gauguin is a masterpiece, and it's time for the public to see it. A painting that magnificent belongs to the world, not a fugitive from international justice. It just isn't fair, Henry!

"Now, I've been thinking about what to do. I decided that if I found someone willing, for a finders fee—let's say ten percent—to donate the painting to the Metropolitan

Museum or, in light of what you've just told me, to a museum in Jerusalem or Tel Aviv, I could—''

"Penny, listen to me. The Gauguin is unknown for now, and has been for years. What are a few more years? It's not as if Crespin and von Rombauer don't know what a treasure they have. It's not as if someone will destroy a masterpiece out of ignorance, as sometimes happens. Cover up the painting and give it to Crespin. The artistic well-being of the world will mean nothing to you when you're at the bottom of Sheepshead Bay,'' he said, mentioning a notorious dumping ground for bodies that needed disposing of.

"You mean cover the painting again?'' she said in a small voice. "Put a covering over the *Tahitian Maiden*?'' Her eyes widened with outrage at his suggestion.

"Yes, that's exactly what I mean! Reapply the overlay you found originally. Put the photo-reproduction back on top, and give Crespin the painting. Wash your hands of the entire episode, and for God's sake, get out of New York. If you're lucky, Crespin will leave you alone as long as you convince him you are completely ignorant of his real business.''

"But I don't want to wash my hands of the entire episode. Too many people have made it their business to ignore evil in this world. You know what I'm saying is true, Henry. You know that's why that Nazi has been living undisturbed in Paraguay all these years. And on a selfish note, I don't want to leave New York,'' she added. "I don't want to go back home, Henry.''

"You told me not long ago you were planning to go back to Iowa, did you not?''

"Illinois,'' she corrected him absentmindedly, already thinking of something else. Her eyes had turned a murky brown and she blew up on her bangs distractedly. Her hair fluttered and settled again on her forehead.

"Iowa, Illinois. What do I know? I am from the Ukraine. You asked me if I knew of people to buy your studio. I asked around, and I found three of my students who want to go into business together. They will buy everything—your equipment, your lease. I will make the arrangements." Henry leaned forward to catch Penny's attention, but she was staring at a spot on the wall behind him, seemingly lost in thought. "Penny, are you listening to me? Do you still have the photograph to put on top of the Gauguin? Is it in good shape?"

Penny snapped her head around to look at Henry. He had given her an idea that was so crazy, so impossible, she could hardly concentrate on his warning. "Yes, Henry, I'm listening and, yes, I still have the photograph. I'll do as you say. I'll cover the painting."

"Good girl! Your life is worth more than the glory of discovering a Gauguin, Penny. Life is everything! *Sic transit gloria.*"

"I think my life is very important, Henry. It's all I've got, after all." *My life and ten percent of an original Gauguin.*

"Good girl," he said again, patting her hand which rested on the table, with enthusiastic approval.

What Henry said was true—the glory of discovering the painting was a dangerous one. What difference did it make if no one knew Penelope Greenaway had actually uncovered the *Tahitian Maiden*? Such egotistic folly could cost her life, a price she might willingly pay, she thought with a shudder, if unimaginable things at the hands of Rocco and his friends preceded its loss.

But there was a way. A way to cash in on her discovery, bring the Gauguin to the world, and eke a tiny revenge from Count von Rombauer, from Crespin, and from their unsavory associates. She needed a backer, she decided, someone with money to burn who could take the heat off Penelope Greenaway, someone willing to see that the Gauguin got into the right hands. For a minor consideration—ten percent, perhaps—a philanthropist could donate the painting to a suitable institution. Penny would make it very clear to the generous benefactor that the *Tahitian Maiden* was not for sale, that it had to be placed where the most people would benefit. There were details to be worked out, of course. Lots of tiny, but vital details. . . .

I'll have my life, the world will have the Gauguin, too, she said to herself. All that was missing from the picture was Andrew Keller.

Andy patted the left pocket of his jacket again as he and Caroline stepped out of a taxi at the corner of Ninety-third Street and Madison Avenue. The small box sat safely in the dark recesses of his pocket.

The ring within the box had cost him nearly two months' salary, an extravagance he could ill afford, but he rationalized his purchase once more, telling himself that Caroline not only expected, but deserved, the tasteful ring—two round, very dark blue sapphires set in simple white platinum on either side of an equally-sized diamond. A classic Tiffany ring in a classic Tiffany box.

His boat account had sunk to a new low, but he knew he would never be buying the schooner he coveted, so what was the difference? Sometimes a man had to let go of his dreams when he reached a certain age. With regret, a man had to move on to new frontiers.

He had chosen the restaurant for that Saturday night's ceremony with equal precision, settling on Devon House, Ltd. after careful thought. He wanted a correct and quiet atmosphere when he gave Caroline the ring, and he knew his choice was right as they descended three steps from the street to enter a handsomely appointed vestibule that led to two small rooms done in robin's egg blue. Superb flower arrangements studded the rooms which had antique mantelpieces against the walls, shirred muslin curtains at the windows, and fine brass sconces protecting the electric candles that provided subdued lighting for the discreetly spaced tables. Devon House, Ltd. seemed more like an elegant private club than a public restaurant, and Andy watched Caroline's brown eyes survey the room appreciatively before she asked him to order her a dry Rob Roy while she made her decision from the limited menu.

"We have some important things to discuss, Andrew," she said, and he felt his heart leap with nervousness. Although the box in his pocket, which he touched once again, was proof enough of his contrition for abandoning Caroline for Penny the previous Sunday, Andy felt he owed Caroline a formal apology for his behavior. In light of the way things had turned out with Penny, no choice remained but to cement his relationship with his fiancée, and he knew he was fortunate the choice still lay open to him. He had acted foolishly with Penny, allowed her to turn his head, and he felt saved from the fire by the quick turn of events that had prevented him from making an irreparable mistake with her.

But his head was filled with confusion nonetheless. He was relieved that circumstances the previous Monday—the presence of the senior Potters, the noise at Studio 54, the excessive alcohol they had all consumed—had made it inadvisable to break off with Caroline at that time, providing him with an opportunity to see Penny for what she really was—dishonest and foolhardy, at best; a compulsive liar and attention-grabber, at worst. Clearly fate had taken a hand in his future. His plans with Caroline had remained intact, had even taken an enormous leap forward in light of the escalation of their relationship that had taken place at Peacock Alley and Studio 54 that evening. Suddenly he had found himself with a new job, a self-contained and lovely fiancée, and prospects for an affluent future.

Why, then, was his stomach so queasy? Why, then, did he feel like asking an invisible executioner for a blindfold and a cigarette, although Andy did not smoke? He supposed all bachelors felt the same sinking sensations in the pit of their stomachs when they planned the one-way leap into matrimony.

"First tell me what you'd like for dinner, Caroline. I've heard service here is on the slow side, although the wait is worthwhile, so we had better order now."

"I know exactly, Andrew. I'll have the veal sweetbreads in puff pastry, carrot and orange soup, and a brace of quail. What about you?"

"The same," he answered listlessly. He had already lost his appetite, although there was no denying that the aromas from the kitchen at Devon House were delightful. "But I'll have *escargots* instead of the sweetbreads." Andy ordered for them both.

"Caroline, I owe you an apology," he began. "That girl who came to my apartment last weekend... That woman, I mean, truly was a client. She's a restorer we hired to fix the shipment of paintings I told you I'm handling, and we've had a tremendous amount of trouble with the entire job. She's a bit of a flake," he went on, feeling guilty at describing Penny that way, although his words were nothing but the truth, "but a well-known restorer, and it's important to NAIU that—"

"Andrew, there's no need to explain," said Caroline kindly, looking at him with her nearly opaque brown eyes and resting one cool, genteelly-manicured hand atop his. "Men will be men. Don't you think I understood exactly how things were between you and that... that tramp?"

She lowered her voice on the final word, although no one seated in the room would have been able to hear the well modulated tones in which she spoke. Her eyes were lowered as well as she glanced down at her drink, so she didn't see the wince of displeasure that crossed Andy's face at her cruel assessment of Penny.

"Oh, you're wrong, Caroline," he interjected quickly. "Miss Greenaway is not a tramp, and there was nothing like what you imply between us! She's a client, or at least she's a jobber hired to please a client, and being an artist of sorts, she's temperamental and flighty. She needed to be cared for at the time, and she came to me for help. What could I do? You of all people know how important it sometimes is to curry the favor of clients. You grew up in that atmosphere with your father, I'm sure."

He felt like a traitor as he mouthed the lies about Penny. Flighty she was, but temperamental? No, not a bit. She was the most placid of women—loving and caring, warm and affectionate. The more he thought of her, the more he wished it were Penny, not Caroline, seated across the table from him, and he wondered where she was on that hot Saturday night in August, and if she were alone or with someone else. He tasted the white wine which had arrived at the table, and found it lacking zest.

He shook his head, reminding himself that he was through with Penny. She was dishonest. She was irresponsible. It was sinful to be even thinking about her while Caroline sat sweetly across the table from him waiting for the Tiffany ring she was almost certain to know was in his pocket.

"Now, there's no need to be stuffy," said Caroline with a hint of rebuke in her voice. "Anyway, it's I who owe you an apology."

"Whatever for?" he asked, genuinely surprised.

"For taking matters into my own hands on Monday when my parents were here. For precipitating the engagement, so to speak. You're a very cautious man, too cautious sometimes. And, although I've known for a long time that you intended to propose formally, I forced the issue on Monday, and I openly admit the fact. Sometimes a woman knows better than a man what's best for them both. Sometimes she has to save a man from his own impetuous self. Do you see my point?''

Andy, who had never considered himself impetuous, who was, in fact, the least impetuous of souls, bristled openly.

''No, I do not see your point, Caroline,'' he said levelly. ''And I don't appreciate your patronizing attitude, either.'' The night wasn't turning out as he had planned.

But Caroline went on, blithely ignoring his pique. ''You've had your little fling with your tootsie, whatever her name is. Now it's time to make plans—''

''Penelope,'' he interjected. ''Penelope Greenaway, and she is hardly my tootsie.''

''All right, Andrew. You had your fling, and I'm not one to begrudge you your fun. I've had my own share of adventures. When you were in Tampa, for instance, I saw a man. Well, it wasn't the first time I'd seen him, but you know how those adventures are—they mean nothing in the overall scheme of life. He's a very sexy man. Macho is the word they use for a man like him, but he's not our kind of people,'' she said, her voice dropping to a confidential whisper, her patrician nose wrinkling just slightly as she spoke. ''Just the kind of man a woman sees once in awhile, on a lark. It always makes a woman appreciate the serious man in her life, don't you think?''

''I wouldn't know,'' he said tightly, staring agog at Caroline who was picking at the mushrooms that surrounded her sweetbreads. Although Caroline obviously enjoyed the food, Andy had lost his own appetite entirely. He felt like some sort of hallucinogenic drug had been slipped into the white Bordeaux in his wineglass. Her words were surreal, and so were the surroundings of Devon House, Ltd.

"Mummy and Daddy are crazy about you, Andrew. They know, as I do, that you and I have so much in common. We have common aspirations for the future, we know the same people, we can always *talk*. I've always felt that talking is such an important part of marriage. This other man—I wouldn't be so indiscreet as to mention his name—is just for sex. Afterward, there's never a thing to discuss, although I always try with his kind in the beginning. God knows, I tried with him, but I've found that kind of man is always the same. None of them likes to talk about anything but himself. That's when I feel so fortunate that *you* are the real man in my life."

"Thank you for the compliment, Caroline." Andy closed his mouth which he realized had been wide open in shock. With a mighty effort to keep his voice steady, he said, "That's always a problem—talking, I mean. Yes, always a problem."

"So, when I saw you with your tootsie, I understood immediately where you were coming from, as they say." She reached across the table and patted his hand once again, not noticing or not caring to notice that his fingers clenched so tightly that his knuckles were turning a yellowish white. "After we're married, you may be certain I'll understand a foray on your part into the gamier side of life. Everyone is entitled to an adventure now and again, Andrew. An adventure keeps life from losing its sparkle, don't you think?" She smiled guilelessly into his eyes.

"Like your father's adventures," he said.

"Exactly. And like Mummy's, as well. Of course, both Mummy and Daddy are extremely discreet," she added. "They're never involved with anyone from our set. That would be tacky."

"I'll say," he concurred. "And you follow the rules, as well? You would never embarrass me with a friend, would you Caroline?"

"Never! How can you ask such a silly thing?" Her laughter tinkled gently from across the table. She leaned toward him. "Andrew, if there's one thing I understand, it's the social order. What's important is to keep life on an even keel. That's one of the things about you that I find so endearing, even though you're not exactly from our set. Even though you weren't exactly Main Line when we met, you've learned a lot in a short time; you understand what's important in life, Andrew." She smiled, showing her perfectly even teeth once again. Inanely he thought that the orthodontia must have cost as much as the newly-purchased diamond and sapphire ring from Tiffany and Company.

Andy patted the ring box in his pocket. "Would you excuse me for a moment? I have to visit the men's room. I'll be back before the quail arrives." He left the table in a rush, his legs weak beneath him. He thought he might be sick before he got to the door of the men's room.

The rest of the evening went by in a blur for Andy. He picked at his quail, which Caroline ate with relish. He did slightly better with the salad course that followed, ate a bit of the cheese and fruit course, and watched with disgust as Caroline put away the apricot tart she ordered for dessert. The most incredible thing was that Caroline was totally unaware that she'd said anything amiss.

When the coffee arrived, he told her they were through. At first he had planned to wait until they got back to her apartment, but the thought of being with her any longer than necessary turned his stomach. Somewhere he had read that a restaurant—a good restaurant—was the place to break off an affair, an engagement, or a marriage. He'd read a woman was less likely to make a scene in public than between the four walls of her own home. Caroline's breeding did not fail her. She listened in silence with her chin held high, and then in a quiet whisper that reached only Andy, she hissed out a string of words he had never imagined she knew, let alone used so freely. When he called for the bill, she went to the ladies' room, and she didn't return to the table.

After a suitable time, Andrew Keller paid and left Devon House, Ltd., stopping to check with the hostess who told him she had seen Caroline into a taxi ten minutes earlier.

He actually whistled as he walked downtown toward his apartment in the East Eighties, fingers wrapped around the ring box in his pocket. He'd return the ring first thing Monday, he decided, thanking his stars it had not been engraved. He felt that an enormous burden had been lifted from his shoulders. He wasn't angry with Caroline for her admission, although his stomach still churned as he thought back on her unbelievable confession. He wasn't even angry with himself for not having seen, in the entire year he had dated her, what Caroline was really like. He still reeled from the disillusion of his ideals, but he felt like a man on death row who'd been given a reprieve after all the appeals were exhausted.

If only Penny weren't such a dangerous flake, he thought. If she were more like Andy, he'd be in a taxi right now on his way to MacDougal Street. She didn't understand ethics. That crazy scheme of hers to pretend she had found a Gauguin was all the provocation Dieter needed to kick Andy out of NAIU once and for all, and Andy wouldn't be able to blame him. Lack of ethics: That was Penny's problem. And without ethics and loyalty, a person was nothing. She had a lot of other problems, too, he reflected, and yet she was adorable, even so. Nevertheless, he considered himself strong. Just because he was finished with Caroline, he didn't intend to put himself back into trouble with Penny. First thing on Monday he'd wind up the restoration case with her. He'd call Mercurio and have everything picked up from Penny's and returned to the warehouse. He had found another restorer in a small town south of Boston to handle the balance of the job. The new restorer was charging more than Penny, but his price was worth it to save problems in the long run.

There was no Caroline in his life anymore. No Gladwyn. No vice-presidency at her father's firm. Did he feel a void already? He shook his head. Yes, he corrected. He did feel a void. But it was Penny he missed, not Caroline.

Oh, well. I still have my position at NAIU, Andrew Keller thought as he crossed York Avenue. Starting on Monday he'd redouble his efforts to climb the corporate ladder. He tried to think kindly of Dieter as he entered the lobby of his apartment building and waited there for the elevator.

But that was Saturday night. By ten o'clock on Monday morning he would think back on that evening, and he would realize that, no matter what he had thought at the time, the disillusionment of Andrew Keller was not yet complete.

Chapter Thirteen

"Come in, Keller," said Dieter early on Monday morning in response to Andy's knock on the open door of his office.

Andy entered the spacious corner room Dieter occupied. His eyes, as usual, were irresistibly drawn to the magnificent view of New York Harbor, and of the Statue of Liberty, guarding its entrance.

He tore his gaze away from the panorama and forced himself to look at Dieter's face, attempting to assess his superior's mood. Was this the moment when Dieter would fire him? Mentally he reviewed the past few weeks of work, certain he had neglected nothing in any of his current assignments. If anything, he had been more conscientious than usual, owing to the uncomfortable climate in the Wall Street office. He scrutinized Dieter's features. The steely gray eyes were stern, but the thin lips were drawn out in the tight line that passed for a rare smile on Dieter's usually scowling face.

Andy allowed himself an inner sigh of relief, his first relaxation since Dieter's summons which he had received shortly after arriving at NAIU's downtown offices exactly at nine. When the glacial face of Dieter showed the crack of a smile, it usually meant that Dieter wanted a favor from someone, so no bad news would follow.

Dieter sat behind his enormous partners' desk, his back to a window, and he gestured for Andy to take a seat in one of the blood red leather wing chairs that faced him. Andy had never been invited to sit down in Dieter's office, and he wondered at the significance of the friendly gesture as he lowered himself into the sighing leather.

"Cigarette?" Dieter slid a rectangular box of nickel silver across the polished wood, opening the lid with one neatly-manicured small hand. Inside its porcelain interior lay an array of filter-tipped cigarettes of various brands.

"No, thank you, sir. I don't smoke."

"Of course." Dieter extracted a small brown cigarette with a gold tip and lit it with ritual slowness, using a table-top lighter. Leaning back in his chair, he exhaled the sweet-smelling smoke up into the quiet air where it hung on a shaft of sunlight that streamed through the eastern window. They sat in silence as Dieter watched the smoke curl and rest in the beam of light.

"Keller," he said at last, "I have called you in this morning because of a bothersome problem that seems to have arisen."

Andy felt the small thrill of fear tighten the muscles of his abdomen. He swallowed, his throat dry with tension.

"A problem, Mr. Dieter? With one of my assignments? I'm not aware of any problems."

"Well. . . Nothing too serious, mind you, and you have not been remiss in the slightest."

"How can I help?" asked Andy with a relieved sigh, releasing some of the tightness in his lungs.

"That shipment of hotel pictures from Germany." Dieter waited for a reaction from Andy. When none was forthcoming, he continued. "One of the crates seems to be missing."

"I'm not aware that anything is missing," replied Andy,

truly surprised at the statement. Certainly Andy would be the first to know if something else had gone awry, and everything had been in order when he left the office on Friday. The shipment seemed plagued with problems.

"Perhaps misplaced is a better word."

"Since when?"

"We think since the break-in at the warehouse. No one seems to know where one particular crate has gone to, and I need you to find out for me."

Andy frowned. He had checked the log in the warehouse and found all the crates accounted for, and now Dieter claimed that one was missing. He could not understand what Dieter meant. Besides, Andy was the only adjustor assigned to the hotel shipment, so who was claiming that one of the crates was gone? Had Dieter been checking up on his work? How, after all, had Dieter been the first to know about the break-in at the warehouse? In the ordinary course of events, the guard would have called Andy who was the warehouse's NAIU contact. That was it—Dieter was trying to catch him in a mistake.

"Who reported the crate missing, Mr. Dieter? I'm not aware—"

"That is no concern of yours, Keller," said Dieter quickly, and a shade too forcefully. "Don't you worry about that matter," he corrected in a friendlier tone. "The point is, one of the crates, one which has, uh—shall we say a greater value than the others?—seems to have disappeared. The company is most anxious to locate the crate."

"What do you mean, a greater value than the others? What's in the crate?" Had there been truth in Penny's wild claims, after all?

"None of your business, Keller. You'll be more comfortable if we keep it that way."

Andy stood quickly. "Of course, it's my business if I'm

to handle locating part of a missing shipment. You can't very well ask me to find something I can't even identify, can you?"

"The crate contains ten reproductions, Keller. That is what we're seeking. Sit down and relax. There's no need to allow your emotions to control your behavior. This matter is routine business, nothing more. Once in a while certain items are shipped from Germany that are not officially declared. For political reasons, you understand. Both the German government and the United States government are aware of the subterfuge; in fact, it is encouraged by the governments in order to avoid—"

"What type of items do you mean?" Andy regained his seat, but he sat on the edge of the red leather.

"Politically-sensitive items—that is all I'm at liberty to say," responded Dieter self-importantly.

Andy closed his eyes for a moment, his thoughts racing. Penny's suspicions, her fantastic story about finding a Gauguin among the reproductions, the accumulation of terrifying incidents surrounding the shipment—all flitted through his mind in the passage of seconds. His heart sank at the thought that his superior, that his company to which he had been so loyal, were involved in a smuggling scheme. A strange, metallic taste lay on his tongue and, for the first time, he understood what was meant by the expression "a bad taste in one's mouth." But, before he had opened his eyes again, Andy realized that Dieter was lying to him. Of that he was certain. Long-established companies like North American International Underwriters did not smuggle paintings in and out of countries with governmental permission. Andy had been in the insurance business long enough to know that much. Politically-sensitive, all right, but not in the way Dieter meant. Both the German and the U.S. governments would make business both embarrassing and difficult for NAIU if the truth came out. NAIU depended upon its impeccable international reputation for its very existence.

"Where is the crate, Keller? According to you, eight crates were in the Christopher Street warehouse and two were at the restorer. I have checked with the restorer who claims to have but one crate. That means one is missing."

"You checked with the restorer? You, yourself?" The doubting words were out before Andy thought about them, and Andy chastised himself mentally, praying he hadn't demonstrated either his closeness to Penny nor his skepticism of Dieter's story by the hasty, challenging question.

Dieter cleared his throat, hesitating just a fraction too long before he replied. "Yes," he said finally.

Penny had never mentioned that Dieter had contacted her, but, of course, it was possible. The way things were going, anything was possible. And if she had already discovered the purported Gauguin when he called, she would never have admitted her find to Dieter. What surprised Andy was that she had told *him* about it. At the time, he had taken her story as a pure fabrication, but now, in the light of Dieter's revelations, he had to believe Penny's claims. And he understood her odd behavior.

"And what will happen if I fail to locate the missing crate?" asked Andy, quite afraid of Dieter's answer.

"You will locate the crate. If not, you'll be very sorry. Very sorry."

Instinctively Andy knew that Dieter meant much more by his threat than a simple matter of being fired. And he knew, as well, that Penny was in greater danger than he. Having failed to locate the crate, Dieter was now playing, in a most civilized manner, his last card. Dieter would not have dared expose himself to Andy if he had not already tried every other avenue open to him—the break-in at the warehouse, the entry into Penny's apartment, her kidnapping, and the subsequent visit of the thug to Penny. If Dieter was desperate enough to approach Andy so directly, whoever was seeking the crate—for obviously Dieter was not alone in his quest—was running out of patience. He must keep these people away from Penny.

"How did you know about the break-in at the warehouse, Mr. Dieter?"

His question was greeted by stony silence. The silence between them grew until Andy realized that Dieter did not plan to answer the question he had posed, nor any other, but rather awaited Andy's response to the problem at hand.

Time. He needed to buy time. Time to think, time to warn Penny. Suddenly he remembered the restorer south of Boston he had engaged to continue the job after he told Penny she was through. "I believe one of the crates was shipped to a specialist in New England," Andy said slowly. "Yes, I'm almost certain the restorer jobbed out one of the crates—she said something about its problems being beyond her expertise. I have not been in contact with the restorer for some time," he lied, lest Dieter suspect he and Penny were in collusion, "but let me talk to her now and see if I can find an answer for you."

"Subtly, you understand." He stared at Andy for a moment. "You may go, Keller. But don't take too long in your inquiries. I am awaiting your answer."

"Yes, sir. I'll have the report on your desk as soon as possible."

"No written report, Keller. Verbal. And to me only," he added, confirming Andy's guess that NAIU itself was not involved, that only Dieter was the cancer in the company. Dieter stood to dismiss him; the thin-lipped smile vanished. "And, Keller, I regret to inform you that your position here has been eliminated. If you complete this assignment to my satisfaction, you'll have a nice recommendation to take with you when you leave at the end of the month. If not . . ."

"I understand, sir," replied Andy. So the ax had fallen, after all. He was not surprised, nor was he as disappointed as he had expected to be. To work with Dieter had been impossible before, but after today's revelations, there was no way Dieter would have allowed him to stay on. Already Andy knew too much.

Although Penny's safety preoccupied him, Andy felt a surge of relief as he went out the door and into the corridor which led to his own office. Automatically he pulled an antacid from the pocket of his suit jacket, but before he had slipped the tiny tablet into his mouth he realized that the reason he had been taking the medication no longer existed. He threw the entire roll into the wastebasket.

Andy stood still while Penny examined him through the peephole of the door to her apartment. The door opened slowly, as if she were wary of the errand that had brought him to her studio at noon on Monday. He would have left the office immediately after his interview with Dieter, but, not caring to use the telephone nor to arouse his superior's curiosity regarding his destination, he had waited until his lunch hour to come uptown to the Village.

He didn't blame Penny for being wary of him; there was no reason for her to expect to ever see his face again. In addition, she was probably afraid that he was in on the deception that Dieter had hatched and greatly regretting that she had told Andy she had the painting. If he were Penny, he'd be fearful.

Penny seemed pale, and dark shadows powdered the freckles that lay across her cheeks, giving her an air of sickness that worried Andy. She wore a pair of vintage blue jeans spattered with paint and a pale blue man's shirt that was tied in a knot around her tiny waist, leaving a patch of skin and the tiny dark mole on her stomach exposed.

"I wasn't expecting you," she said dully. "I was expecting Mercurio to pick up the crates. He was supposed to be here at nine, according to the telephone call from your secretary on Friday. There was no need to have your secretary call me, Andy. I can still speak civilly to you." The tone of voice belied her words, however, indicating a barely-contained anger.

"Mercurio's not coming," said Andy. "May I come in?"

She stood back to let him enter, and he walked into the studio, his jacket held casually under one arm. A blue-and-red striped tie dangled haphazardly from one pocket and dragged on the floor.

"Your tie is going to get dirty," Penny said. "There might be some paint on the floor."

"I don't care," said Andy. He tossed the jacket and tie on the Hollywood bed and sat heavily.

"How come Mercurio isn't coming? Off meeting some girl somewhere?" Penny seemed nervous. She rubbed her palms on the sides of her jeans.

"I told him not to come. Penny, I had nothing to do with this painting business. You know that, don't you? You really have a genuine Gauguin?"

"Genuine! And, of course, I know you weren't involved! Why would I have told you about it otherwise? Foolish I may be, but foolhardy, no."

"They're looking for that painting. You're in danger, real danger."

"Yes, I know. I've already told you that, but I thought you didn't believe me. What made you change your mind?"

"Dieter. Remember him?"

"No, who is he?"

"He's my boss, the man with the thick German accent. The man who called you trying to locate the missing crate."

"He never called me. I don't know what you're talking about, Andy."

"He told me he'd talked to you about the missing crate. But he never called you?"

"No, never. I would have remembered, believe me!"

"Then he's definitely involved with those men who've been bothering you. Definitely. Penny, you're in grave danger."

"No kidding," she said sarcastically. "Don't worry; I'm safe for a while. It doesn't surprise me that someone in your office is involved. There are probably more people involved, too. Someone in Germany had to coordinate the shipment of the original painting, after all. There were a great deal of technical points to be considered." She looked at him sharply and then away. "I've told only you and one other person that I have the painting, and neither of you knows where it is. You haven't told anyone at the office, have you?"

"No, thank God! I never told anyone. You believe me, don't you?" He searched her face.

"Of course, I believe you. I can't imagine you ever telling a lie," she replied.

"I was worried that you would think I was involved with Dieter and his scheme, whatever it is."

"No, I never thought that of you," she answered dully, implying by the emphasis of her statement that she had thought other, equally unflattering things in its stead. She had taken a seat on a wooden stool which sat in front of the easel he had seen before. Although pretending not to stare, he looked at her carefully, noting that red paint blotched the heel of one of her hands. His eyes traveled from the small hand to the canvas on the easel, and he realized he had interrupted her in the process of painting a still life of apples in a wooden bowl. She was painting from life; there was a bowl of apples on her worktable, and a light shone over the arrangement. The painting disappointed him slightly. Not that he thought Penny was perfect—he knew she was far from perfect—but he had believed she was a much better painter than the mess on the easel demonstrated. Even Andy's unschooled eye told him the painting was not very good.

However, his silent criticism of the painting didn't change the feelings he had for her, which was one of his problems that afternoon. If she would show him the slightest warmth, if she would just look into his eyes for one short moment, she'd see the agony this visit was costing him.

"I owe you an apology," he said. "You were right about something."

She did look up then, glancing at him with a mixture of emotions on her face. Curiosity he recognized, but there was something else, something Andy did not understand. There was an apprehension or an expectancy, almost as if she were waiting for something.

"Something you said," he concurred. "You said the company didn't give a damn about me, and you were right. I was fired this morning."

He could see by the stunned look on her face that he couldn't have said anything more surprising or more pleasing to her.

"Fired? Why? You're probably the most conscientiously boring insurance man in downtown New York," she said bitterly, shifting her eyes away once more. "I can't imagine they'd fire you for anything short of debauchery on the premises. What did you do?"

Andy winced at her accurate and deliberately insulting words. Even though he'd known the news of his sacking would warm her, as well it might have, after all the self-important things he had said to her when they quarrelled, nevertheless he hoped for a little more sympathy. She was usually so warm and compassionate. He kicked himself for having brought up the matter. He had come only to warn her and to prevail upon her to return the painting before something terrible happened to her. He should have known that they went too far when they exchanged angry words the previous week, and that this entire errand could have been accomplished on the telephone. He'd been a fool to come to see her again.

"What's it to you if you're fired? You have your job with Caroline's father. They'll take good care of you. You'll be fat and rich before you're forty." She hooked her feet behind a rung in the stool, allowing the sandals she wore to drop to the floor.

"I've called it quits with Caroline," he replied.

"Why?" She looked at him again. Was that a spark of interest in her eyes? No, she was sizing him up, doubt written all over her features, her lips pursed tightly and her eyes cold. She'd heard this story before, after all.

A lot of reasons, he wanted to say, Caroline's confession of promiscuity being the least of them. *Because I love you. Because I don't want to live with anyone else, even though you're crazy and unpredictable. Even though...* Well, enough of such thoughts, he mused. Penny wasn't open to such admissions from him. She sat stonily on the stool with her arms crossed protectively over her perfectly-shaped breasts, looking as if she couldn't wait for him to quit her presence.

"I just did," he said simply. "There's nothing in the Potters' life that appeals to me."

"Money? Position? High society? Those things mean nothing to you all of a sudden? My, you've certainly had a change of heart, Andy." *Tell me another one,* the green eyes said clearly.

"It's true, my eyes have been opened lately," he said. "You had a lot to do with it, too."

"In what way?"

"What you told me about your father, for instance. His life seems sad and empty to me."

"My father has everything," said Penny. "Two gorgeous houses, a boat on Lake Michigan, a Mercedes Benz—all the things you can have with Caroline. My mother came from a wealthy family just like Caroline's, you know. She could have bought all those nice things for him, but she made him earn every bit of them in other ways. He's still paying."

"I know he is. I'm not willing to pay such a high price for security."

"I see." Penny was looking at her toes now, wiggling them nervously. "So now what? Another insurance job?"

"I suppose. I'll start looking tomorrow."

"Why don't you buy the sailboat you've always wanted?" she asked suddenly. "Throw it all over, and do something different. This could be a great opportunity for you. An ill wind that blows no good, as they say."

"Really?" He looked up, touched that she remembered his dream and had brought it into the conversation, despite the awkward words they exchanged. Their eyes met for a moment before he quickly looked away. "No, it would never work," he said.

"Why not?"

"I just couldn't, that's all. I have hardly enough for a down payment on a small boat, and as I told you before, you need a source of income to swing a loan." Even when he returned the ridiculous sapphire ring to Tiffany's, there wouldn't be enough money in his savings account to brag about.

"So you charter the boat in the winter season. Take customers, and let their money pay the bank."

"I can't swing a boat big enough to charter, Penny. With what I have, I can't swing much of anything."

Penny stared down at her foot again, looking worried and pensive, as if she were weighing what to say next. A long moment went by in which Andy studied the soft, fluffy curls on the top of her head and remembered how those curls had tickled his nose. He wanted very much to go to her, to run his hand through her hair, to kiss her lips just one more time. How beautiful and desirable she was. He made himself sit still on the bed and wait for her next words.

"Tell me exactly what this man Dieter said to you this morning," she said at last. This time her voice was gentle and so low he could hardly hear the words she spoke.

"He said he was looking for a crate that seems to be missing, a crate which was much more valuable than the rest. He said he had checked with you, and that you don't have it."

"And what did you tell him?"

"I told him I thought you didn't have the crate, that you'd mentioned that you might job out some of the work to a specialist in New England. I didn't know what else to say."

"That was a good answer. That gives me a little time."

"A little time for what?" he asked.

"Shhh," she said. "Just be quiet for a minute."

She looked at him again. Her eyes were probing, seeking something from him that he couldn't imagine. He waited while she weighed her next remarks, knowing that some sort of struggle was going on within her.

"Do you believe in me?"

Andy acknowledged that Penny was reaching out to him in some way, but her reaching out was a thread so fragile that a wrong word might easily snap it. "Of course, I believe in you. But what are you talking about?"

"And you swear you didn't tell anyone at all about the painting?"

"I never thought to mention the conversation to anyone." That was the truth. There hadn't been time for any discussion of the case whatsoever, nor had there been reason to repeat Penny's claims before the meeting with Dieter. And after Dieter had begun to talk, the torturers of Torquemada could not have dragged the information from him.

She took a deep breath, and then said, "There's a way you can have your boat and your dreams, Andy. Sell everything you own, and then you'll have enough. I'll go with you if you want me. I'll throw my money in with yours, and we can make a big down payment on a big boat. I love you." She looked at him with wide eyes that entreated him not to hurt her for baring so much of her soul.

"What?" He wasn't at all sure he had heard her correctly. In fact he was certain her words were a hallucination. "What did you say?"

She stood quickly from the stool and turned her back to him. "I said," she whispered, but loudly enough that he heard her, "that I love you."

"That's what I thought you said." He was behind her in a flash, his arms around her waist, and his nose buried in the curls of her hair. "I love you, too. I love you like crazy!" He made her pivot to face him and was touched to see how shyly she looked up into his eyes. "I've been longing to tell you how much I love you, but you seemed so angry and hurt, I felt like a fool! Penny, I—"

"You're a wonderful lover, Andy. You're not a pompous ass—well, sometimes you are, but I love you anyway. I didn't mean those terrible things I told you. I was so angry about Caroline, about the way you acted like I was crazy or something. I'm so sorry," she said.

"I deserved everything you said."

"No, you—"

Leaning down, Andy silenced Penny with a tender kiss. When he finally broke away, he said, "Tell me how long you've loved me," he said.

"Almost from the beginning," Penny whispered as he slipped his arms around her waist and held her tightly. "I thought there was something wrong with me. After all, you represent everything I've spent my life trying to get away from. What about you? Do you really love me? All this time I've been thinking that you and Caroline—" He silenced her with two fingers on her lips.

"I've loved you from the beginning, too," he told her. "At first I didn't realize it was love. I guess...I guess I never knew what love felt like before. I've been trying to put you out of my mind all along, but you kept coming back. Even when I was sitting across from Caroline with an engagement ring in my pocket, all I could think of was you. I wanted to marry you, not her."

"I'll marry you," said Penny.

"Really! Penny, I can't believe it. There's nothing I want more in the world. But you just said I represent—"

"On one condition," she interrupted. Her green eyes were deadly serious.

"What's that?"

"That you quit insurance and buy a boat. After all the trouble I've gone to, I'm not settling down in the suburbs with an insurance man. I want to live on the high seas," she said dramatically. Then, immediately practical, she added, "I'll help with the down payment."

"You don't have any money," he said with doubt all over his face.

"Yes, I do. I've just made a deal to sell my company and all my equipment. The buyers and I sign the papers next week. How big does a boat have to be?"

"It should sleep six, at least. But then we'll have nothing if it doesn't work out," he said. "We'll be completely broke and have to start over."

"And that's a risk you're not willing to take," said Penny with disappointment. "I should have known."

"It's not a question of taking risks," he said. "It's facing reality." A woman like Penny deserved much more than bumming around harbors all over the world. She was a hopeless romantic, a person who didn't understand that one had to plan for the future. "I love you. I don't want you to live from hand-to-mouth. I want to give you nice things—a decent place to live, no worries about the future, a—"

"So I can be a middle-aged widow and clip coupons? No, thanks, Andy. I want you to do what you've always dreamed about. I don't want to be a millstone around your neck, even if you want to act like a workaholic."

"But, Penny, you don't understand. You aren't the most practical person in the world."

"Horse feathers, Andy. There's such a thing as a calculated risk. You insurance people take calculated risks all the time. Tell me you'll buy a boat, or I won't marry you. I come with a substantial dowry," she added with a smile that made her eyes crinkle at the corners.

"I bet. You can't cook, what you know about keeping house you could put in one tube of that paint over there, and your clothes are weird," he laughed. "Some dowry."

"All I need is a bathing suit and a pair of shorts for the Caribbean."

"That's true."

"And you're a much better cook anyway, so why should I cook?"

"You've got a point. If there's one thing I like, it's a woman who bows to a man's greater talents."

"And how hard can it be to keep a boat clean?"

"You'll be surprised. A boat is nothing but maintenance. Work, work, work all the time. On the other hand, I think you're up to it," he said.

"So you'll do it? We'll buy a boat?"

"If that's what you want, Penny, but I can't help telling you, I worry about the future. I'm a pretty cautious man, and I don't like jumping into a situation without weighing the risks." What made him say that? he wondered. In one sentence he was throwing away habits of a lifetime, just to be with her. But wasn't she what he wanted more than anything in the world? Wasn't she, really, why he had come there that afternoon?

"You mean the risk of marrying me?"

His mouth came down hard on hers before he answered. "No. That's not a risk. That's a sure thing," he said, nuzzling into her neck which caused her to shiver with delight. He felt the slight trembling in her body. Then she kissed him, with her arms around his neck, her lips parting willingly to meet his tongue.

"Then what's worrying you?"

"How we're going to live."

"Like I said, we'll make money from the charters."

"We'll never have enough to save a penny. What if we hate it? What if we want to start a family? What if—"

"Lord, Andy! You can be such a bore sometimes." Penny broke away from his embrace and walked to the Hollywood bed where she plumped herself down with evident irritation. She stared at the floor, lost in thought for a moment, chewing on her lower lip. She was weighing an answer again. Andy felt himself tense. She couldn't give herself to him, and then pull herself away so quickly, could she? Was she serious about her condition for marriage?

"Are you angry with me?" he asked. "I can't help if I worry about things like the future. You can be so impractical, Penny." He came and sat by her on the bed, throwing one arm around her shoulder and pulling her toward his body as he spoke. "You're so romantic about life, but reality is reality. You have to understand."

She blew up on her bangs, took a deep breath, and plunged. "No, I'm not angry. I've got a proposition to make," she said. "I've got a Gauguin worth millions of dollars. You could work your whole life adjusting claims for oil tankers and never make what that painting is worth, but together we can turn this painting into a new boat and still have money left over to put in the bank. We can strike a deal with the appropriate parties for ten percent of its worth, free and clear. I've got it all worked out. I've already spoken with a well-known philanthropist who—"

"There you go with your Gauguin again," he said lightly. "That painting is going to get you killed, you know. Show it to me."

"With pleasure," said Penny, jumping up from the bed. "Look around you. It's right here in the room."

Andy's eyes roamed the four walls of the studio and finally came to rest on the only visible painting, the canvas propped up on the easel.

"*That's* a Gauguin?" he said skeptically.

"I swear," Penny replied.

"No one would ever believe that's a Gauguin, Penny. Even I know it's not."

"That's what you're supposed to think," she said.

"You painted that painting, yourself. I don't mean to insult you, but it's not exactly good."

"You're right on both counts. I didn't have enough time to do my best work," she said without taking offense. "I've only had a few hours' sleep since Friday. I must look a sight." She touched both hands to her hair.

"I don't understand," he said. "Are you all right?"

"I'm perfectly fine," she assured him. "That's a Gauguin—I've had it authenticated, and it is genuine. Not only that, the painting doesn't belong to your hotel chain, or a museum, or anything. It wasn't stolen before, but it is now. Well, not really stolen," she clarified. "Temporarily in the process of changing ownership is a better way of putting it."

"What do you mean?"

"I mean that I have 'liberated' this magnificent masterpiece from the Count von Rombauer and his flunky, Steven Crespin," she said, explaining quickly who the men were. "I don't see why a Nazi who's wanted for war crimes should own a Gauguin when it really should belong to the people. Especially when Penelope Greenaway and now Andrew Keller can be compensated for making certain that the world knows of its existence. Do you? All we have to do is get it safely out of here and into the hands of the right people."

"How do you plan to—"

"Simple. They know the painting is in the crate of Seurats, and they're waiting for me to tell them when the Seurats show up. They broke into the warehouse to find that one particular crate, but it wasn't there. Then they broke into my studio, but the crate wasn't here either."

"Where was it?"

"In Mercurio's van. The NAIU van was towed for illegal parking, and the Seurats were over on the West Side with the impounded cars. When Mercurio brought me the crate, I didn't have room in the studio for it, so I had him leave it upstairs at Winnie's and since I found the Gauguin, I've kept it hidden up there, right on the wall over the fireplace. It's a good thing, too. That man, Rocco—one of the men in the Cadillac—burst in here one day and looked around. They're watching me—not all the time, but enough to be seen every so often, just to make me know that they're watching. They're outside now.''

"How do you know?"

"Look out the window," she told him. "There's a gray Cadillac with two men in the front seat parked down the street. They've been there an hour or so. After awhile they'll drive away, but they'll be back tomorrow. They always come about this time, and they don't care if I see them. It's psychological warfare, I guess."

He had noticed the Cadillac, he realized, not just today, but another time he had come to the apartment. He had even noticed the burly man who was usually reading the *Daily News* or the *New York Post* in the passenger seat. He had seen the car before, too, parked in front of the warehouse that Saturday Dieter had called him after the break-in, but until Penny pointed it out, he had not made the connection.

"I saw that car with Dieter one day," he said out loud.

"That's the same bunch that grabbed me the night I arrived at your apartment. You remember that night. . ."

Of course, he remembered that night. That was the time he had actually made his choice of Penny over Caroline, although he'd been too stubborn and suspicious to stay with the courage of his conviction.

"Is Dieter a German?" Penny asked, breaking into his thoughts.

"Yes, but he's been living in South America for years," replied Andy, confused.

"That's it, then!" she cried. "He's a friend of that Nazi in Paraguay! He fired you because he was afraid you would become suspicious of all the strange things surrounding the shipment.''

"He fired me because I already know too much,'' said Andy. "And so do you. You'll never get away with stealing that painting. Never.''

"Oh, no?'' she asked.

Andy looked at the still life of apples again. "But—''

"But that mess of apples doesn't look like a Gauguin. Is that what you're going to say?''

"Yes. What's your plan, Penny? You're going to get yourself killed. Get us both killed.''

"If you're really in on this with me, come upstairs, Andy. I'll show you something else.''

He followed her up the stairs to Winnie's apartment. As soon as Penny opened the door, he saw an unmistakable Gauguin above the fireplace, its warm, lush colors dominating the room. He was certain the painting was the same he had seen Penny working on in her studio, the one she had told him she painted herself. A young native girl, her eyes lit with a seductive innocence, held a basket of red flowers.

"*That's* the Gauguin,'' he said with assurance.

"No, that's the copy,'' she corrected. "I painted that picture. It took me all weekend.'' She didn't mention that the most difficult part was finding a suitably old canvas. But she had managed.

"I don't understand.''

"When that painting is dry, I plan to cover it with the Seurat reproduction, put it back in the crate, and give it to Mercurio. What happens after I do my part...,''

"And what about the apple still life?''

"*That's* the Gauguin,'' she said. "I painted the apples over the Gauguin to hide it.''

"It's ruined!''

"No, the painting is safe. I did the same thing the smugglers did. I covered the painting with a water-soluble gelatin and chalk ground, applied rice paper tissue on top, and then sealed with a very thin varnish. Over that I put gesso, and I painted the apples."

"You're not a very good painter, Penny. But you're a very good copyist."

"Yes, I know," she said, staring up at her copy of the *Tahitian Maiden*. "It's too bad we can't have the genuine article hanging around. You'll have to learn to live with the apples. Until we can strike a deal with the government of Israel."

"What do I care about apples? Having you is all I care about," said Andy. He had to admire her. Penny was more practical, and a lot more courageous than he had given her credit for in the past. She was willing to take on unscrupulous smugglers to do what she wanted. "What do I have to do?" he asked.

"We'll go on with the restoration commission as if everything were normal because we need time. Go sell everything you own," she said with a delightful laugh that reminded him of the tinkle of crystal wind chimes on a warm, gentle breeze. "Everything! We need money to buy a boat. I'll take care of everything else!"

Chapter Fourteen

After stalling for several days, Andy explained to Dieter that the sought-after crate had been sent, as he had hinted previously, to a second restorer near Boston and that he had requested, through Miss Greenaway, its return, untouched, to her premises. Miss Greenaway had agreed to recall the crate, he told his superior, but regretted to inform him that the Boston restorer was out of town on an assignment and would not be back until the last week of August, at which time she would make certain that he shipped the crate back to New York. At Andy's suggestion that to probe further might arouse suspicion and interest better left sleeping, Dieter had accepted the news.

By the end of two weeks, Andy turned his file over to Dieter and left the offices of NAIU for good, informing his superior that he had taken a position in Philadelphia and was to be married to a local girl there.

Penny finished the assignment for North American International Underwriters in record time. At a telephone call from Penny, Mercurio brought a new crate to inspect and repair every five days, and she worked long hours to finish the job, explaining to Andy she wanted to complete the commission to everyone's satisfaction so there would be no question of calling in another restorer to work on the reproductions. For nearly three weeks she barely left her studio, allowing Andy to do all the marketing and cooking, and to help her where he could with the assignment.

Andy broke the lease at his apartment and sold its entire contents to a small company that specialized in liquidating homes. A pair of blue garters was found behind the areca palm by the woman who came to appraise the furnishings of the apartment, much to Andy's blushing embarrassment. He moved in with Penny, coming and going as he pleased from the studio, since Rocco and his friend had never seen Penny and Andy together, and they were careful to keep matters that way.

Penny sold her business intact to the three graduates of Henry's restoration course, who agreed to take possession the week before Labor Day and to feed Winnie's cat until Winnie returned from Europe. She didn't receive as much as she had hoped for her studio and its contents, but she was so happy to have buyers with cash in hand just when she needed them that she accepted their second offer, leading Henry to tell her that she had capitulated too soon in the bargaining process. Penny had merely smiled at Henry's comment. She informed Henry that she had taken his advice: The Gauguin was covered once more and would be returned to the insurance company.

On Thursday of the third week, convinced that her Gauguin copy was thoroughly dry, Penny covered the fake with rice paper and affixed the Seurat reproduction to its surface. She replaced everything in its frame and, with Andy's help, nailed the crate together once more.

Finally she was ready. She called the NAIU office and asked that Mercurio pick up the last crate of the shipment.

"Mercurio, have I got a girl for you!" said Penny when the messenger came to her apartment at noon the next day.

"Yeah? Where? What's her name?"

"Finish loading the crate upstairs, and I'll give you all the information. She has eyes as big as saucers—dark brown, like velvet. She has long, black hair, and the greatest legs since Betty Grable's."

"Who's Betty Grable?" he asked as he followed Penny up the stairs up to Winnie's apartment. "I'd like to meet her, too."

"Sorry, she's dead."

"Then tell me more about the girl who isn't."

"Do your work first."

"Okay." Mercurio was whistling as he loaded the crate containing the Seurats onto his dolly. "Five minutes," he said. "I'll be done in five minutes. I'll come back, and you can give me all the particulars."

Back downstairs Penny shoved the last of what she needed into her purse. She gave one final look around her studio. She would miss the old place, she decided. She and Janie had spent some good times there. And she would miss MacDougal Street, too—all the Village, in fact.

Yes, she would miss life in New York, but not enough to stay her hand from the plan she was about to put into operation. She and Andy had a wonderful future before them, but not if they stayed in New York. They had to leave, but since they wanted to go, she would never feel like an exile.

Satisfied that everything was in order in the studio, she went to the wall where the still life of apples hung. She looked at the painting one more time, almost gagging at its lack of expertise. She could have done worse only by painting the apples on black velvet, she decided. Its colors were garish, its perspective amateurish at best, and it's conception was that of a Sunday artist who had no formal training whatsoever. But there had been no time to be fancy.

"Well, I never called myself an artist," she said aloud, removing the painting from its hook and tucking it under her arm. Butterflies bumped against her rib cage. She had assured Andy she could handle her plan. She had insisted she was capable of carrying off the most important deception of her life. He had been so nervous. Not distrustful of her ability, to be certain, but terribly concerned for her safety. He was so sweet, she decided, so hopelessly sweet and old-fashioned. She was the one to carry this off, not Andy whose face read as clearly as a road map at high noon.

She went to the window with the canvas under her arm and peered up to the street through the bars. Mercurio was still loading the wooden crate into the van which was parked illegally next to a fire hydrant, and down the street she saw Rocco and his driver sitting in the front seat of the Cadillac. Rocco was reading what appeared to be the *Daily News*.

She went out the door and into the sunshine of the street, approaching the van. Mercurio was just slamming the double doors in the back as she arrived, and his face had a look of nervous impatience. She went to him, standing so he would have to face her with his back to the door, because she had noticed what he apparently was too preoccupied with Penny's promise of matchmaking to have realized: The keys still dangled in the lock. Not that she needed the keys left behind for the wheels of her scheme to turn smoothly, but their presence was a fortuitous touch.

"So this girl," he said with enthusiasm. "Tell me about the girl. How and when can I meet her?"

"The interesting thing is she's dying to meet you, Mercurio. She's been watching you all month while you delivered the paintings, and she asked me about you a long time ago," fibbed Penny convincingly. She wasn't even certain Mercurio and the girl would be able to converse, but, after all, she told herself, when sparks fly, the language of love is universal. "I told her I'd introduce you as soon as I could. Would you like to meet her now?"

"Are you kidding, Miss Greenaway? Take me to her."

"She's just down the block in the coffee shop. Her name is Maria; she's the waitress behind the counter. I can't go with you, though. I have to deliver this painting. Why don't you just go in by yourself, and tell her I sent you?"

"I'm on my way!" He was halfway across the street before the words were out of his mouth. For fear he would look back, Penny quickly shifted her stance so he couldn't see that he had left the keys in the lock of the van's back door. She watched him walk quickly toward the Parthenon Palace, and she waited until she saw him go up the two steps to its entrance.

"Adios," she said under her breath. She hoped he wouldn't be fired when he told the people at NAIU what had happened. She felt a pang of guilt, but she realized everything was at stake for what she was about to do, and Mercurio's job was a small price to pay for her safety, and Andy's as well.

Even if she hadn't arranged the present deception, she knew her life was at stake anyway. She knew too much; the Whisperer and his men would hardly let her go back to the placid life she had led before she met them. And, now that Andy was involved, their very lives depended on the outcome of the next few minutes.

She shifted the canvas to her right arm, making certain the painting itself showed, and she began to walk down the street as if she had an errand to do. It took a lot of strength not to run past the Cadillac, and she had to take two or three deep breaths to steady herself as she neared the open window of the car. Rocco's massive forearm stuck out the door.

"Hi, Rocco. How're you doing?" she said in a friendly

tone, although she could hear her own pulse throbbing, and her throat was so dry she had to clear it before the words came out normally.

His eyes squinted at her in surprise. "Uh, fine." He was as transparent as Andy, she decided. She could see the effect her everyday words had on him. After all, the last time they had actually spoken, he had terrorized her, and now she was standing placidly at the side of his car and smiling. He twisted his features in suspicious curiosity.

"I'm just on my way to the gallery around the corner to sell this painting I did."

He hesitated for a moment, as if he hadn't quite decided what she was up to with her sudden friendliness. Then he glanced at the misshapen apples and said, "Hey, that's real nice," he said. "How much would you get for something like that?"

Relief flooded through her. Rocco, it seemed, had decided she was merely making conversation, and that she had accepted the inevitability of his presence on MacDougal Street, which must have meant to him that she was going to cooperate with his boss's wishes.

"Do you like it?" asked Penny. "I'm not certain I do, but then I'm not a very good artist. I just paint for fun sometimes. The gallery will probably give me fifty dollars or so."

"For fifty bucks, I'll buy it from you," he said. The features of his lumpy face moved together in an odd way, and Penny realized he was giving her what passed for a smile. Inadvertently she shivered, despite the heat of the day. She'd hate to see him actually angry.

"Thank you, Rocco. That's very flattering. If you like, I'll do another for you sometime, but this one is already promised to a buyer. Just stop in at my place in two weeks or so, and you can tell me what you want."

"Whadda ya mean, two weeks or so?" The dark scowl was back as he darted his narrowing eyes sideways at her. Penny felt a thrill of fear shoot through her legs while underneath her sun dress pinpricks of perspiration burst forth to cover her chest and her midriff. For a moment she thought she couldn't go through with the conversation; she thought, in fact, she might faint.

"I'm going away on vacation. But I'll be back soon," she said calmly, and she even found the strength to smile.

"You can't go away," he barked out, their quick-lived friendship over as soon as it had begun. "We got unfinished business, missy." He scowled in the most threatening manner and opened the door of the car, ominously unfolding his hefty body from the front seat of the Cadillac.

"No, we don't Rocco. Our business is over for good. See that van parked in front of the fire hydrant back there? The pictures you want are in the van, the driver's down at the corner having a cup of coffee. And Rocco," she lowered her voice, "the keys are in the back door lock."

The opposite door of the Cadillac opened, and Rocco and the driver began to run down MacDougal Street toward the van. On weakened knees, Penny walked quickly, being careful not to run, in the opposite direction. She knew her Gauguin copy was extremely well executed. Even when they peeled off the photo-reproduction that hid the painting from view, Dieter and the Whisperer would probably never realize the switch had been made. She wondered if their potential buyer would have the painting authenticated. An expert would, of course, recognize the painting for what it was—a fake, but by then, the painting would have been through so many hands... There were more than enough people to suspect of making the switch along its circuitous path from Nazi Germany to the walls of a collector's home... Besides, to whom would one complain? Certainly not to the police.

Penny shrugged and quickened her step. Rounding the corner, she saw a yellow Checker cab with its back door open and Andy's worried face leaning forward watching for her through the window. She ran to the taxi and jumped into the back seat.

"Penny, is everything okay? Lord, I've been so worried." The frown between his eyebrows seemed to be etched into his skin. She propped the painting up against the back of the seat, and edged herself closer to him. He took one of her hands, squeezing it tightly between his fingers.

"I know just the way to get rid of those lines, Andy," she said, kissing his nose and rubbing at the puckered skin with one finger. "What you need is an extended cruise in the southern sun. Kennedy Airport," she ordered the driver with a laugh bubbling up within her. Lovingly she touched one hand to the edge of the canvas.

Penny had both hands in warm, soapy water, and was scouring the last of the wild rice from the inside of a saucepan. She reached for the plastic bottle of detergent that sat in its assigned niche in a spot nearby in the miniature kitchen which she, with difficulty, was learning to call a galley. Everything was nearby in the tiny confines of the kitchen, and she wondered how Andy was able to turn out the gourmet meals for four that he regularly prepared. That afternoon's lunch had been cold boiled lobster, wild rice, and some of the crisp dry white wine he fancied lately.

The boat rocked gently, kissed by the wavelets in the harbor. She would have a nap after she finished the luncheon dishes, she decided, if she could find a bit of shade.

Andy had taken the Zodiak, their rubber dinghy fitted with an outboard motor, and gone to Saint-Pierre to replenish their supplies, the current guests being unexpected afficionados of their store of bourbon which had given out early in the week of their charter. She hoped Andy would buy half a case of bourbon, at least, although American whiskey was devilishly expensive in Martinique, imported as it was from the States. But then Andy never made mistakes; he had an unerring eye when it came to sizing up the customers. He knew exactly what drink to offer, what type of delicacy would tickle their guests' palates, when to suggest pills for seasickness, and when to break out the suntan lotion. He was absolutely cut out for the life of a charter captain.

She also hoped Andy wouldn't forget to look for a copy of a New York newspaper in Saint-Pierre so she could continue to follow the Stephan Crespin art forgery case. How foolish of Stephan to try to sell a fake Gauguin to the Metropolitan Museum of Art! Why, even an art student would have known the oil was a fake, the New York district attorney had been quoted as saying. What greed did to some dealers! Stephan would have a long time to reconsider his avarice when he was convicted, as Penny was certain he would be, and a long time to live in fear of retaliation from von Rombauer who was probably exceedingly angry to have lost part of his bloodstained nest egg.

Penny dried her hands on the skimpy, white shorts she wore and, in bare feet, she went up the first two companionway steps until her head just peeked into the open cockpit. Before her, lay the sleepy harbor of Saint-Pierre, and behind the town, mist-shrouded Mount Pelee, the volcanic mountain which had erupted with such disastrous consequences in 1902, killing thirty thousand people, and covering the northern tip of Martinique with ash and lava.

Pelee was quiet today, as it had been since the late twenties. Wispy, white clouds hovered around its deceptively innocent peak, belying the volcano's tempestuous core. Its placid surface reminded her of her husband, she mused—all proper on the exterior, a raging volcano when aroused. Not Andy's temper, but his sensuality which had been too long hidden under his Brooks Brothers suits and his Dunhill ties.

Penny couldn't remember the last time she had seen Andy in a suit. It must have been on the day they were married in San Juan, she thought, but certainly not since. All they owned between them now was a wardrobe of jeans and shorts, and perhaps three sweaters that they shared for an occasionally cool night.

Andy hadn't worn a tie since their rushed and secret trip to Israel in October. There, at the side of a well-known New York real estate magnate, they had quietly watched as the government accepted the anonymous donation of a previously unknown painting by Paul Gauguin. In memory of those who did not survive, the philanthropist had stated, bringing tears to everyone's eyes.

Penny blew up to flutter the hair of her bangs. As she stood in the doorway—companionway hatch, she corrected herself silently—she became aware of the murmur of voices which a gentle breeze carried to her ears from the foredeck. Their customers—Andy kept reminding her to call them guests—lay tanning themselves forward. They had spent the previous evening in Fort-de-France, the capital of Martinique, dancing the night away, and had not returned to the boat until almost two in the morning. Penny had known that breakfast would be delayed the next morning, lunch would be later than usual, and the entire day would be planned to accommodate the guests' hangovers.

Penny didn't care. The Kellers had no schedule and, in fact, she had sold her watch long before, knowing there was no longer a reason to own one.

She and Andy had begged off the previous night, and the guests had gone into Fort-de-France without them. They had been happy to have a rare night alone during the busy winter season on their schooner which slept six people, a sailboat they had bought used and rechristened *The Tahitian Maiden* for reasons they never explained.

They ate on the deck at sunset. In the west, the sun dropped over the horizon with the spectacular, split-second, green flash that lights up the Caribbean sky like the iridescent tail of a peacock. Afterward, they went below and made love twice, and then she brought him a glass of the wine they had drunk with dinner, and a late-night snack of a wonderful French blue cheese she had found in the Fort-de-France market that afternoon. They shared the cheese on pieces of a *baguette* while sitting naked on the berth in their tiny stateroom, having given over their larger quarters to the paying guests for two weeks. Afterward, they had gone up on deck and watched the Caribbean stars above while Andy told her the names of the glowing lights that seemed to hang almost within reach above their heads, and he had made love to Penny yet again in the soft, velvet air that surrounded *The Maiden* which rocked gently under their movements.

"Penny and Andrew are such a perfect couple," the woman was saying. "So carefree, so much in love."

"This is the way to live, Edith!" agreed the man. "This beautiful boat, every detail of it perfect, everything polished to a fare-thee-well." Penny was gratified to hear that the man had noticed the polished brass. Polishing was her responsibility. Andy did most of the sailing, but he was teaching Penny how to navigate, and he did all the cooking since they both agreed he was much, much more adept in the galley than Penny could ever hope to be. She did the bulk of the marketing, all the clean-up, and she took care of the reservations paperwork. "They must have worked their tails off to buy this boat," the man was saying. "He told me they sold everything they owned to make the down payment. I don't understand kids." Penny could just picture the man shaking his bald head. "They never think about putting anything by for the future."

"No, Paul, there's money behind them, I can always tell," replied his wife. "They have a certain air about them, an air that comes from having security. Besides, she told me they owned the boat outright. Something about buying it with the proceeds of a finder's fee. I don't remember her exact words. You don't suppose they discovered a hidden pirate's treasure somewhere?"

"More likely it's a case of rich parents or a giant portfolio of stocks somewhere. Yes, I see your point. Put a little lotion on my back, will you, Edith? I'm starting to cook."

"The only discordant note on the whole boat is that horrid apple painting in the main cabin. Did you notice?"

"He told me his wife painted it, and they keep it as a souvenir of their courtship," said the balding Paul. "I guess he thinks it's beautiful."

"Love is blind, Paul. It must be if you still love me," said Edith with a little laugh.

"And what about me? You'd better put some lotion on my head, too, my dear, or I'll look like the lobsters we had for lunch."

Penny smiled a secret, happy grin.

"Some people just don't understand art!" she said out loud, but the wind blew her words across the turquoise bay where they were lost on the gentle breeze.